W9-AFD-897

FEARLESS™

Double Edition #1
Fearless (#1) & Lost (#25)

FRANCINE PASCAL

SIMON PULSE

New York   London   Toronto   Sydney   Singapore

HAYNER PUBLIC LIBRARY DISTRICT
ALTON, ILLINOIS

If you purchased this book without a cover, you should be aware that this book is stolen property. It was reported as "unsold and destroyed" to the publisher and neither the author nor the publisher has received any payment for this "stripped book."

This book is a work of fiction. Any references to historical events, real people, or real locales are used fictitiously. Other names, characters, places, and incidents are the product of the author's imagination, and any resemblance to actual events or locales or persons, living or dead, is entirely coincidental.

First Simon Pulse edition January 2003

Fearless text copyright © 1999 by Francine Pascal
Lost text copyright © 2003 by Francine Pascal

Cover copyright © 2003 by 17th Street Productions, an Alloy Inc. Company

SIMON PULSE
An imprint of Simon & Schuster Children's Publishing Division
1230 Avenue of the Americas, New York, NY 10020

All rights reserved, including the right of
reproduction in whole or in part in any form.

Fearless™ is a trademark of Francine Pascal.

Printed in the United States of America
10 9 8 7 6 5 4 3 2 1

ISBN 0-689-85811-6

Fearless and *Lost* are also published individually.

AEI-22 34

Double Edition #1
Fearless (#1) & Lost (#25)

FEARLESS

*To my daughters, Jamie Stewart,
Laurie Wenk, Susan Johansson*

Losers with no imagination say that if you start a new school, there has to be a first day. How come they haven't figured out how to beat that? Just think existentially. All you do is take what's supposed to be the first day and bury it someplace in the next month. By the time you get around to it a month later, who cares?

When I first heard the word *existential,* I didn't know what it meant, so I never used it. But then I found out that no one knows what it means, so now I use it all the time.

Since I just moved to New York last week, tomorrow would have been my first day at the new school, but I existentialized it, and now I've got a good thirty days before I have to deal with it. So, like, it'll be just a regular day, and I'll just grab my usual school stuff, jeans and a T-shirt, and throw them on. Then just like I always do, I'll take them off and throw on about eighteen different T-shirts and four different pairs of jeans before I find the right ones that hide my diesel arms and thunder thighs. Not good things on a girl, but no one else seems to see them like I do.

I won't bother to clean up when I'm done. I don't want to trick my new cohabitants, George and Ella, into thinking that I'm neat or considerate or anything. Why set them up for disappointment? I made that mistake with my old cohabitants and . . . well, I'm not living with them anymore, am I?

George Niven was my dad's mentor in the CIA. He's old. Like fifty or something. His wife, Ella, is much younger. Maybe thirty, I don't know. And you certainly can't tell from the way she dresses. Middle of winter she finds a way to show her belly button. And she's got four hundred of these little elastic bands that can only pass for a skirt if you never move your legs. Top that with this unbelievable iridescent red hair and you've got one hot seventeen-year-old. At least that's what she thinks. We all live cozy together in Greenwich Village in a brownstone—that's what they call row houses in New York City. Don't ask me why, because it isn't brown, but we'll let that go for now.

I'm not sure how this transfer of me and my pathetic possessions was arranged. Not by my dad. He is Out of the Picture. No letters. No birthday cards. He didn't even contact me in the hospital last year when I almost fractured my skull. (And no, I didn't almost fracture my skull to test my dad, as a certain asshole suggested.) I haven't seen him since I was twelve, since . . . since—I guess it's time to back up a little. My name is Gaia. Guy. Uh. Yes, it's a weird name. No, I don't feel like explaining it right now.

I am seventeen. The good thing about seventeen is that you're not sixteen. Sixteen goes with the word *sweet*, and I am so far from sweet. I've got a black belt in kung fu and I'm trained in karate, judo, jujitsu, and *muay thai*—which is basically kick boxing. I've got a reflex speed that's off the charts. I'm a near perfect shot. I can climb mountains, box, wrestle, break codes in four languages. I can throw a 175-pound man over my shoulders, which accounts for my disgusting shoulders. I can kick just about anybody's ass. I'm not bragging. I wish I were. I wish my dad hadn't made me into the . . . thing I am.

I have blond hair. Not yellow, fairy-tale blond. But blond enough to stick me in the category. You know, so guys expect you to expect them to hit on you. So teachers set your default grade at B-minus. C-plus if you happen to have big breasts, which I don't particularly. My friend from before, Ivy, had this equation between grades and cup size, but I'll spare you that.

Back in ninth grade I dyed my way right out of the blond category, but after a while it got annoying. The dye stung and turned my hands orange. To be honest, though (and I am not a liar), there's another reason I let my hair grow back. Being blond makes people think they can pick on you, and I like when people think they can pick on me.

You see, I have this handicap. Uh, that's the wrong word. I am hormonally challenged. I am never afraid. I just don't have the gene or whatever it is that makes you scared.

It's not like I'll jump off a cliff or anything. I'm not an idiot. My rationality is not defective. In fact, it's extra good. They say nothing clouds your reason like fear. But then, I wouldn't know. I don't know what it feels like to be scared.

It's like if you don't have hope, how can you imagine it? Or being born blind, how do you know what colors are?

I guess you'd say I'm fearless. Whatever fear is.

If I see some big guy beating up on a little guy, I just dive in and finish him off. And I can. Because that's the way I've been trained. I'm so strong, you wouldn't believe. But I hate it.

Since I'm never afraid of anything, my dad figured he'd better make sure I can hold my own when I rush into things. What he did really worked, too. Better than he expected. See, my dad didn't consider nature.

Nature compensates for its mistakes. If it forgot to give me a fear gene, it gave me some other fantastic abilities that definitely work in my favor. When I need it, I have this awesome speed, enormous energy, and amazing strength all quadrupled because there's no fear to hold me back.

It's even hard for me to figure out. People talk about danger and being careful. In my head I totally understand, but in my gut I just don't feel it. So if I see somebody in trouble, I just jump in and use everything I've got. And that's big stuff, and it's intense.

I mean, you ever hear that story about the mother who lifted the car off her little boy? That's like the kind of strength regular people can get from adrenaline. Except I don't need extra adrenaline because without fear, there's nothing to stop you from using every bit of power you have.

And a human body, especially a highly trained one like mine, has a lot of concentrated power.

But there's a price. I remember once reading about the Spartans. They were these fantastic Greek warriors about four hundred something B.C. They beat everybody. Nobody could touch them. But after a battle they'd get so drained, they'd shake all over and practically slide to the ground. That's what happens to me. It's like I use up everything and my body gets really weak and I almost black out. But it only lasts a couple of minutes. Eventually I'm okay again.

And there is one other thing that works in my favor. I can do whatever I want 'cause I've got nothing to lose.

See, my mother is . . . not here anymore. I don't really care that my dad is gone because I hate his guts. I don't have any brothers or sisters. I don't even have any grandparents. Well, actually, I think I do have one, but she lives in some end-of-the-world place in Russia and I get the feeling she's a few beans short of a burrito. But this is a tangent.

Tangent is a heinous word for two reasons:

1. It appears in my trigonometry book.

2. Ella, the woman-with-whom-
I-now-live-never-to-be-confused-
with-a-mother, accuses me of
"going off on them."

Where was I? Right. I was
telling you my secrets. It probably all boils down to three magic
words: I don't care. I have no
family, pets, or friends. I don't
even have a lamp or a pair of
pants I give a shit about.

I Don't Care.

And nobody can make me.

Ella says I'm looking for
trouble. For a dummy she hit it
right this time.

I *am* looking for trouble.

He lay sprawled in a half-conscious pile, and she was **walking** tempted to **trap** demand his wallet or his watch or something.

DON'T GO INTO THE PARK AFTER
sunset. The warning rolled
around Gaia Moore's head as
she crossed the street that bordered Washington Square Park
to the east. She savored the

The Point

words as she would a forkful of chocolate cheesecake.

There was a stand of trees directly in front of
her and a park entrance a couple hundred feet to
the left. She hooked through the trees, feeling the
familiar fizz in her limbs. It wasn't fear, of course.
It was energy, maybe even excitement—the things
that came when fear should have. She passed
slowly through a grassy stretch, staying off the
lighted paths that snaked inefficiently through the
park.

As the crow flies. That's how she liked to walk.
So what if she had nowhere to go? So what if no
one on earth knew or probably cared where she
was or when she'd get home? That wasn't the
point. It didn't mean she had to take the long way.
She was starting a new school in the morning, and
she meant to put as much distance between herself
and tomorrow as she could. Walking fast didn't
stop the earth's slow roll, but sometimes it felt like
it could.

She'd passed the midway point, marked by the
miniature Arc de Triomph, before she caught the

flutter of a shadow out of the corner of her eye. She didn't turn her head. She hunched her shoulders so her tall frame looked smaller. The shadow froze. She could feel eyes on her back. Bingo.

The mayor liked to brag how far the New York City crime rate had fallen, but Washington Square at night didn't disappoint. In her short time here she'd learned it was full of junkies who couldn't resist a blond girl with a full wallet, especially under the cover of night.

Gaia didn't alter the rhythm of her steps. An attacker proceeded differently when he sensed your awareness. Any deception was her advantage.

The energy was building in her veins. Come on, she urged silently. Her mind was beautifully blank. Her concentration was perfect. Her ears were pricked to decipher the subtlest motion.

Yet she could have sensed the clumsy attacker thundering from the brush if she'd been deaf and blind. A heavy arm was thrown over her shoulders and tightened around her neck.

"Oh, please," she muttered, burying an elbow in his solar plexus.

As he staggered backward and sucked for air, she turned on him indignantly. Yes, it was a big, clumsy, stupid him—a little taller than average and young, probably not even twenty years old. She felt a tiny spark of hope as she let her eyes wander through the bushes. Maybe there were more . . . ? The really incompetent dopes usually traveled in packs. But she heard nothing more than his noisy, X-rated complaints.

She let him come at her again. Might as well get a shred of a workout. She even let him earn a little speed as he barreled toward her. She loved turning a man's own strength against him. That was the essence of it. She reversed his momentum with a fast knee strike and finished him off with a front kick.

He lay sprawled in a half-conscious pile, and she was tempted to demand his wallet or his watch or something. A smile flickered over her face. It would be amusing, but that wasn't the point, was it?

Just as she was turning away, she detected a faint glitter on the ground near his left arm. She came closer and leaned down. It was a razor blade, shiny but not perfectly clean. In the dark she couldn't tell if the crud on the blade was rust or blood. She glanced quickly at her hands. No, he'd done her no harm. But it lodged in her mind as a strange choice of weapon.

She walked away without bothering to look further. She knew he'd be fine. Her specialty was subduing without causing any real damage. He'd lie there for a few minutes. He'd be sore, maybe bruised tomorrow. He'd brush the cobwebs off his imagination to invent a story for his buddies about how three seven-foot, three-hundred-pound male karate black belts attacked him in the park.

But she would bet her life on the fact that he would never sneak up on another fragile-looking woman without remembering this night. And that was the point. That was what Gaia lived for.

"WHO CAN COME TO THE BOARD AND

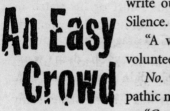

write out the quadratic formula?" Silence.

"A volunteer, please? I need a volunteer."

No. Gaia sent the teacher telepathic missiles. *Do not call on me.*

"Come on, kids. This is basic stuff. You are supposed to be the advanced class. Am I in the wrong room?"

The teacher's voice—what was the woman's name again?—was reedy and awful sounding. Gaia really should have remembered the name, considering this *was not* the first day.

No. No. No. The teacher's eyes swept over the second-to-back row twice before they rested on Gaia. *Shit.*

"You, in the . . . brown, is it? What's your name?"

"Gaia."

"Gay what?"

15

Every member of the class snickered.

The beautiful thing about Gaia was that she didn't hate them for laughing. In fact, she loved them for being so predictable. It made them so manageable. There was nothing those buttheads could give that Gaia couldn't take.

"Guy. (Pause) Uh."

The teacher cocked her head as if the name were some kind of insult. "Right, then. Come on up to the board. Guy (pause) uh."

The class snickered again.

God, she hated school. Gaia dragged herself out of her chair. Why was she here, anyway? She didn't want to be a doctor or a lawyer. She didn't want to be a CIA agent or Green Beret or superoperative *X-Files* type, like her dad had obviously hoped.

What did she want to be when she grew up? (She loved that question.) A waitress. She wanted to serve food at some piece-of-crap greasy spoon and wait for a customer to bitch her out, or stiff her on the tip, or PINCH HER BUTT. She'd travel across the country from one bad restaurant to the next and scare people who thought it was okay to be mean to waitresses. And there were a lot of people like that. Nobody got more shit than a waitress did. (Well, maybe telemarketers, but they sort of deserved it.)

"Gaia? Any day now."

Snicker. Snicker. This was an easy crowd. Ms.

What's-her-face must have been thrilled with her success.

Gaia hesitated at the board for a moment.

"You don't know it, do you?" The teacher's tone was possibly the most patronizing thing she had ever heard.

Gaia didn't answer. She just wrote the formula out very slowly, appreciating the horrible grinding screech of the chalk as she drew the equals sign. It sounded a lot like the teacher's voice, actually.

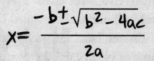

$$x = \frac{-b \pm \sqrt{b^2 - 4ac}}{2a}$$

At the last second she changed the final plus to a minus sign. Of course she knew the formula. What was she, stupid? Her dad had raced her through basic algebra by third grade. She'd (begrudgingly) mastered multivariable calculus and linear algebra before she started high school. She might hate math, but she was good at it.

"I'm sorry, Gaia. That's incorrect. You may sit down."

Gaia tried to look disappointed as she shuffled to her chair.

"Talk to me after class about placement, please." The teacher said that in a slightly lower voice, as if the rest of the students wouldn't hear she found Gaia unfit for the class. "Yes, ma'am," Gaia said brightly. It was the first ray of light all day. She'd demote herself to memorizing times tables if it meant getting a different teacher.

Times tables actually came in pretty handy for a waitress. What with figuring out tips and all.

HE SAW HER RIGHT AFTER THE seventh-period bell rang. She seemed dressed for the sole purpose of blending in with the lockers, but

Not Cloying

she stood out, anyway. It didn't matter that her wide blue eyes were narrowed or that her pretty mouth was twisted into a near snarl—she was blatantly beautiful. It was kind of sick the way Ed was preoccupied with beautiful girls these days.

There weren't many people left in the hall at this point. He, of course, had permission to take his own sweet time getting to class. And she was probably lost. She cast him a quick glance as she strode down the hall. The kind of glance where she saw him without actually seeing him. He was used to that.

He felt a little sorry for her. (He was also preoccupied

with finding ways of feeling sorry for people.) She was new and trying hard not to look it. She was confused and trying to look tough. It was endearing is what it was.

"Hey, can I help you find a classroom or anything?"

She swiveled around and glared at him like he'd made a lewd remark. (Was she some kind of mind reader?)

"Excuse me?" she demanded. She wasn't afraid to give him a good once-over.

"You look lost," he explained.

Now she was angry. "This is not what lost looks like. This is what annoyed looks like. And no, I don't need any help. Thanks."

It was the spikiest, least gracious "thanks" he'd ever heard. "Anytime," he said, trying not to smile. "So, what's your name?"

"Does it matter?" She couldn't believe he was prolonging the conversation.

"Mine's Ed, by the way."

"I'm so happy for you." She gave him an extra snarl before she bolted down the hall to the science wing.

He smiled all the way to physics class. He almost laughed out loud when he passed through the door and saw her shadowy, hunched-over form casting around for a seat in the back.

She was in his class; this was excellent. Maybe she'd call him a name if he struck up another conversation.

Even curse him out. That might be fun. God, he'd probably earn himself a restraining order if he tried to sit next to her.

He was so tired of saccharine smiles and cloying tones of voice. People always plastered their eyes to his face for fear of looking anywhere else. He was fed up with everybody being so goddamned nice.

That's why he'd already fallen in love with this weird, maladjusted, beautiful girl who carried a chip the size of Ohio on her shoulder. Because nobody was ever mean to the guy in the wheelchair.

September 23

My Dearest Gaia,

I saw a mouse race across the floor of my apartment today, and it made me think of you. (What doesn't make me think of you?) It reminded me of the winter of Jonathan and your secret efforts to save his little life. I never imagined I'd think longingly upon an oversized gray field mouse whose contribution to our lives was a thousand turds on the kitchen counter, but I grew to love him almost as much as you did.

Oh, Gaia. It feels as if it's been so long. Do you still love rodents and other despised creatures? Do you still carry a pocket full of pennies for luck? Do you still eat your cereal without milk? Do you ever think about me anymore?

I write it and think it so often, it's a mantra, but

*Gaia, how desperately I hope you'll forgive me someday.
You'll understand why I did what I did, and you'll know
it was because I love you. I have so many doubts and
fears, my darling, and they seem to grow as the days between us pass. But I know I love you. I'd give my life for
you. Again.*

Tom Moore lifted his pen at the sound of the
beeper. God, he hated that sound. He didn't need to
look at the readout to know who was summoning him.
It wasn't as if he had friends and family swarming
about—it was his self-inflicted punishment that if he
couldn't be with his daughter, he would be alone.

He snatched the wretched little device from his
desk and threw it across the room, mildly amazed at
his own rare show of temper as the beeper bounced
off the windowsill and skittered across the wood floor.
It was always the same people. It was always an emergency. By tomorrow he'd be in a different time zone.

Before he picked up the phone, he walked to the
ancient aluminum filing cabinet and opened it. He
thumbed through the files without needing to look.
Locating the thick pile of papers, he placed the letter
at the front, just as he always did with all the others,
unsent and locked in the drawer.

MacDougal and

LaGuardia—

bzzzt—slashing

victim, female

African American

in her **stupid**

thirties—

bzzzt—

hobby

young male

perpetrator—

bzzzz . . .

a

"HELLO, CEEENDY."

"Hi, Zolov. What's shaking?"

"Shakeeeng?"

Gaia laughed. "How are you playing?"

Zolov worked his mouth. He drew his wrinkly brown hand over his lips, thinking about the question seriously. "I beat everyone."

"Of course you did," Gaia said loudly. "You're the best."

He nodded absently. "Tank you. You are a good geerl."

In spite of the fact she was practically shouting at him, Gaia could tell he was reading her lips and that it was tiring for him. He sat back in the sunshine, ready for his next opponent, who would very likely not show. His favorite chessboard was set. As always, it was presided over by one of the Mighty Morphin Power Rangers, a red, helmeted action figure he'd probably picked up in somebody's garbage. He never played without him.

Gaia would have sat down across from him if she'd had more than twenty cents in her pocket. Instead she lay back on the bench and closed her eyes.

This park, these chess tables, was Gaia's favorite place. It was her home in New York more than George and Ella's house ever

24

would be. Zolov was at least ninety years old and thought her name was Cindy, but even so, he was her favorite person.

Who says I have no life? she mused as she stretched her arms behind her head, feeling the fabric of her gray T-shirt creeping over her belly button. She inhaled the scent of sugary nuts roasting in a pushcart nearby. This was her favorite place, and that was her favorite smell. It was so sweet and strong, she could practically taste it. One of these days she was going to buy a big bag of those nuts and scarf them down without even pausing to breathe.

She felt a shadow come over her face and squinted one eye open. "Hey, Renny," she said. "You ready for 'dimes of demonstration'?"

Renny was a thirteen-year-old Puerto Rican boy—Gaia's second-favorite person. He was a self-proclaimed poet and such a whiz at chess he hustled great sums of money out of almost anybody who was dumb enough to sit down across from him. Today his face didn't light up with its usual bravado.

Gaia sat up and put a hand over her eyes to block the sun. "You're scared I'm going to steal your money and make you cry?" she taunted. She scanned the tables for a free board.

As she did, her eye snagged on a new piece of graffiti splayed on the asphalt just to the left of Zolov's usual table. A swastika. It was at least a foot across, and the white paint was as fresh and bright as a new pair of sneakers. Gaia's stomach was filled with lead. Could it be for her benefit? she wondered. Could somebody possibly know how the Holocaust had decimated her mother's family and made her grandparents into heroes? No. Not likely. She was being paranoid. How would anyone know about her Jewish background? In fact, when she told some people, they acted all surprised—like if you had fair hair and blue eyes, it wasn't possible. That really annoyed her.

Her eyes flicked over the ugly shape again. Had Renny seen it? Had Zolov? Did they think anything of it?

For some reason Renny wasn't jumping in with his usual rhyming insults and eager put-downs.

"Gaia, you oughtta go home," Renny said almost inaudibly in the direction of his sneakers.

This was odd. "What's up, Renny?"

"It's gonna get dark," he noted.

"Thanks, Ren. It usually does." He was wearing a stiff new jacket that advertised its brand name from three different spots. He licked his lips. "You oughtta, you know, be watching out," he continued.

"For what?" she asked.

He considered this question a moment. "The park is real dangerous after dark."

Gaia stood, impatient. She swept a strand of hair behind her ear. "Renny, cut the bullshit. What's the matter? What are you talking about?"

"Did you hear about Lacy's sister?" His face was slightly pink, and he wasn't meeting her gaze.

"No, why?"

"It was on the news and everything. All the kids are talking about it. She got slashed in the park last night," Renny explained. "She had to get sewn up from her eyebrow to her ear."

"God, that's awful," Gaia said. "What kind of blade?"

"What?"

"What kind of blade?"

Renny gave her a strange look.

"Was it a razor blade?" Gaia persisted.

"I guess. I don't know." He looked up at her a little defiantly. "How am I supposed to know?"

"Just asking, Renny." She softened her tone. "Thanks for warning me. I do appreciate it."

He nodded, his face growing pinker. "I was just . . . you know, concerned about you." He tried to look very tall as he shuffled away.

Gaia swung her beat-up messenger bag over her shoulder as she watched him. She had a bad feeling about this. She sensed that Renny was no longer satisfied with the insular world of chess misfits. He was starting to care what the big boys thought—those stupid boys who hung around the fountain, trying to look tough. Renny was smarter and funnier and more original than they'd ever be, but he was thirteen. He was at that brutal age when many kids would sell all the uniqueness in their character for the right pair of shoes. She longed to tell him not to spend so much time in the park, to go home to his mother, but who was she to talk?

Yes, Renny might be concerned about her. But not as concerned as she was about him.

She herself loved this misfit world, Gaia mused as she surveyed the tables. Curtis, a fifteen-year-old black kid, was sitting across from Mr. Haq, a Pakistani taxicab driver who appeared to like nothing more than parking his yellow cab on Washington Square South and killing an afternoon over a chessboard.

She loved that people who couldn't begin to pronounce each other's names played and talked for hours. She loved that a forty-something-year-old cabdriver and a fifteen-year-old from the Manhattan Valley youth program had so much in common. She loved getting a break from the stupid hierarchy of high school.

She loved that there weren't people like . . . well, people like . . . h i m.

The him was walking by slowly, looking confidently over the boards in play. His hair was light in color—a tousled mixture of blond and brown and even a little red. His chinos were cuffed, and his preppy gray jacket flapped in the autumn breeze. Gaia felt her stomach do a quick pitch and roll. She felt queasy and strangely alert at the same time.

You didn't find people who looked like that . . . as in, stunningly, astonishingly good. People like him sipped coffee at Dean & Deluca or swing danced on Gap commercials or spouted Woody Allen–style dialogue on *Dawson's Creek,* where they belonged.

So what *the hell* was he doing lingering over chessboards with the freaks and geeks? She had half a mind to walk right over and tell him to get lost.

This was her favorite place, and he had no business here, reminding her of things she would never be.

Don't Be Afraid

"Thank you, Marco, you're a sweetheart."

Marco nodded at the woman, making sure to tilt his chin so she had a good look at his left side, the side where his broken nose hardly showed at all. "No problem." He kept his voice deep and smooth. She probably thought he was like twenty-five or something.

She took a long sip from the bottle of Coke he'd brought her, exposing her pale neck. She lifted one leg to rest on the low wall of the fountain, revealing several more inches of thigh under her stretchy aqua miniskirt. He tried not to stare. Or did she want him to stare?

He stopped breathing completely as she slowly, slowly brushed her fingers over his upper arm. "What happened here?" she asked.

He glanced at the purplish bruise. He paused before answering and cleared his throat, trying to make certain his voice didn't come out squeaky. "Nothing much. I got jumped last night. These three big guys thought they were real tough. Probably black belts in karate or something."

Her eyes widened in just the way he'd hoped. "You're okay? Did you call the police?"

"Uh-uh. That's not how we—how I—do things." Marco ran a hand through his dark hair. It had come out perfectly today. "I've got some friends who will back me up if those guys ever come back here." Marco loved the way she watched him when he talked. So he kept talking. He wasn't even listening to what he was saying.

Man, she was gorgeous. She was older than he, twenty-something at least, but sexy as hell. Like some kind of goddess with her straight red hair and green eyes. And the legs on her. He couldn't look away.

He'd first noticed her at the beginning of the summer. All the guys noticed her—it was hard not to. She lived around here, he guessed, because she walked by this fountain almost every afternoon. He wasn't the only one who magically turned up each day around four o'clock to watch the show.

Lately he'd noticed she'd started returning his looks. Just a glance at first, but then her eyes stayed longer. Last week she'd said hello to him, and he'd practically peed in his pants. Today she'd been late, so most of the guys had wandered away, but some kind of crazy instinct made him stay.

He took his eyes off her breasts for a moment to see if he spotted anybody he knew. He would love for any one of his buddies to see him right now.

Just then she reached toward his collarbone and rested her index finger on the pendant that lay there. The electricity from her touch surged through his chest and seemed to throw his heart off rhythm. "What is this?" Her voice was almost a whisper. "I've seen this before."

He studied her face before he answered. He wasn't sure how much to tell—how much she really wanted to know. "It's, uh, it's called a hieroglyph—you know, like ancient Egyptian writing? It's the symbol for . . . uh, power."

"Where have I seen it before?" Her green eyes fixed on his.

His glance darted around the fountain. "I don't know. Maybe you saw one of the other guys wearing it. Maybe a tattoo on somebody's arm. It's kind of a . . . I don't know . . . kind of a . . ."

His voice trailed off awkwardly. He didn't want her thinking he was some kind of thug. He sure didn't want anybody to overhear him telling her secret stuff.

"A mark?" she supplied. "Some sort of identification?" She didn't appear wary the way most girls he knew would. Her eyes were wide and intense, fascinated.

"Yeah, like that."

"Ah. I see. Are you part of—"

Marco sucked in his breath. Suddenly this didn't seem so cool. What if she was an undercover cop or some kind of informer? He'd heard of stuff like this. He backed up, putting a few feet between them. "I gotta be going. It's, like, after six, and I—"

With two steps she closed the distance. "Marco. Don't be afraid of me." Her fingers fluttered over his cheek. "Don't tell me anything you don't want to. I'm just . . . interested, that's all. I'm interested in everything about you."

All the blood in his body seemed to pool in his

32

head. He felt dizzy. "You're not, like, a cop or anything?" He was pretty sure she'd have to say so if she were.

She laughed. "No. Most definitely not." She gave him a look. It was a mischievous, sexy kind of look. "*Definitely* not."

GAIA SMACKED THE SHORTWAVE RADIO

Rapunzel Monkey

that sat on the table next to the bed. Her bed. She had trouble thinking of anything in this house as hers.

"Piece of crap," she murmured. She'd picked up the radio at a junk shop on Canal Street. She'd gotten it to tune in to the local police frequency, but the damn thing emitted almost nothing but static. She rearranged the antenna she'd rigged until she heard a break in the fuzz. She rolled off the bed and walked to the window. Ah, that was good. She could decipher various bleeps that sounded almost like words. She stood by the door. Oh, it liked that. Now she could actually understand the words.

Bzzzzt—MacDougal and LaGuardia—*bzzzt*—slashing

victim, female African American in her thirties—
bzzzt—young male perpetrator—*bzzzz . . .*

Dammit. She tried jumping up and down.

—lost him in the park—*bzzzzzzzzz . . .*

Shit. Gaia grabbed the radio and threw it off the table. What a stupid hobby. Why couldn't she just watch *Roswell* like a normal girl?

Well, for one thing, because the television was in the so-called family room. It would mean walking past, possibly even fraternizing with, George and his bimbo bride. It wasn't that she didn't like George. She did. He was trying really hard to make her feel comfortable. He tried so hard, in fact, that she found it awkward to be around him. He put on this peppy voice and asked her about her classes or her friends. What was she going to say, "I see my math teacher through crosshairs"? "My best friend has Alzheimer's"? George wanted something within the universe of normal, and she simply couldn't give him that.

Ella was another story. Stupid, vain Ella she genuinely disliked. There were Ella's fingernails, her passion for Victoria's Secret catalogs, her love of Mariah Carey. That was about it for Ella. How in the world had a sensible man like George fallen prey to a tarty thing like her? And God, he had fallen.

Gaia really needed some air. She strode to the door

of the room and listened for signs of life. What sucked was that her room was on the fourth floor of the four-story house. She hid up there during the little time she spent in the house because she hated walking past every other room on her way in and out. She was like a latter-day Rapunzel except her hair was only a few inches below her shoulders, slightly fried, not all that blond, and furthermore, who the hell was ever going to climb up to give her a hand? The guy in the wheel-chair from school?

What she—and Rapunzel, frankly—needed was a decent ladder.

Gaia opened the door slowly. Hopefully George was still at work and Ella was—who ever knew where Ella was? By profession Ella considered herself a pho-tographer, but Gaia had a hard time taking her seri-ously. It gave Ella an excuse to saunter through hip downtown neighborhoods with a camera slung over her shoulder. Apparently she got the odd commission to photograph somebody's dog or living room or something. Her "work," as George called it in his pious way, was displayed over most of the wall space in the house—mostly arty black-and-white pictures of dolls' heads and high-heeled shoes.

Thank God for the automatic camera that makes it all possible, Gaia thought sarcastically as she crept through the hallway and down the stairs.

At the second landing she was faced once again

by "the photograph." Most days she averted her eyes. Although Ella hadn't taken it, it was by far the most upsetting in the house. It was a picture of an eleven-year-old Gaia with her parents, snapped by George the week he visited them at their country house in the Berkshires. Once Gaia looked at the photo, she found it hard to look away and, after that, hard to get her mind to cooperate with her.

The Gaia in the picture made her think of a little monkey, clinging to her dad with long skinny arms, her wrists circled by several filthy friendship bracelets, her narrow shoulders lost in the beloved brown fisherman's sweater he'd bought for her on a trip to Ireland. Gaia's smile was big and exuberant, so pitifully unaware of what the next year would bring.

Now Gaia moved her gaze to her mother, even as she willed herself not to. If Gaia's face in the picture was all embarrassing openness, her mother's was pure mystery. No matter how many times Gaia searched it, no matter how clearly she saw those features, she felt she couldn't tell what her mother really looked like. She *needed* something from that face that it never gave. The same miserable questions started their spiraling march through Gaia's brain: *Why am I holding Daddy and not you? Why aren't I beautiful like you? Did you love me, anyway? Did you ever know how much I loved you?*

And then, as always, the thoughts got so unfathomably sad, they didn't even come in words. Her throat started to ache, and her vision swam. She couldn't pull enough air into her lungs. Without exactly realizing what she was doing, her hands shot out and yanked the framed photograph off the wall.

"What are you doing?"

Gaia spun around. Her heart was bouncing in her chest, and it took her a moment to focus her eyes on Ella. She cleared her throat. She took a deep breath. She tried to rearrange her posture into something less rigid.

"I am removing this picture from the wall."

"Can I ask why?"

"Sure."

Ella waited impatiently. "Okay, why?"

Gaia placed the picture facedown on the bookcase. She glanced at her watch. "I didn't say I'd answer."

Ella got that eye-rolling martyred look. "Gaia, you know George loves that picture. He put it up for you."

Gaia cleared her throat again. She tried shrugging, but it didn't come off with the indifference she was aiming for. "If George put it up for my benefit, he won't mind if I take it down."

Ella's hands found their way to her hips as they mostly did within a few minutes of starting a conversation with Gaia. "I swear, Gaia, George does so much for you. I would think you could at least—"

Gaia tuned out the shrill voice as she made her way

down the rest of the steps and out the front door. She knew every word of the speech. There wouldn't be any vocabulary words or clever turns of phrase. Ella wasn't going to surprise her.

Gaia took the sidewalk at a near run. She felt like she might explode. The sky was darkening as she turned left on West 4th Street, leaving bustling outdoor cafes, overpriced little restaurants, all-night delis, her favorite subterranean record shop behind her in a blur.

She headed straight for the park. No one was going to scare her out of her shortcut. And certainly not tonight, not in the mood she was in. And in fact, she hoped they'd try. Let them find her instead of some kid or some old guy who wouldn't know how to handle it. Maybe if she did this enough, those creeps would learn that everyone who looked vulnerable wasn't necessarily so. What a gorgeous lesson to teach them. After all, wasn't that what her gifts were all about? Power to the little people!

She spun
around,
instantly
accosted by
strange
blurred
images.
A flash of
chrome. Two
large
wheels.

mr.
valiant

THREE MORE STEPS. OKAY, FIVE MORE

steps. Okay, ten more. Just to
the maple tree. Okay, not that
one, the one behind it.

A Force for Good

She was a little nuts. She knew
it. Skulking around Washington
Square Park for three hours and
twenty-three minutes, counting
steps (and okay, seconds), looking for trouble. It could be
called entrapment. That's exactly what she wanted to do,
entrap those lowlifes.

Gaia lingered under the tree, feeling drops of sweat
sliding down her spine. Wasn't New York City supposed to be getting cool in September? The smell of
late season pollen was so thick, it felt like paste in her
nostrils. Please, somebody. Anybody. She'd come here
with the secret hope that one of the notorious slashers
would have a go at her, but now she'd grown desperate. She would take absolutely any criminal, from
petty shoplifter to ax murderer; she
really wasn't choosy. Hey, who even needed a criminal? She was ready to pounce on the strength of a big
mouth or a bad attitude.

But she wouldn't. Gaia would never attack anybody unprovoked. She would never do more harm
than necessary. That was the code, and as much
as she hated her father, she was still bound to honor it.
It was bred into her, just like her blue eyes that seemed

to change shade with her mood, the weather, the color of her shirt. Just like her love of sweets. She had to use her Miraculous Gift (that's what her father always called it) as a force for good. Her mission was to draw out violent behavior and squash it, not to produce more violence.

But sometimes carrying out her mission felt more self-indulgent than honorable. Did it count as a good deed if you enjoyed yourself? She liked to think she thrived on self-defense. But there were times, really upsetting times, when she saw the line between defense and offense as clear as day and barreled toward it. Hey, she had an extraordinary talent, and she wanted to use it.

What if one day she crossed that line that separated good guys from bad guys? It would be easy. There was only a hair's width between them. Why hadn't anyone warned her that inside the crucible of real anger, good and bad were so nearly the same?

Worse yet, what if one day she'd stop being able to see the line at all? She wouldn't know anymore if she was good or bad or crazy or sane. Maybe Gaia didn't know the meaning of scary, but that sounded an awful lot like it.

Gaia made a slow loop around the maple tree. She had to get out of this park, but she really didn't feel like going back to George and Ella's. God forbid

George would put on that earnest face and try to talk about "her loss" as he often did after Ella complained about her.

She didn't feel like walking on Broadway—the street was mobbed with NYU students, tourists, and shoppers at every hour of the day. Instead she turned south on Mercer Street. She loved the deserted, `canyonlike feel` of the narrow street and the sound her steps made on the cobblestones. She'd walk straight down to Houston Street and see what was playing at the Angelika.

Suddenly, as if in answer to a prayer, Gaia heard voices behind her. She stopped and fumbled through her backpack as if she were looking for something. Jeez, what a girl had to do to get mugged in this city.

The voices turned into whispers, and then she heard footsteps, slow. Oh, *yes*. Finally. She turned toward the noise, pasting what she hoped looked like a terrified expression on her face. Inside, her heart was leaping with anticipation.

There were three of them, and they looked young—around sixteen or seventeen. Two of them had shaved heads. The smallest brandished a razor blade. `Gaia detected more than a hint of nervousness under his swagger.` She backed up (fearfully, she hoped), wanting the situation to escalate. She hated herself, but there it was.

The little thug was up front, covering the ground

between them with a menacing lurch. The other two were hanging back, present to witness this feat of loyalty. It was becoming obvious to Gaia what was up here, and it pissed her off.

Come on, boys, she silently encouraged them. *Come and get me.* Her mind hovered on the swastika she'd seen painted on the ground in the park. That coupled with the shaved heads and the leather jackets gave her the strong suspicion that these assholes were some kind of neo-Nazi white supremacist outfit.

Her concentration was so keen, she had to remind herself to keep breathing. She couldn't let her anger get the best of her. She had to play this just right. If she struck back too quickly, she might scare them away. The kid was trying hard to look tough, but his toughness went about as deep as the sheen of sweat on his upper lip.

Now. He was right on her, razor blade lifted. She screamed helplessly as she drew back her arm for a sharp blow to his wrist. And just as she balanced her weight to deliver the strike she heard a thunderous shout and a commotion behind her.

Suddenly noise was coming from every direction. Her adrenaline was rising fast, but her focus was thrown. She spun around, instantly accosted by strange blurred images. A flash of chrome. Two large wheels. She jumped back to try to make sense of it.

"Get away from her!" a familiar voice shouted.

Gaia's razor-blade-wielding attacker fell back in confusion.

Equally confused, Gaia swiveled her head.

"It's okay, Gaia! Go! Run!"

She watched in perfect amazement as Ed, the guy in the wheelchair from school, rolled into the fray. Her very own knight in shining armor come to save the day.

"You've got to be joking," she muttered under her breath.

But no, there he was. Mr. Valiant.

Now what was she supposed to do? She couldn't just burst into action with Ed sitting on the sidelines. He'd see everything. He'd know far more than he was allowed.

It was one thing showing an attacker her tricks. Every time she did this, she made a wager that her attacker wouldn't confess to being pounded by a girl, and she'd never been wrong. But Ed was a different story. Ed would tell the nifty adventure to everybody in school. They'd probably recruit her for the judo club or something.

The adrenaline was surging through her veins, and the primary person she wanted to strangle was Ed.

The three attackers had been as surprised as she by Ed's arrival, but they were now regrouping.

Okay, fine. She'd take a couple of hits. She wouldn't

let the razor blade near her, but that would be easy enough to dispose of in a stealthy way. They'd hit her. She'd scream. Somebody would hear the noise and call the cops. The three losers would feel manly and dangerous and go away. The little one would earn his initiation on somebody else.

It was disappointing as hell, but she'd deal.

ED FARGO PUSHED HIS WHEELS AS

One Small Problem

fast as he could. He sailed over the curb and bumped along the cobblestones. He'd often dreamed of running over somebody with his wheelchair, but he'd never actually done it before. His lungs ached for air and his arms ached with exertion as he plowed through the low bushes and into the guy with the razor blade. Thank God he'd been coming along Mercer just then. Thank God he'd heard the scream.

He heard the powerful meeting of metal and shin bone.

"Ahhhhhhh!" The attacker fell backward.

"Gaia, get out of here!" Ed shouted again. He'd never felt quite so important in his life.

She looked stunned. Why the hell wouldn't she get her ass out of there? Was she paralyzed with fear? So traumatized, she couldn't move a muscle? Thank God he'd arrived when he had. "Please go!" he commanded.

The guy with the razor blade fumbled back up to his feet, and his two accomplices came closer in for backup. Ed realized he didn't have much time. Panic was taking hold of his chest. He looked at Gaia's frozen form. He looked at the three hoods gathering for attack. Oh, man. This time their vicious eyes weren't focused on Gaia; they were aiming directly at him. Oh, oh, oh.

His brain was spinning. His heart was pounding at least five hundred times a minute. The obvious thing to do was get out of there as fast as his arms would carry him, but he couldn't. He couldn't just leave Gaia standing there. She'd be slaughtered.

"What is wrong with you?" Ed bellowed at her. "Get the hell out of here *now!*"

Three big angry thugs were closing in and that stupid girl wouldn't move. Panic was now weirdly tinged with resignation. He was dead. If they wanted to kill him, that is. Maybe they'd be satisfied just mangling him or slashing him to ribbons.

The biggest of the three took hold of the armrest of his wheelchair and gave it a powerful shove. Ed collided hard with the street and rolled from the toppled chair.

This was sad. It sure would have been handy if his legs worked right now. He looked up at the stripe of night sky between the old cast-iron buildings, waiting for the first blow. He put his arms over his face for protection.

Slam! He heard the sound of a foot connecting with hard flesh and then a deep moan. Was that him? Had he made that noise? He heard another searing blow. Jesus, was he so far gone, he couldn't even feel the pain?

He moved an arm away from his face and cracked open one eye. He heard a groan and then a barking shout. Strange. He was pretty sure his mouth was shut. He opened the other eye and sat up. Then he shut both eyes again. Had he gone into cardiac arrest and died already? God, that was quick. Weren't there supposed to be a lot of warm feelings and long tunnels and a bright light?

He simply could not have seen what he thought he saw. He was dead. Or hallucinating. Maybe that was it. His mind was dealing him some truly mind-bending hallucinations. Awesome ones, as it happened. He opened his eyes again. His mouth dropped open.

Gaia Moore, the lovely girl with the slim frame and sullen expression who haunted the back of his physics class, had suddenly transformed into Xena, Warrior Princess, only blond and even more beautiful. She crushed the jaw of Thug 1 with a roundhouse kick.

She struck Thug 2 in the chest with such violence, he was left gasping for breath. Thug 3 came swinging at her from behind, and she spun around and neutralized him with a stunning kick-boxing move he'd only ever seen executed by Jean Claude Van Damme.

Holy shit. Could this actually be real? Gaia's dauntless, intense, angry face looked real. The thonk of her sneakered foot in Thug 1's belly sounded real.

Unbelievable. Gaia was a superhero. Hair flying, limbs whirling, she was the most graceful, powerful martial artist he had ever laid eyes on. Her every move was a mesmerizing combination of ballet and kung fu. And not only was she magical, she was lethal. Thug 1 was writhing on the ground, Thug 2 was ready to flee. Although Thug 3 appeared to be rallying, Ed almost pitied him.

Suddenly Ed sucked in the moist night air. A chill began in his fingertips and crept up his wrists and arms. He saw only a flash at first, and then the image resolved itself. Thug 3 had a knife. Ed saw it clearly now glinting in the streetlight, looking awfully real.

Oh, my God.

Did Gaia see the knife? Did she realize what was coming? He certainly couldn't tell by her expression. Her eyes revealed not even the tiniest hint of fear. Jesus, she was tough. That or paranormally stupid.

"Gaia!" he heard his own voice bellowing. "He's got a knife!"

Her gaze didn't flicker. She stood there motionless as Thug 3 went after her. She looked as if she were in some kind of deep meditation.

Ed was hyperventilating. He didn't care how tough Gaia was; she couldn't defend herself against an eight-inch blade. Presumably her skin was made of the same stuff his was. He had to do something.

He supplied his seizing brain with some oxygen, then dragged himself toward his wheelchair. He pulled it upright and set his sights on the slouching back of Thug 3. Ed's legs might be useless, but his arm strength was formidable. He launched the chair like a missile.

Strike! The chair hit its mark, and Thug 3 staggered forward. Ed briefly registered the look of surprise on Gaia's face as Thug 3 careened into her and sent her sprawling backward. His stomach clenched. Oh, God. That hadn't been his intention at all.

Now the guy retrieved his knife and leaped on top of Gaia. Worse yet, from Thug 2's cowardly hideout behind a parked car, he saw the tide turn and was racing back to join the fight. Ed dragged himself toward Gaia as fast as he could, his eyes fixed on her vulnerable throat and the knife hovering over it. "Stop!" he roared. "You're going to kill her!" He felt tears stinging his eyes.

It happened so fast, Ed wasn't sure he'd actually seen it. Gaia delivered a powerful kick exactly to the groin of Thug 2 and almost simultaneously struck Thug 3 in the side of the neck with her hand. Thug 3 rolled over, unconscious. His knife skidded along the stones. Thug 2 pitched to the ground, screaming in pain.

Gaia was instantly on her feet. She scooped up the knife and stepped over the prone body of Thug 3. Suddenly Thug 1 and Thug 2 seemed to forget their pain and sprinted for safety like jackrabbits in traffic.

Ed was watching Gaia, his heart overflowing with relief and admiration, when she surprised him again.

She got to the sidewalk and collapsed. Her legs literally crumpled under her body, and without a noise she fell in a heap on the pavement.

GAIA BREATHED DEEPLY AND WAITED

for it to pass. She wouldn't struggle to move or attempt to get to her feet. She knew by now it wouldn't work. The only thing to do was wait.

That Old Kryptonite

Pretty much right on

schedule, she heard a noisy approach and felt a hand on her shoulder. Argh. She didn't need to open her eyes to see the worried, eager face.

Once he'd reached her, she heard him collapse beside her. Listening to his labored breathing, Gaia's heart was pulled forcefully by two equal and opposite desires:

1. Her desire to hug Ed for his valiant, misguided efforts on her behalf.
2. Her desire to murder him for being such an unbelievable pain in the ass.

"Are you okay?" He touched her shoulder again. She could hear the fear in his words.

She would have really liked to rouse herself right then. It was unthinkable that he should see her in this state of weakness—to see what happened to her after one of these episodes. And yet there was just no way around it short of killing him, which, though tempting, didn't seem all that sporting under the circumstances.

"Gaia? Gaia?" His voice was rising with panic.

"Mmmm," she mumbled.

"Oh, God, are you hurt? Did they hurt you?"

A yellow cab cruised past them, slowed for a stop sign, then drove on. If anyone in the car saw them, they apparently hadn't felt the need to get involved. That was New York City for you. Its inhabitants set a high standard for unusual.

With great effort she fluttered open her eyes and very slowly, by inches, shook her head. The sidewalk made a really bad pillow.

"What's the matter? Should I call for an ambulance?"

She gritted her teeth. If she'd had any energy left, she would have rolled her eyes. "Mm. Mmm." After another pause she reinforced it with another slight shake of her head.

"No? Are you sure?"

She wasn't accustomed to anyone seeing her like this, and it was irritating. She found the strength to open her eyes for real and concentrate on Ed's face. It had suddenly become a much more significant face—the face of the guy who knew her secrets.

Holy shit. How had she let this happen?

It was so ironic. So ironic and pitiful and stupid and weird, she wanted to laugh. For some reason this guy had become her self-appointed guardian angel and nearly gotten her killed in the process. How typical that her guardian angel would be a slightly scruffy ex-skate rat in a wheelchair who caused so much more trouble than good. How strange it was that he suddenly knew more about her than anyone else on planet Earth. (Except her father, of course.)

Gaia had been so careful over the years to keep

everything secret. It was another of her father's curses: *I'll make you into a freak and not let you tell anyone.* Not like she was going to tell, anyway. She had no confidant and meant to keep it that way. Besides, the strange facts of her life were all connected. Telling a little would ultimately mean telling a lot.

"Gaia? Please tell me you're okay?"

It always seemed that when her body sank into this state of paralytic exhaustion, her mind zoomed into overdrive. She summoned the energy to move her lips. "I'm fine," she whispered.

"You don't look so fine."

Patience, Ed, she asked of him silently. She felt the energy returning to her muscles. It was tingly at first, as if her whole body had fallen asleep. She groaned a little as she sat up. She studied Ed. Worried, terrified, astonished, concerned Ed. She couldn't help but smile a little.

"I'm fine," she said. She paused for breath. "Except for the fact that I may have to kill you."

To: L
From: ELJ
Date: September 25
File: 776244
Subject: Gaia Moore
Last Seen: Mercer Street, New York City,
10:53 P.M.

Update: Subject observed in fight with 3
suspected gang members, one armed with
knife. Attack complicated by appearance of
young man in wheelchair. Motive unclear.
Confirmed subject's mastery of jujitsu.
Subject displayed other martial skills previously documented. All 3 attackers subdued.

Subject appeared injured but later observed to walk from incident unharmed.

To: ELJ
From: L
Date: September 26
File: 776244
Subject: Gaia Moore

Directives: Identify and create file on young man in wheelchair.

Issue immediate instruction: Subject not to be injured under any circumstances. Repercussions will be severe.

There is this other really freakish thing about me. I've never told anyone. I'd be way too humiliated.

Humiliation, by the way, is a truly terrible emotion. It's at the bottom of the pile. Much worse than fear, I bet. Since I don't have to have fear, why do I have to have humiliation? If only I could toss it wherever fear went. And while I was at it, I'd get rid of anger, hurt, compassion, betrayal. And self-ishness. Oh, and guilt. Definitely guilt. It's out of there. Without all of those things, I think I could imagine maybe being happy someday.

Hey, that's it. I, Gaia Moore, have discovered the secret to happiness. People have been searching for it since the begin-ning of time, but it took me, a seventeen-year-old with no philo-sophical, medical, or psychologi-cal training, to discover the truth:

Lobotomy. You don't have to
feel anything at all.

You heard it here first,
folks. And a full frontal lobotomy probably costs no more than
the average nose job.

Okay, where was I? Oh, yeah. No
wonder I'm digressing—I don't feel
like putting this into words.

I'm a virgin.

No, no. It's way worse than
that. I wish it were only that.

I've never had a boyfriend.

True, but nope. That doesn't
convey the depth of this particular humiliation.

I've never kissed anybody.

Okay, there you have it. Can
you say "loser"?

Let me try to soften this information with an excuse or two.
When I was twelve, I had something approaching a boyfriend, in
a preboyfriend kind of way. His
name was Stephen, and he lived
around the corner. He was the one
with the right kind of hair
(light brown, straight, no

cowlicks), the right kind of bike (specialized, like you care), the right kind of jeans (Gap, at the time). His parents had the right kind of car (red Jeep, good stereo) and a very large pool. For these reasons the popular girls sought him out. I liked him because he was secretly just as weird as me. We both played chess and knee football. We concocted these elaborate fantasy games set in Camelot or a mile under the sea, long after imaginary games are socially acceptable (age four, roughly). We were nerdy enough to watch Bill Nye, the Science Guy, but cool enough not to admit that to anybody but each other.

Hold on. Wait just a second. Why am I telling you all this? Am I really so desperate that I'll try to pass off a neighbor without underarm hair as some kind of romantic conquest? This represents a new low.

But it points to something

real, which is that I'm stunted. My love life got left behind with the rest of my life the autumn after my twelfth birthday. Eventually, when the moving van came, I told Stephen I hated him, just so as not to leave any threads dangling.

My life ended then, but I keep growing.

I usually pride myself on the fact that I don't care about being a freak or a misfit. I don't care what people think of me. But for some reason this kissing business, this lack of kissing business, bothers me, and I can't pretend it doesn't.

That's the very worst thing about it, really. How much it bothers me. How much I think about it.

I'm going to be brutally honest right now, and hopefully afterward I can snap back into some more comfortable state of denial.

Ready? Okay.

Of all the terrible things

that have happened in my life—my
mom, my dad, the life I lost—I'm
such a vain, petty, and selfish
person that I am most ashamed of
the fact that nobody has ever
kissed me.

This thought drives me to more
than the desire for a lobotomy.
This drives me to something
worse.

Yo, Rapunzel. Forget the ladder. There's a faster way down.

Ten years from now Heather's awfulness would have caught up with her, **bitch** and she'd be a **queen** disgruntled wretch pining for the glory days.

"I STARTED THINKING/NOT DRINKING

was better for me/so it got me to thinking/about getting a lobotomy..."

So Sweet, You'll Puke

"What did she just say?" Gaia was sitting behind a very large, very expensive mug of coffee across from Ed and squinting at the band that was playing in the far corner. Gaia was happy to ignore them. She'd seen plenty of unplugged garage bands in her day. But these weird snippets of songs kept floating into her consciousness and sticking there the way raspberry seeds stuck in her molars.

"Huh?" Ed asked.

"That singer. Did you hear the words?" Gaia asked.

Ed strained to listen over the clink of spoons and the hissing of the cappuccino machine. "Something about a lobotomy."

"You're joking," Gaia declared.

Ed gave her a puzzled look. "If so, it wasn't a very funny joke."

"No, I mean, she didn't actually say lobotomy."

"Okay, she didn't." Ed shrugged. "Why does it matter?"

Gaia stirred her coffee. "Never mind." She studied the singer. She looked a little like Ashley Judd before the makeup went on. An East Village version, anyway, with a wool stocking cap, hair so messy it was coagulating into dreads, and a tattoo of a spider that perched on her collarbone.

Gaia fidgeted in her chair. She didn't want to leave too much silence because Ed might bring up what happened last night and she really didn't want him to.

"You know what the problem is with these fancy brown sugar packets?" Gaia held one up. "The granules are too big. They don't dissolve. They just hang around in the bottom of your mug, so your coffee isn't as sweet as you want it to be until you get to the last sip, which is so sweet, you want to puke."

Ed looked both puzzled and slightly amused. "Huh. Hadn't thought of that." He gestured at the counter. "They have regular sugar up there."

Gaia nodded. Why had she gone for coffee after school with Ed?

Because he'd asked her, mainly. Because he'd tried to save her life, even though she'd ended up saving his. She should have remembered, before she'd accepted, that going for coffee with someone usually meant talking to them.

Ed was looking at her a little too meaningfully. He stretched his arms out in front of him. "Listen, Gaia, I just wanted to tell you that I—"

"I don't want to talk about it," Gaia jumped in quickly.

"Sorry?"

"I don't want to talk about it."

"What is *it*?"

Now he really was going to think she was a wacko. "It. Anything."

"You don't want to talk about anything?" Ed asked carefully.

Gaia tugged at her hair awkwardly. "I don't want to talk about last night. I don't want you to ask me any questions."

Ed nodded and digested that for a minute. "Hey, Gaia?"

"Yeah."

"I'll make you a promise."

"That sounds heavy."

Ed laughed. "Just listen, okay?"

"Okay."

"I promise that I won't ever ask you any questions, all right?"

Gaia laughed, too. "I think that was a question."

"Fine, so it was the last one."

"Fine."

Gaia was starting to sense too much friend-liness in the air, so she stood up. "I'm going to, um, get that regular sugar. I'll be right back."

"Good."

"Okay."

She walked to the counter with her mug. This

was so cozy and normal seeming, she felt as if she were inhabiting somebody else's body. Absently she dumped two packets of white sugar into her coffee.

Oh, yes, she was just a happy girl in the West Village, having coffee with a friend.

A troop of familiar-looking people streamed in. They were from school, she realized. The self-designated "beautiful people." There were three girls and two guys, and they were laughing about something. Their manner and wardrobe screamed, "Put me in a Banana Republic ad right now!" One girl in particular was quite beautiful, with long, shiny dark hair, slouchy chinos, and a collared shirt that was whiter and crisper than anything Gaia had ever owned.

Much as she wanted to dismiss them as they swarmed around her at the counter, ordering various combinations of lattes, au laits, con leches, and mochas in pretentious Italian sizes, Gaia couldn't help imagining some alternate universe where she was one of them.

What if she were witty and well dressed and carefree? What if her biggest dilemma in life were whether to order a grande latte or a magnifico mocha? What if that fairly cute one, the boy in the beat-up suede jacket, called her all the time? She studied his dark hair, so pleasantly dilapidated, and his hazel eyes. She allowed herself a look at his lips. What if he'd kissed her? Not just once but hundreds of times?

She felt a weird tingling in her lower extremities as the fantasy evolved in her mind. He'd be standing next to her, studying the coffee board, as familiar to her as a brother, and he'd reach for her without really thinking about it. She'd be wearing a cute little lavender sweater set and crisp khakis instead of these oversized drawstring army pants and her faded blue football tee. He'd loop an arm around her hips and draw her a little closer and order something she knew he'd order because he always ordered it. Then he'd order for her, too. Not because he was an asinine pig, but because he knew she loved hazelnut mochaccino even though it did cost six dollars. Then he'd pay, even though she'd tell him not to. And she'd say something so funny and adorable that he'd look at her, really look at her, and remember how beautiful she was and how much he loved her. Then he'd lean toward her and kiss her on the mouth. No tongue or anything. That would be tacky in the middle of a cafe. His kiss wouldn't be long or filled with questions or expectations because he could kiss her anytime he wanted and he didn't have anything to prove. It would be soft and real and simple, yet mean a thousand loving things. She would kiss him back, but not in a way that was desperate or inexperienced. And then—

Gaia suddenly realized that the boy she was kissing in her mind's eye had transformed. Gone were the dark hair and the suede jacket, replaced by ginger-colored hair that curled around his temples and a preppy gray twill jacket with a corduroy collar. And then she realized that this person who'd barged right into her fantasy was none other than him, the guy from the park—the guy who'd wandered by the chess tables. How did he get here? she demanded of herself stridently. Who invited *him?*

"Gaia?"

She was so startled and unnerved that she forgot she even had hands, let alone a steaming mug of coffee in one of them. In horror she watched the mug sail from her grasp and the brown sugary stuff leap out of it and land all over the front of that very white, very crisp shirt of her alternate-universe best girlfriend.

The girl screamed.

"Oh, shit," Gaia muttered.

Suddenly everybody burst into motion: The fairly cute boy was grabbing up napkins, the girls were buzzing all over their friend, the other boy was plucking pieces of mug from the mess on the floor.

Of course, Gaia knew that the right thing to do was

apologize a lot, hand the girl a few napkins, make a self-deprecating remark, and offer to get her shirt dry cleaned. But for some reason Gaia did none of those things. She just stood there, gaping like a complete moron.

The offended girl turned on her with narrowed eyes. "*Excuse* me, but you just poured boiling coffee down my shirt."

"I—," Gaia began.

"What the hell is your problem? Are you some kind of idiot? Could you at least apologize?" The girl didn't look so pretty anymore.

"I just—I—I'm really—"

"Hel-*lo?*" the girl demanded. "English? Do you speak English? *Habla español?*" This was apparently humorous to herself and to her friends.

Gaia really had been working up to a sincere and heartfelt apology, but this girl no longer deserved it. "Bitch," Gaia said under her breath. It was completely the wrong thing to do. The worst thing to do, but Gaia had a talent for that.

The ex–pretty girl stiffened. "*What?* Did you just say what I think you said? Who the hell do you think you are?"

Gaia turned away at this point. It was the only thing to do. Gaia heard the girl railing and threatening as she returned to the table and a shell-shocked-looking Ed.

"Gaia, can I ask you one question, just one, and this is really the last?" Ed didn't wait for her to respond.

"Do you get in fights *everywhere* you go?"

"MARCO! OVER HERE."

There's This Girl

Marco glanced around the Chinese restaurant casually, as if he hadn't noticed her the instant he'd walked through the door. Man, she was hot. She was wearing dark denim jeans today and a formfitting pink sweater.

"Hey, how's it going?" he said, treating her to his most charming smile and sitting down across from her.

She returned his smile and for a moment laid her hand on top of his. She was making him dizzy again.

A waiter hustled by and dropped two menus. The place was still noisy, but the after-school crowds were clearing out. Marco checked his hair quickly in the mirror that coated the restaurant's side wall. He was glad he'd refused to shave his head like the other guys. He consulted the filthy laminated menu. Was he supposed to order something? He suspected she hadn't asked him to meet her here because she was hungry.

"So, Marco, tell me how you've been." She was studying him intently and ignoring her menu. She leaned close. He felt a gentle foot on his.

Yes, dizzy. Really dizzy. "I've been, uh, pretty cool." He swallowed.

"What's been going on in the park?"

Shit. Was he supposed to be able to think when she was doing that with her foot?

"Not much," he said. "Couple of my buddies got beat up last night."

She looked more interested than concerned. "Who did it?"

"I'm not sure. Some real tough guys, I guess. Some guys who know how to fight." Now her foot was gone, and he really wanted it back.

"You'll get them," she said confidently.

He liked the way she said it and the way she looked at him. He nodded real slow, the way his buddy Martin's older brother did. "Bet your ass," he said.

"I need to ask you something," she said.

Where was her foot? Had he done something wrong? "Yeah?"

"There's this girl, a friend of mine. She likes to hang out in the park. I know there's a lot of stuff going on. You know, slashing and whatever."

"I heard about that," he said, his look just as knowing as hers.

"I want to make sure nobody touches her, okay? She's a real sweetheart, and I don't want her getting hurt."

The foot was back. Marco felt a `dull buzz` in his ears. "Right. Okay. You point her out to me in the park, and I'll take care of it."

The restaurant was nearly empty now. The waiters were sitting at a round table at the very back, eating their own snack. Marco felt a hand on his knee under the table. He had to stifle a groan. He leaned toward her and snaked his hand around the back of her neck. He kissed her hard, and she kissed him back. Her sweet smell combined with the heavy scents of fried wontons and cabbage. Her soft, blissful tongue explored his while the brown Formica table jammed into his stomach. God, he wanted to do it `right here`.

Suddenly her tongue and her hands were gone and she was standing. "Come on." She gestured at the door. "I know a place we can go."

Who's Heather?

ED SAW HER THE FOLLOWING AFTERnoon, sitting at a chess table near the southwestern corner of the park, and his heart sped up a little. The late September breeze was blowing her blond hair out of its messy ponytail and around her face. She'd shed her rumpled jacket to reveal a sleeveless white T-shirt and lithe, sculpted shoulders. Her muscles were defined, but long and graceful. In the sunshine he noticed a few freckles along the bridge of her nose. Her eyes looked less stormy gray and more Caribbean turquoise in this light.

Her opponent at the chessboard was a man in his thirties wearing a baseball cap and a pair of expensive sneakers and appearing to concentrate about ten times harder than she was.

She was wearing an expression he hadn't seen on her before—sort of wide-eyed and distracted. She gazed around. She examined her fingernails. She even appeared to giggle while losing a pawn. Was this actually Gaia?

Ed's legs were for crap, but his eyes were excellent. It was definitely Gaia. Either that or her ditzy twin sister.

He watched in surprise as she lost two more pawns and a knight. Her opponent was looking pretty pleased with himself. He was also allowing his eyes a few breaks from the board to gawk at Gaia. *Pervert*, Ed thought irritably.

Gaia lost another pawn. She might be able to take Bruce Lee in a fight, but she sure sucked at chess. She giggled again. It was a weird sound. Like a parakeet mooing or something. What was up with her?

Gaia's opponent snatched up her rook, and suddenly her manner changed. She focused with a slight frown on the board and started making moves rapidly. The man was smiling at her when she looked up from the board again. He looked so patronizing and full of himself that Ed suspected he was about to ask her out. He hoped Gaia would break his jaw.

Instead she said, "Checkmate," in a matter-of-fact way. Ed read her lips more than actually heard her say it.

Ed watched with blossoming pleasure as the man's face fell and his mouth snapped shut. He looked confused, then a bit suspicious, and then downright sour as he pulled out his wallet and handed over a twenty. As he walked away with his *New York Times* tucked under his arm, his overly youthful baseball cap looked even more absurd. Maybe he was in his forties.

"Go, Gaia," Ed said, wheeling over.

She turned toward his voice, her eyebrows connecting over angry eyes. "What, are you spying on me?"

"No, I'm strolling through the park and stopping to say hi to a friend," he countered. "A paranoid friend." He *was* basically spying, but she didn't need to know that.

Her fierce eyes relented a bit. "Oh."

"I see you discovered how to play chess right there in the middle of the game. Wow."

She cocked her head and almost smiled. "Gee, yeah. Lucky timing, huh?"

"And you made twenty dollars to boot," Ed added.

"Poor bastard didn't know what hit him."

"So you were spying," Gaia accused, but she didn't look mad anymore.

"Maybe a little," he admitted.

She sighed. "You know, Ed, if you learn any more of my secrets, I really will have to kill you." She stood and slung her weather-beaten messenger bag over her shoulder.

He shrugged. "Okay. I guess."

She started walking toward Washington Place, and he followed her.

"But before you do," he continued, "I was wondering, will you go to a party with me tonight?"

She stopped and turned on him, her eyebrows drawing together again. "Are you joking? Of course not."

Since his accident Ed had become a near professional button pusher, but nobody's buttons gave him quite the thrill that Gaia's did. Most people pretended to be civil for far too long. Gaia got spitting mad right away.

"Come on, it's a school party. Allison Rovitz is having it—you know, Heather's friend?"

"Who's Heather?" She was walking again.

"The girl you, uh, met over coffee yesterday," Ed said, quickly catching up with her.

Gaia shook her head in disbelief. "Boy, you sure do make it sound tempting."

Ed nodded. "It might be fun. Besides, it would be

good for you to meet some people," he suggested brightly.

Gaia stopped short and glanced around her. "What is going on here? Are the cameras rolling? Are we secretly starring in an after-school special? *Wheelchair Boy Befriends Angry Orphan Girl*?"

Ed laughed genuinely. "So I'll meet you there at nine? I'll leave the address on your answering machine."

"No!" Gaia almost shouted.

"Why not?" Ed persisted. "You don't have anything else to do."

"Yes, I do," she shot back.

"Like what?" Ed demanded.

She was silent for a few seconds. "Okay, I don't." Gaia glared at him. "Rub it in."

Ed loved the way she pressed her lips together. He loved the way she stood with one hip stuck out. He tried not to be obvious when he admired the way her hair fell perfectly, framing her face and stunning eyes, no matter how hard the wind tore at it. He had heard of this mythic species, beautiful girls who were not conscious of the fact that they were beautiful. He'd seen them represented in movies and on TV—unconvincingly for the most part. He'd read about them in books. But he'd never actually met one in person until Gaia.

"I know why you won't go," Ed said suddenly.

Gaia's patience was waning. "Why?"

"Because Heather's going to be there. You're scared of Heather," Ed stated confidently.

Gaia put her hands on her hips. She looked like she really did want to kill him. "Ed. I am not *scared* of Heather. Trust me."

WHAT IN THE WORLD WAS SHE doing? Gaia walked extra fast along Seventh Avenue, past Bleecker, past the duplex psychic shop blazing with neon, past the shop (one of many) that pierced you anyplace you could think of, past the bustling gay bars on Christopher Street.

Klutz Girl Strikes Again

As much as she despised getting railroaded into a stupid party full of people she was sure to hate, there was a small but unsquashable part of her that was happy to be out on a Saturday night with someplace to go.

She was going because she wasn't afraid of Heather and because she really didn't have anything else to do.

But she was mostly going because Ed had asked her. He was the first person in her entire high school career who'd cut through her defenses long enough to ask her to a party. He was the first person she hadn't succeeded in scaring off, in spite of her usual efforts.

The party was at 25 West Fifteenth Street. West meant west of Fifth Avenue, but not by much, so she hung a right at Fifteenth. Weeks ago, before she'd even moved here, she had committed a map of lower Manhattan to her near perfect visual memory.

She glanced down at her dark jeans and trashed sneakers. It would be impossible to tell from looking at her that she had spent over an hour getting dressed. She'd put on some mascara, then washed it off. She'd tried on three pairs of nearly identical jeans before finally closing her eyes and grabbing a pair randomly. She'd even changed her socks. Her one lasting concession to beauty was buried under shoes and (carefully chosen) socks—toenail polish in a hue called Cockroach.

As the address grew near, she spied one of the things she most disliked about New York residential life: a doorman. How much did you have to pay a guy to dress up in a butt-ugly polyester suit and embarrassing hat and open your damn door? And where were the door*women*, anyway? She hadn't seen a single one since she'd been here. Maybe she'd change her life's ambition from waitress to doorwoman. "Doorwoman." It sounded like some postmodern urban superhero.

Of course, this particular doorman wanted to know her name and whose apartment she felt privileged enough to visit. "Ed Fargo," she told him. "Visiting Allison Rovitz in apartment 12C."

The doorfellow gave her a once-over. "You don't look like an Ed."

"Tell my parents that. It's a real burden," she told him.

He shook his head, as though wishing he never had to speak to another scruffy, attitude-wielding seventeen-year-old as long as he lived.

He consulted his list, then waved a hand toward the inner lobby. "Go ahead."

"Why aren't there any doorwomen?" she nearly shouted after him as the elevator door closed.

The party in 12C could be heard throughout 12, from what Gaia could tell. She felt her muscles tense at the shrieks of laughter and loud buzz of conversation spilling into the hallway. This was kind of a momentous event. Although her capacity for nervousness was nil, her capacity for insecurity was all there. She tucked some hair behind her ear. She took a deep breath and pushed open the unlocked door.

What was she expecting exactly? Some deeply

narcissistic part of her thought everybody in the place would know that even though she was a junior, she had never been to a real high school party before. They would fall silent and turn to stare at her.

In fact, the only difference between before she had come and after was that there was one more beating heart in a very crowded apartment.

Okeydoke. Yes, here she was. Suddenly she was sure she'd been born with an extra gene for social awkwardness. Time to find the real Ed Fargo and hope he still thought she was entertaining.

She squeezed past a knot of people in the foyer who didn't care about her at all. In the living room she recognized a girl from her history class, a couple of guys who had lockers near hers. Every flat surface was covered with soda cans and beer cans in about equal number. A lot of people were smoking—mostly girls. On a table in the corner were raw carrots and dip and some unappealing chips and salsa. The meager food table was quickly being taken over by cans and cans and cans and makeshift ashtrays. Were anybody's parents here? She'd heard that New York City parents let their kids drink at parties because nobody drove anywhere afterward.

The sweet, suffocating smell of marijuana made its way over. She zeroed in on the little clutch of people passing around the joint before she turned and walked in the opposite direction. She had less than no time for that. Were those kids really so confident in their sanity, they could tempt fate?

When she finally caught sight of Ed's wheelchair in the dining room, she stifled the strong urge to sprint over to him and give him a hug. She walked toward him as slowly as she could manage, as though expecting to encounter hordes of friends and acquaintances along the way.

Gaia was shy. She'd forgotten that about herself, but she was. She was more comfortable beating the crap out of somebody than chatting about the weather. She could be sullen and obnoxious and irritable all day long, but she couldn't think of a single way to start a friendly conversation.

"Hi, Ed," she said lamely, once she was near.

"Gaia! Holy shit!" He smiled big. "You actually came."

"I never miss a party," she said wryly.

"Wow. You look great," he said.

"No, I don't."

"Okay, you don't. Hey, this is Claire." He pointed at a long-haired Asian girl he'd been talking to. "Claire, this is Gaia."

Claire waved and smiled. She was smoking a cigarette.

"And this is Mary. Mary, Gaia, et cetera."

Mary was tall, with wavy red hair. She waved in a

perfunctory way and took a swig of beer.

"You're new, right?" Claire asked.

"Yes," Gaia answered.

"Where are you from?" Claire wanted to know.

Ed shifted in his chair.

Gaia cleared her throat. "Uh. Memphis." It was a lie. She didn't want to play the "oh, really, do you know . . . ?" game about anyplace she had actually lived.

"Really? I have a cousin in Tennessee," Claire responded predictably. "In Johnson City."

"Oh?" Gaia nodded blankly.

Suddenly there was a swell of noise from the direction of the front door. All eyes turned.

"Hey, Gaia, check it out," Ed said. "It's your best friend."

Gaia gave him a mean look. It was Heather and friends—the same group from the cafe plus a couple of Hollywood extras. Heather really was beautiful when she wasn't snarling. Judging from the energy she and her crowd brought into the apartment with them, the party had only started at that moment.

Claire studied the group carefully. "I guess Heather didn't bring her boyfriend. Too bad. That guy is altogether hot."

Mary looked unimpressed. "He's a big college man. He goes to NYU. What's his name again? Carrie says he doesn't like coming to high school parties."

Of course Heather would have a gorgeous, snotty boyfriend who was in college. Of course. Gaia could only imagine what kind of asshole the guy must be to choose Heather as a girlfriend.

"I guess we're blessed even to have Heather," Gaia mumbled, instantly cursing herself for being snide.

Mary glanced at Gaia appreciatively. "Yes. I mean, who better to make the rest of us feel `fat and friendless`?"

Gaia laughed and felt a surge of . . . something. Optimism, was it? Hope? Social acceptance? She wasn't sure exactly—it was so unfamiliar. But here she was, `maladjusted freak-thing` Gaia Moore, gabbing with people who could very easily have been her friends. It was utterly alien, but not in a bad way. Only now she had to try to think of something else to say.

Heather led the wave of party energy through the living room toward the dining room and, no doubt, the kitchen, where the beers were waiting. Gaia wondered a bit warily if Heather would recognize her.

As it turned out, she did.

"Oh, my God!" Heather shrieked, wheeling around to face Gaia straight on. "It's Klutz Girl! What are you doing here?"

Suddenly all eyes really were on Gaia. Her social success was evaporating quickly.

"I would watch out for this girl," Heather warned loudly. "Don't give her anything to eat or drink, or you'll end up with it on your shirt."

Heather's friends tittered loyally.

"Who let you in here?" Heather demanded.

Gaia studied the small place on the girl's neck just below her chin. She could deliver one swift blow to that spot and put her out.

"I invited her," Ed said, filling the awkward silence at least momentarily.

"Excuse me, *Ed*," Heather said nastily. "I didn't realize it was your party."

"I didn't realize it was yours," Ed responded.

Allison, the actual party giver, was watching the scene unfold with the rest of them. Heather turned to her.

"Al, did you realize this bitch was coming to your party?"

Poor Allison looked frightened.

"Don't worry about it, Allison. I'm going," Gaia said. She strode through the apartment without looking back.

It didn't matter so much that she was back on the outside, Gaia consoled herself as she opened the front door and passed through it. This was Heather's time. Let her have it. Ten years from now Heather's awfulness would have caught up with her, and she'd

be a disgruntled wretch pining for the glory days. Let her have high school. Gaia was holding out for something better.

Gaia stood sullenly at the elevator bank and punched the down arrow. Mercifully the elevator doors opened right away.

At least she was back in her comfort zone.

Some things I like:
Chess
Slurpees
Road Runner cartoons
Eye boogers
W. B. Yeats
Ed

Some things I don't like:
Heather
Ella
Skim milk
Butterflies
Baking soda toothpaste
Myself

A thing I hate:
My dad

Rain plastered
thick dark
cords of hair
to his fore-
head. **meeting**
Now that it
was no longer **sam**
perfect, **moon**
she could see
it was
beautiful.

"HI, ZOLOV."

The old man squinted at Gaia for a few seconds before he recognized her, then he smiled.

People Like Him

"Hey, Curtis," she said to Zolov's opponent. "Where's Renny?"

The fifteen-year-old chess fixture shrugged. "He hasn't been coming around anymore."

Gaia nodded and looked for a free table. She was happy to be there, even without Renny. She was glad that the bleak sky threatened rain and that the air was finally turning cold. All that warm sunshine seemed to demand perkiness and pastel-colored clothing.

She watched Curtis leaning far over the board, studying Zolov's sequence. She almost laughed to herself. She couldn't believe she was watching an ancient Jewish man in a threadbare wool overcoat teaching the Ruy Lopez opening to a black kid dressed head to toe in Tommy.

She turned her affectionate gaze to the right, and suddenly her mood went into free fall.

Him.

What the hell was *he* doing here?

God, he was good-looking. He was wearing that same gray jacket, this time with a pair of jeans and just the right shade of dark, perfectly scuffed leather shoes.

Go away, she ordered him silently. Go back to where you belong.

He didn't go away. Instead he came very close, and her mouth felt dry. Why did she all of a sudden care that she hadn't run a brush through her hair that morning? So she looked like a homeless person. What was it to him?

Oh, shit. He was looking at the board set in front of her. His eyes glanced over the empty chair across from her.

He was stopping!

He was sitting down!

He was staring right at her!

Then she felt mad. What, was he on some kind of field trip from normal-people land? Was he the Jane Goodall of the popular set, here to take notes?

It didn't help that just a few days before he'd appeared *uninvited* in her romantic fantasy and *kissed* her, for God's sake. "Do you want to play?" he asked, just like that.

He wanted to play her! What! Didn't he know that it was illegal in a cosmic sense for a guy who looked like him even to get near a board? The gods of social stratification would zap him but good.

Fine. If he insisted on turning the world upside down, what could she do? She'd play him. She'd point out to him which pieces moved which way as though she'd only recently learned herself, and then she'd hustle as much money out of him as possible. She could probably get two or three fast games out of him before the rain began to fall.

"Hello?" He scrunched down a little in his chair to try to gain eye contact.

"What?" she blurted out irritably.

"Do you want to play?"

She was so flustered, she couldn't pluck one arrow from her quiver of hustling tricks. "Fine."

"Don't feel like you have to."

Oh, wasn't he just honorable.

"No, it's fine. I only just started playing myself." God, she sounded wooden. Her acting really needed some work.

"Okay. You start, right?"

"No, I mean, I think. Well, we usually—" Dammit. She took a black pawn and a white one and mixed them up behind her back. She enclosed each in a fist and stuck them out toward him. "You pick."

He pointed to her left hand, and she produced a white pawn.

"You go first," she said.

He looked tentative. "It's kind of a custom to play for money here, isn't it?"

Custom? Yes, it is, O Great Doctor of Losers.

"Usually," was what she said.

"How much?"

"I dunno. Twenty?"

He blew out his breath. "Wow. Okay."

"Okay."

What was it about him that bothered her so? That he was the kind of guy who'd never look twice at a girl like her? Okay, well, there was that.

She couldn't find major fault with his wardrobe. It wasn't like he was wearing a Rolex or anything.

She didn't hate him just because he looked like . . . that. Even she wasn't quite that shallow or `rabidly judgmental`.

What was it, then?

He was so . . . confident. That was the big problem. Here, in her place, where he had no right to be, he was so goddamned sure of himself. He probably had no sense of humor, least of all about himself.

She couldn't wait to kick his ass.

The Fire Hose Test

SAM MOON WASN'T SURE WHAT TO make of this girl. He'd sat down at her board because she was new, and that always represented an opportunity.

Well, okay. That wasn't the only reason. Another reason

was that in spite of her somewhat disastrous personal hygiene, she was pretty. A pretty girl at a chessboard wasn't your everyday sight. He hadn't even realized just how pretty until he was within a couple of feet and had a chance to really look.

Some friends of his from high school used to rate a girl's attractiveness by what was known as the fire hose test. If the girl's looks were all about makeup and hair and clothes, she'd look like crap if you shot a fire hose directly in her face from point-blank range. A genuinely pretty girl would still look good. Now, this girl here looked as though a hose actually had blasted her, so there was no leap of imagination necessary to know that she passed the test. Passed it with an A, he decided as she bit her lip and tapped impatiently on the queen's pawn.

"Okay, here goes," he said, thumping to E4.

She predictably took E5.

Pretty as she was, though, she was annoying. She obviously thought she knew what she was doing— under her truly flimsy pretense that she didn't. Maybe she'd won some high school tournament or something. Whoop-de-do. She had no business taking over a table here.

And why was she glaring at him like that? What had he done to piss her off?

He'd give her hope for a few

minutes and then shut her down. He could really use the twenty bucks.

He flinched a little as a clap of thunder roared overhead. The air felt heavy with coming rain. He'd give her a very few minutes.

SHE WAS SURPRISED. NOT ALARMED

The Rain Starts

or anything. Just a little surprised.

She hadn't expected him to respond so adroitly to her opening. They'd progressed quickly to the midgame, and she'd achieved almost no advantage. Now the wind was blowing in soot-colored clouds and thunder rolled through the sky and she was looking at the possibility of a complicated endgame.

He wasn't the doofus she'd imagined. That much she had to admit. She hadn't thought it possible to have perfect orthodonture and a good haircut and also be great at chess, but then, she was only seventeen. There had to be a few things left to learn.

She wasn't pretending anything anymore. She was too focused on the board. All attempts at inane, gee-whiz posturing had fallen away.

His manner had changed, too. His concentration on the game was so full, he let out these tiny, almost inaudible grunts every so often. He had this funny tick of drumming his fingers against his bottom lip before he made each move. She couldn't exactly remember what about him had seemed so self-satisfied.

She unintentionally knocked her knee against his under the table. He glanced up.

"Sorry," she mumbled. Her face felt warm. She prayed it wasn't actually turning pink.

His hair had fallen over his forehead. She couldn't read the expression in his eyes.

She commanded her own eyeballs back to the board.

A fat, cold raindrop landed on her scalp. Damn. Why couldn't she just finish this up?

TINY DROPS OF SWEAT WERE collecting in his hairline, bleeding into the raindrops slapping on his head. Drops dribbled down his neck, and **More Rain** his sweater was starting to smell funky. He was concentrating too hard to care.

The girl moved her king's bishop.

Ugh. He closed his eyes briefly in disgust at himself. Why hadn't he seen the pin? What was wrong with him?

He was forced to defend with a knight. That was a tempo lost.

The main thing wrong was that this girl was totally shocking. She was not good. She was very, very, very good. Where had she come from? She couldn't be from around here because he felt sure he would have met her in tournaments before. She had to be an internationally ranked player. Either that or he suddenly stunk.

He'd sacrificed material to no avail. She'd dismantled one of his most trusted combinations. But even so, it was a really exciting game. Her play was not only smart and challenging, but unorthodox. Who had taught her? Who was she?

He glanced up at her. Her light hair was soaked flat with rain. Her blue eyes darkened to mirror the sky, and they were steady with concentration. She was somewhere around sixteen or seventeen years old. He hadn't detected any accent, which would have at least helped to explain how she was so good. It seemed like foreign players always dominated in competition.

The harsh, defiant set of her face had dissolved now. Self-consciousness had fallen away as her focus intensified. Her eyes were lovely, rimmed with long, dark (wet) lashes. Her cheekbones were exceptionally prominent for a person her age. Her face was open now and almost sweet. Raindrops stood on her bare arms, and her T-shirt was . . .

She snapped her rook into the center of the action.

Okay, better not to look anymore. He was screwing up here. Lucky for him there weren't many beautiful girls who played chess, or he'd probably be bowling right now.

His heart was speeding with nervousness and excitement. He could feel warmth radiating from her legs, so close to his. His palms felt tingly.

Think about chess, you idiot, he ordered himself.

YES, ALARMING. IT WAS NOW officially alarming. He was up a knight and coming on strong. How had she misjudged him so badly?

He was probably the best person she had ever played except for her father, maybe, and Zolov, who was nuts.

She studied his face. He was older than she, but not by much. Maybe twenty. He had to be an international master at least. She wasn't on the chess circuit, but she knew an extraordinary player from a good one.

And as he played he was becoming real to her. His

little ticks were so peculiar. The skin around his fingernails was ragged from being picked at too much. Tiny blue veins zigzagged under the surface of the transparent skin beneath his eyes. Rain plastered thick dark cords of hair to his forehead. Now that it was no longer perfect, she could see it was beautiful.

Suddenly she had this powerful urge to touch the pale skin above his wrist, where she could see `his pulse thumping`. She stared transfixed at that spot, feeling that her own heart was beating out the same rhythm.

Oh, Gaia. She almost groaned out loud. Get ahold of yourself, girl.

This was an inexplicable reaction she was having to him. Was she profoundly low on sleep, maybe? When had she last eaten?

Another bolt of lightning blazed through the sky. Maybe it was the plunging barometer? The electricity in the air?

When she looked back at the board, she felt dizzy and disoriented. A chess game like this one meant holding a million teetering moves and possibilities in your mind, and here all at once she'd dropped them. The crowd of pieces left on the board had gone from a `thrillingly complex and significant battle` in one second to a meaningless jumble the next.

Blood rushed to her face. She tried to kick-start her

memory, to patch together her lost strategy. But it was as though the whole thing had existed in someone else's mind.

Rain blanketed them. Steam rose from the surrounding pavement. Goose bumps pricked up and down her arms. Why had neither of them suggested giving up this ridiculous contest and going inside?

He was looking at her. Not silently, impatiently demanding her next move, as she would expect. Just looking. Looking for something. Rain dotted his eyelashes with diamonds, formed rivers down his cheeks.

His eyes had taken hers, and she couldn't look away.

Then she felt something grab hold of her chest. It wasn't fear. It couldn't be. But what was it? She had to get out of there.

With a flick of her index finger she felled her precious king. "I'm sorry," she murmured. "I have to go." She got to her feet, reaching into her bag for her wallet. He stood, too. She fumbled the wet leather and pulled out a twenty-dollar bill, then jammed it in his palm.

"No. No," he told her. The bill fluttered to the ground, but neither of them stooped to get it. She was already walking, and he was hurrying alongside her, confused, surprised, stammering for a word.

"W-Wait. Please," he whispered.

She was almost running. In her sneakers the water squished around her toes. The rain was so loud, it filled up all of her senses.

She hurried from him and from the strange perception that a million frozen feelings were about to thaw and the flood would certainly drown her.

HE WATCHED HER GO, FEELING A

Bottomless

terrible tightness in his throat. What had she done to him?

It had all happened in that moment, when he'd met her eyes and, like a mystic, seemed to see her past and future. Her past was haunting, marked by bottomless wounds, and the future was terrifying because it included him.

For the last
twenty-four
hours his
mind had
behaved
more like a
badly
trained
dog on a
too long
leash.

**no
bad
dogs**

"I WISH MY NAME WERE FARGO."

The Right to Ask

Gaia was walking so fast, Ed Fargo was having a hard time keeping up with her. Her movements were strangely jerky, and her mouth was going a mile a minute.

"Why is that?" he had to practically shout at her because she kept getting ahead.

"It's a cool name," she said.

"You could marry me if you asked really nicely," he proposed.

"Yeah, right."

"What's the matter with Moore?" he asked as they rounded the corner of Charles Street and Hudson.

"I don't know." Gaia's eyes weren't quite focused. She wasn't completely paying attention to what she was saying or where her feet were going. "Moore . . . Less," she mused absently. "Hey, Gaia Less. Guileless. I like that."

He was getting annoyed. "Gaia, would you please slow down? I'm kind of in a wheelchair here."

She glanced back at him. "Oh. Sorry," she mumbled.

In her expression Ed saw traces of impatience but no embarrassment, no pity. He loved her.

"Guileless," he continued. "What does it mean?"

"You know, without guile."

"What does guile mean?"

"Deceit, duplicity, dishonesty."

He slowed down a bit more. "Gaia, how do you know these things?"

She shrugged. "I'm smart."

"And modest, too."

"Modesty is a waste of time," she pronounced.

"I'll keep that in mind."

They passed Zuli's bakery and the tiny store that sold homemade ravioli. A woman passed them, pushing a toy poodle perched in a baby carriage. Gaia didn't even seem to notice.

"For somebody so smart, you sure bombed the physics quiz today," Ed pointed out.

"Yeah, well. Parabolas are so simple, they're boring."

Ed laughed. "I'll have to remember that excuse to tell my parents the next time I get a D."

Suddenly Gaia stopped and grabbed his shoulder. "What's that?"

"Ouch," he said, and she lessened her grip on his clavicle. "What?"

"That music." She yanked him around the corner. "Do you hear it? Where's it coming from?"

He pointed across the street. "That band we heard at Ozzie's. They practice in the basement of that building."

"How do you know?"

"Because I'm smart."

Gaia rolled her eyes. "What's the name of the band?"

"Huh?"

"The name of the band?"

"Fearless. They're always playing around the neighborhood. Ozzie's on Friday afternoons, Dock's on Wednesday evenings, and fully amplified at The Flood most Saturday nights. Our local OTB takes bets on when they'll actually get signed."

Gaia had completely tuned out.

"Ha-ha. That was a funny joke," Ed pointed out.

Gaia nodded dumbly. "Fearless?" she asked. "No way."

Ed shrugged. "No reason to lie." He was bored with this conversation.

Gaia paused for another moment as slow lyrics drifted up to the street.

". . . And I'm a stone/falling deeper/into your black, black ocean/let me drown . . ."

Gaia was off again like a shot.

"Where are we going now?" he asked, almost breathless in his effort to catch up.

"I don't know. We're strolling."

"Oh."

They strolled for a while in silence.

"Hey, wait a minute," he said, slowing down warily as they sailed past Sixth Avenue without a pause.

"What?"

"I have a feeling we're strolling to the park."

"So?"

"I don't want to go to the park."

Gaia looked annoyed. "Why not?"

"Because innocent people are getting slashed there practically every day. Because there are evil bald guys carving swastikas into trees. Do you watch the news?"

"Ed, it's broad daylight."

"That doesn't stop you."

"Stop *me*? Stop me from what?" she asked.

"From finding people to get into fights with," he responded.

She looked slightly abashed.

"Let's walk down Broadway toward Soho," he suggested.

Gaia was quiet, fidgeting with the threads hanging off the bottom of her jacket, but she did follow him at least.

"What's the matter?" he asked.

"I'm trying to think of a way to apologize for the other night," she explained.

"What do you mean?" he asked.

"For ruining that party you invited me to."

"You didn't ruin it," he said comfortingly. "We all had a perfectly good time after you left."

She kicked his wheel.

"Gaia, Jesus!" He regained control of his chair. "I was just kidding. I left right away. I tried to catch you, but you were too fast for me."

She slowed down a little. "Really?"

"Yeah. Anyway, it wasn't you. It was Heather who was out of control."

"You think so?"

He laughed. "For once, yeah."

"She's such a raving bitch," Gaia declared.

Ed shook his head thoughtfully. "There's actually more to her than that."

"You know her well?" Gaia asked, clearly surprised.

"Sure. I went out with her for a few months."

Gaia stopped cold in the middle of Bleecker Street. A truck honked loudly.

"Gaia, go!" Ed commanded, and she did.

"No way," she stated when they were safely on the other side of the street.

Ed looked at her peevishly. "You say that too much."

"Sorry. But I mean it. No way."

Ed held up his hands. "It's true. Heather and I went out for a while before my accident."

"Wow." Gaia was obviously struggling to absorb this. They walked for three blocks in silence.

"Hey, Gaia?" he asked finally.

"Yeah?"

"Are you ever going to ask me why I'm in a wheel-chair?"

"No," she said.

"Why not?"

"Because if I do, you would have the right to ask

where I lived before, or why I'm a black belt in karate, or what happened to my parents."

"Oh," he said. "Okay."

And they kept walking.

That Girl

SAM WASN'T WALKING THROUGH THE park because he wanted to see that girl. He didn't want to see that girl. She was trouble.

And he had a girlfriend. That was the more important point. He had a girlfriend, and he was late to meet her, and even though it was almost dark and he knew he shouldn't be cutting through the park with all of the crap that was going on, he was doing it anyway.

But not because he wanted to see that girl.

Although he was running late, he could count on the fact that Heather would be at least twenty minutes later and that she would show up with a noisy entourage. She would be all out of breath and apologize fervently for being late, as though her lateness depended on such a rare and extenuating matrix of once-in-a-lifetime circumstances that it could never possibly happen again. And the next time she would be just as late.

He should just tell her it bugged him. He was basically a punctual person, and he didn't appreciate all the dramatic entrances. He didn't love the entourage, either.

But if he did tell her, she would probably listen and stop, at least for a while. And then where would he be? What could he complain about? What reason would he have for breaking up with her?

Ooh. That last bit just slipped out. He hadn't totally meant to have that thought.

Heather was gorgeous. Heather was smart. Heather was confident and funny. Heather, though only a senior in high school, was the envy of all his college friends. Heather was even capable, when she let go of her own mythology for a few minutes, of being a decent person.

But these were not good reasons for going out with a person, and he knew that in his heart. So why did he stay with her?

That was complicated. It hinged on a lot of stuff about his old life and his old self, and he didn't feel like thinking about it just now.

His thoughts wandered back to the girl. *The girl.* He'd certainly never thought so much about a person whose name he didn't know. His mind slipped back to her every time he gave it a moment's freedom. He kept picturing her eyes, infinite as the sky. His mind used to be so obedient, so precise. For the last twenty-four hours it had behaved more like a badly trained dog on a too long leash.

Did she live in the neighborhood? Where did she go to school? Would she come back to the chess tables in the park? If she did, would he try to talk to her? Would he ask her to play again?

His heart rate was rising at the very thought.

Okay, enough.

He was so distracted, he veered off the path and nearly crashed into a sign. He looked up at it.

Curb Your Dog, it said.

IF SHE SAW HIM, SHE WOULD

A Mistake

just change course. Gaia's eyesight was good. She would spot him before he spotted her, before any interaction needed to take place.

Strictly speaking, walking through the park wasn't the smartest way to avoid him. But it was the fastest way to get home after she dropped Ed off at his house. And now that it was dark, it was by far her best chance for getting jumped or slashed by one of those neo-Nazi bastards.

She wasn't going to go out of her way for this guy.

Usually the park was still busy at this hour when the weather was good, but tonight it was nearly deserted. People were spooked by the reports of slashing. Lots of kids had been talking about it in school that day.

Gaia paused to take off her jacket and tie it around her waist. Slashing was such a random, mean-spirited brand of violence and the whole Nazi mythology so profoundly hateful, she was particularly eager to draw it out. She liked to think of herself as a trap. A walking trap.

As she dawdled in the wooded area near the dog run, she heard whispers. Oh, man. Could it be this easy? She strained her ears to hear and ambled a tiny bit closer. She couldn't really make out the conversation, but she did see the flash of a knife. Not a blade this time, a real knife. Four guys were huddled together, probably plotting their next attack.

Me! Me! Choose me! she thought. Jeez, what a wacko she'd become. She made as much noise as possible while still appearing naive and oblivious. She really hoped none of them would recognize her from a previous run-in.

She walked as slowly as she could without actually stopping and yet within moments found herself on the open, brightly lit sidewalk of Washington Square West untouched. So it wasn't her lucky night. Maybe tomorrow.

She felt sulky and suddenly quite alone. It was weird, this business of having a friend, she decided, thinking of her long, aimless walk with Ed. It made being alone less fun.

Gaia looked up and saw a figure crossing the street toward her. It was a girl, and she appeared to be heading straight into the park. Gaia's mind flashed to the knife she'd just seen, and she bent her steps toward the girl. She didn't realize until she was a few feet away exactly which girl it was.

"Is that Gaia?" a not-friendly voice demanded.

It was Heather. This really wasn't Gaia's lucky night. Gaia was immediately struck by the fact that Heather was alone. Where was the famed boyfriend? Where were the adoring, fashionably dressed friends?

"Listen, Heather," she began matter-of-factly, "you probably shouldn't—"

Heather bristled and walked on. "Leave me alone, bitch."

Gaia wasn't sure what to do. Follow her? "Heather, I really don't think—"

"Get away from me," Heather snapped. "I don't care what you think."

Gaia had intended to be helpful, but now she was angry. Let the stupid girl get slashed. It wasn't Gaia's responsibility. If anybody deserved it, Heather did.

Gaia's temper smoldered as she continued across the

street. She was just about to turn onto Waverly when she spotted more familiar faces. They were all three Heather acolytes. One was named Tina, she believed. The other was a girl whose name she didn't know, and the third was the good-looking guy from the cafe.

This time she was just going to keep walking, but one of them stopped her.

"You're Gaia, right?" the non-Tina girl asked.

"Yeah."

"Have you seen Heather, by any chance?"

Gaia looked from one to the next. This didn't seem like a trick or anything. "Yeah, I just saw her about a minute ago. She was cutting through the park." Gaia gestured in the general direction.

"Thanks," they all said. They weren't oozing warmth, but they seemed perfectly friendly.

"Hey, uh . . . Tina," Gaia called over her shoulder.

They all stopped and turned.

"You really shouldn't go through the park. There's a bunch of whacked-out guys in there, and at least one of them has a knife."

Tina and her friends looked surprised and alarmed in varying degrees. "Shit. Okay. Right."

"Thanks," the guy said again.

Gaia watched with satisfaction as they skirted the park, staying on the lighted sidewalk.

See? She'd done her good deed. She wasn't a bad person. She could go home in peace.

Sometimes I dream I'm
skating. Not a ramp or half pipe
like one of those Mountain Dew
commercials. My feet are planted
on a board, and I'm steaming
along straight and steady. First
it's maybe a sidewalk and then a
street and then it becomes a
highway of at least four lanes.
Then the board transforms into an
airplane, and I'm in the cockpit.
It's a passenger plane, I guess,
but I'm not aware of having responsibility for any passengers.
I have this sense of excitement
and anticipation as I accelerate,
gaining intense, powerful speed.
Fast, fast, faster. I feel sure
I've passed that speed you need
to leave the ground. But I'm
still on the highway. I'm still
zooming past houses and fields
and forests.

The highway bends slowly into
a curve. It curves again. I become conscious of road signs—Deer
Crossing, Boulders Falling, you
know those. And I begin to pay

attention to them. I realize I've
adjusted my speed from about a
million miles an hour to just a
few above the speed limit. I peer
into the side mirror of my airplane to check for cops.

After a while it's a forgone
conclusion that I won't be taking
off. Just a plain fact, like any
of the others we learn to live
with. I'll be following signs on
the highway in my jumbo jet,
built to fly thirty-five-thousand
feet above our blue Earth.

And she
followed
them through
the exit,
distinctly
aware of **no**
the huge **peace**
cloud of
hate
behind
her.

BEFORE HE PASSED THROUGH THE

An Angry Place

school entrance the next morning, Ed knew there was something wrong. The halls were extra crowded, but not loud enough. Kids were gathered in little clots held together by hushed voices. A lot of eyes were darting around. The air had that heightened energy, that guilty pleasure of tragedy.

"What's going on?" he asked the first person he came to, a vaguely familiar girl with a magenta crew cut.

"God, it's so scary," she said. He could tell she was trying to rein herself in to project the right amount of sobriety. "Heather Gannis got shot in Washington Square last night. She's in the ICU at St. Vincent's."

"Jesus," Ed muttered. That sick zingy feeling, as if his blood were suddenly carbonated, started under his stomach and spread through his limbs. "Do they know who did it?"

The girl was already gone, so he wheeled up to the nearest group. "What happened? Who did it? Is she going to be okay?" he burst in loudly. He didn't feel like being measured and coy.

The five faces above him were practically caricatures of gravity. "The police claim they have suspects, but there hasn't been an arrest," a black-haired girl answered. "Nobody knows exactly what happened. They think it was some kind of gang activity—this white supremacist group—connected to the slashings."

"But it was a shooting," he argued.

"No, it wasn't. It was a stabbing," a guy said.

"A stabbing?" Ed asked.

At least two of them nodded.

"She's in ICU?" Ed continued, feeling impatient. He needed this information to slow his speeding heart. He actually cared about the facts and their implications, unlike most of the rumormongers.

"In a coma," another girl added.

He sighed in frustration. "We're talking about Heather?"

Black-Haired Girl's face closed in annoyance. "Obviously," she snapped.

Ed wheeled away, shaking his head. He had a feeling that if he talked to every one of the groups in the hallway, he would get a slightly different story from each.

This was surreal and terrifying. Heather wasn't the kind of girl who got shot or stabbed or stepped into a hospital for any reason but to visit her grandmother after elective surgery. He couldn't help but think of Heather's parents and sisters.

His experience on Mercer Street with Gaia came

back to him in full detail—the knife, the fear, the chaos. How had the world become so malignant? New York City was transforming from the eccentric but comfortable place where he'd grown up into the dangerous, angry place he'd always heard about.

"Attention, students." Principal Hickey's voice came blasting through the loudspeaker. "There will be an all-school assembly this morning directly after homeroom. Attendance is mandatory." Even the principal's solemnity sounded phony and exaggerated.

Ed wheeled slowly to homeroom, his mind ricocheting from big, appropriate thoughts about crime and death and police investigations to weird little inappropriate thoughts like whether Heather was wearing one of those hospital gowns that tied in the back, and, if so, who had undressed her. Then he felt guilty about having that second category of thoughts and tried not to have them, which took up a certain amount of mental energy in itself.

He was sitting in homeroom, trying not to have any thoughts at all, when he overheard Gaia's name mentioned. He didn't turn because he didn't want to disrupt the conversation.

"Gaia Moore saw what?" asked Becca Miller, a girl with long, supercurly hair who always sat behind him.

"She saw the guy with the knife in the park," responded Samantha something, a friend of Becca's, in a voice hushed but intoxicated with the thrill of conveying important information.

"What are you talking about?" Becca asked.

"Gaia was in the park just a few minutes before Heather got slashed, and she saw the guys who did it."

"Tell me you're kidding. How do you know this?" Becca demanded.

"Tina Lynch told Carrie she was with Brian and Melanie last night and they saw Gaia, right outside the park. Gaia told Tina she'd just seen Heather going into the park. But Gaia warned Tina and those other guys not to go into the park—that she'd just seen a guy with a knife."

Ed's mind was spinning with the number of names and personal pronouns, but also with the ramifications of what he was hearing. Gaia was involved. Of course she was. If trouble was magnetic north, then Gaia's head was a huge chunk of iron. In the short time Ed had known her, he'd almost gotten killed, watched three thugs get demolished, witnessed two catfights, seen one slashing victim's family crying on the news, and now learned his ex-girlfriend was in a coma.

Of course Gaia was there. How could it be otherwise?

But what had she done, exactly?

He couldn't trust these girls or really anybody but Gaia to tell him what had happened. And Gaia would give him the unvarnished truth. He and Gaia were alike in that way. They both took special satisfaction in telling you the one true thing you really, really didn't want to hear.

GAIA HADN'T PAID MUCH ATTENTION

to all the whispering at first. She had learned to be good at ignoring it. In her experience whispering either:

A Smelly Monster!

1. Didn't include her

   or

2. Was about her

And in neither case could she take part.

So it wasn't until the assembly that she heard the news.

"As many of you know, a tragedy befell our school community last night," Principal Hickey intoned to the enormous, totally silent all-school assembly. Gaia should have known right then that something was seriously wrong by the simple fact that people were actually listening to the guy. "Heather Gannis was slashed in Washington Square Park last night. She lost a great deal of blood before she was discovered by friends and fellow students. She is in critical condition at St. Vincent's Hospital. I know you all join me in sending Heather and her family our . . ."

He kept talking, of course, but Gaia didn't hear. An ugly, evil creature with smelly fur and sharp fangs was gnawing on her intestines, and that was hard to ignore.

Her thoughts from the previous night returned to her word for word.

Let the stupid girl get slashed. If anybody deserved it, Heather did.

But I didn't mean that, a small, panicky voice inside Gaia claimed pitifully. I meant to warn her. I was going to, but—

Shut up! Gaia screamed at her own mind. If she'd had a tire iron, she would have clubbed herself with it. She'd heard too many excuses in her life. She couldn't stomach them, especially not from herself.

The principal was droning on about safety precautions now, and the attention he'd commanded was lost. Kids were talking, whispering.

Gaia realized when she looked up that hundreds of eyes were bouncing around and landing on her again and again. What could she expect? She had known exactly what Heather was walking into, and at least three other people in this very auditorium knew that she knew. She could have saved Heather, and she didn't. She let a petty, stupid conflict, probably based more on her own jealousy than anything else, destroy another person's life.

The fanged creature devoured several more feet of intestine and moved on to the lining of her stomach.

Everybody was standing up and milling around. Gaia guessed that the assembly was over. Numbly she got to her feet and let herself be moved along by the crowd. Just beyond the doors, in the lobby of the auditorium, the puffy, tear-stained face of Tina Whats-her-name bobbed into view.

Gaia stopped.

If only shame were part of fear. If only self-loathing were part of fear.

If Gaia were a better person, she would have offered some comforting words. She didn't. She remained the person she was.

"What *happened* last night?" Tina asked her in a voice tinged with hysteria. "What was Heather *thinking* going in there alone? Did you talk to her? Did you tell her what you'd seen in the park?"

Gaia realized Tina wasn't judging her. Not yet. She was inviting Gaia to commiserate, to take part in the why-oh-why-oh-why that churned her restless mind. She wanted to think the best of Gaia.

Other people had gathered. Some were comforting,

others being comforted. Several friends clutched Tina supportively.

"I—I didn't," Gaia said stiffly. "I didn't warn her."

Tina's face took a few moments to register this. "What do you mean?"

Gaia had to remind herself to breathe. "I mean I didn't tell Heather about the guy with the knife."

"Why not? Why didn't you?" Tina's shiny doe eyes turned into slitted bat eyes.

The crowd of people readied their looks of horror but held off, waiting for an explanation.

A part of Gaia wanted to describe to all these eager sets of ears how Heather told her off, called her names, but she knew it would sound just like the lame excuse it was. She deserved the blame for this. She would take it without flinching. "I just didn't."

Tina was crying now. "God, what's the matter with you? You warned us but not her? Do you hate Heather so much that you wanted her to get killed?"

Amid the loathing, judging faces, Gaia suddenly spied blue. Dark blue uniforms, dark blue hats. The fragments resolved into two policemen.

Could you actually get arrested for failing to warn someone? Gaia wondered irrationally. The faces parted to let the police come through. The hum of voices in the lobby grew to a roar.

"Are you Gaia Moore?" one of them, a tall black man, asked.

123

"Yes," she answered. Were they going to handcuff her right here, in front of the entire student body?

"Would you please come with us to the precinct? We have some questions to ask you."

The man asked it like a real question, not a rhetorical one. He waited for her answer; he didn't slap on any handcuffs.

"Yes," she said. "Of course." And she followed them through the exit, distinctly aware of the huge cloud of hate behind her.

That was one plus about profound self-loathing. Nobody could hate you worse than you hated yourself.

Different but the Same

"AND AT APPROXIMATELY WHAT hour did you see Heather Gannis approaching the park from the west side?"

Gaia couldn't quite pull her eyes from that vague middle distance to focus them on the detective sitting across from her.

"About seven forty-five, I guess."

"You guess?"

"I wasn't wearing a watch at the time. I'd dropped off a friend at First Avenue and

Fourth Street at seven-thirty and then walked directly to the park on my way home. I figure it would take roughly fifteen minutes to walk from First and Fourth to Washington Square West," Gaia replied. She was on auto-answer. It felt to her that she'd already fielded at least a hundred thousand questions, and they hadn't even gotten to the meaty part.

"Fine. And what exactly happened when you saw Heather?" the detective asked. Detective Anderson was his name. He was in his forties probably, with thinning medium-brown hair, slightly pocked skin, and pale eyes. He looked just as tired and harassed as detectives always looked on those realistic cop shows.

Gaia let out her breath slowly. Did he really want the catty details? "I—um—sort of stopped her, and she—uh—" Gaia broke off and glanced at the detective. "See, Heather and I weren't exactly on friendly terms. A few days ago I spilled hot coffee on her, and since then—"

"Since then?" he prompted.

"We've had, uh, words, you could say," Gaia explained.

"I see." The detective nodded. "So you disliked Heather, did you?"

"I was told she is still alive."

"Excuse me. I'm sorry. Yes." Detective Anderson looked genuinely awkward. "You dislike Heather," he amended.

"That's a tough thing to say about a girl in a coma, sir," Gaia pointed out.

"Right. Yes. Okay." He sighed and shifted in his chair. "But as of yesterday evening, you and Heather were enemies?"

"Am I a suspect in this case?" Gaia asked, staring him dead in the eye.

He cleared his throat and shifted again. He moved his mouth a few times before any sounds came out. "Uh, no. You're not."

"Okay." She settled back in her chair. She knew she wasn't a suspect, because she knew they'd assembled a police lineup, because she'd overheard it being discussed when Detective Anderson was hunting around for cream for his coffee. She knew he was trying to pretend like she was so he could `manipulate and intimidate` her more easily.

"So, back to the story," she said, chilly but helpful. "Heather told me to leave her alone, and I did. Less than a minute after walking past her, I ran into her friends—Tina and two other people whose names I don't know. I think you know the story from there. After that I walked home. You have all that information already."

Detective Anderson looked even more harassed and tired. "Right. Now am I to understand that you did not warn Heather as to what you'd just seen moments before in the park?"

"No, sir."

"But you did warn the three people you saw subsequently?"

"Yes, sir."

He waited for an explanation that didn't come. After a while he stood up. "All right, Gaia, that's it for the moment. Would you come with me? I'd like you to look at a lineup."

She followed him through the precinct to the viewing room, listening to directions, warnings, assurances associated with a lineup. She felt floaty and distant as she took in the hodgepodge of beat-up office furniture, papers, files, boards, maps, clippings, notices, charts, the pathetic set of twigs on a windowsill that had probably been a live plant a decade or two ago.

It was so different in particulars, but so generally the same as the precinct where she'd spent the night as a twelve-year-old in San Rafael, California, after her mother was murdered, when they couldn't figure out anyplace else to put her.

"GAIA! GAIA! ARE YOU OKAY?"

Her Fault

It was Ed, waiting outside the police station for her, and she wasn't happy to see him. Who ever said misery loved company? Her misery did not love company. Her misery loved to be alone. Her misery threatened to bludgeon company.

"I'm fine." She hardly stopped. Another funny thing about having friends was that they expected things of you. They made you want to not be a terrible, awful, execrable person. They made you feel even worse when you were one. It was a lot easier not to have any friends.

"Gaia, wait. What's going on?" He rolled along after her.

She was tempted to find a quick set of stairs to ascend. Jesus, she really was an awful person.

"Haven't you heard from the angry hordes at school? I put Heather in the hospital. Didn't they tell you?"

"They—I—I mean—," Ed stammered.

"Come on, Ed. They did, didn't they?"

"But Gaia, you know it's not true," Ed argued, breathless from rushing to keep up with her. "You are not responsible for Heather. Even if you had warned her to stay away from the park, she would have cut through, anyway. She wouldn't have listened to you. There's nothing you could have done."

Gaia made a sharp turn onto West Fourth. Ed's tires practically left skid marks.

"Gaia, are you even listening?" Ed demanded.

She didn't bother to stop at the light on Seventh Avenue.

"Gaia! Come on!"

She practically sprinted all the way down Perry Street and pulled up short in front of George and Ella's house.

"Listen to me. What happened to Heather was scary and horrible, but it was not your fault."

Gaia walked up all fifteen steps of the front stoop before she turned around to look at him. "Ed Fargo. Thank you for trying beyond all possible reason to be my friend," she said quietly. "But it was my fault."

She turned her key in the door, went inside the house, and shut the door firmly behind her. She went up three flights of stairs with the grace of a robot. Once in her room she walked straight to the vintage turntable she'd recently hauled from the garbage and set up on the mantel. She reached behind the pile of records she kept in the nonfunctional fireplace to the LP in the very back.

She'd long ago memorized every centimeter of the faded, brittle record cover, memorized every word. She took out the record gingerly and set it on the player. She didn't need to study the grooves to know exactly where to set the needle.

The music filled the room, loud enough to destroy the speakers, to infuriate Ella, to explode her own head.

It was the second movement of the Sibelius violin concerto, the darkest, saddest piece of music on the planet. It was her mother's favorite—her weird, beautiful Eastern European mother with the embarrassing accent. Her mother knew all of Tchaikovsky, Rachmaninoff, Sibelius, and Prokofiev and nothing of Nirvana or any music Gaia held to be important at the time. She'd been so annoyed at her mother for that.

But now the soaring, wailing violin touched Gaia's cracked heart, and she did something she only allowed herself once or twice a year.

She lay down on the floor and cried.

He needed
to pull
himself
out of
this
trance,
to get a
little
distance.

the opposite of love

SAM SAT IN THE WAITING ROOM OF the intensive care unit, rhythmically whacking his heel against the foot of the couch. It was just like hospital waiting rooms were supposed to be: genuine Naugahyde couch and chairs, plastic side tables displaying magazines you wouldn't have wanted

Not Thinking of an Elephant

to read in the late eighties when they came out. A mounted television showed some wretched soap opera that might as well have been filmed and closed-captioned in that very hospital.

He hadn't seen Heather since last night, and he felt nervous. Finding her in the park eighteen hours before, white as the moon in a dark puddle of blood, was such a potent jolt to his system, he was still breathing, moving, thinking too fast.

God, she'd looked so fragile and broken. He'd thought she was dead until he detected the faintest, slowest flutter of a pulse in her wrist. After that everything exploded into sound and motion. Screaming ambulance sirens, police sirens, people hurrying every which way.

He hadn't slept since, of course, so his senses were oddly distorted—colors were too bright, noises too shrill, smells too acrid. `Time was disjointed.` For example, hadn't it been at least two hours since Heather's parents had disappeared with a doctor into Heather's room, telling him they would be out in ten minutes?

What little peace he had would be shattered when Heather's sisters arrived from their colleges and Heather's friends stormed the place the moment school let out. A bunch of those friends had already `camped out in the waiting room through their lunch period, spewing millions and trillions of words.`

But Sam would suffer them. He would deprive himself of food and drink and sleep and continue to torture himself with this ridiculous soap opera as punishment, laughably slight though it was.

What was the punishment for? For contemplating a breakup with Heather not half an hour before she nearly bled to death. For sitting here, his skin intact as a newborn's, while Heather lay slashed in a coma. For thinking nonstop of *that girl*.

Mistake. Big mistake. Better not to think of thinking about her because then suddenly he was thinking of her. No. Stop. Heel. New thought.

New thought . . . He dragged his mind back to an absorbing topic, one he could worry and fiddle with obsessively, like a bloody hangnail. `What was that girl's name?` The one Tina and Co. had blathered on about for a solid hour? Maia. No. What was it? Gaia? Something like that. How he hated her. Loathed and despised her. What kind of person would let an innocent girl walk straight into a situation they knew was deadly? How petty and small and cowardly this girl Gaia must be.

Of course, the knife-wielding devil who attacked Heather deserved the real blame. But he was beyond hating. He was beyond imagining. Gaia, on the other hand, was a classmate. She was one of them.

Ah. This was good. Righteous indignation got him back on course every time. If he could just keep this focus, keep railing loyally against Gaia, he wouldn't have to think for minutes at a stretch of *that girl.*

GAIA DREADED THIS WORSE THAN she would dread a group hug with Ella and George or thirty-three simultaneous root canals or even trying out for the cheer-leading squad. But she would make herself do it. She would drag herself right up to the

The Boyfriend

eighth floor of this hospital, past the bevy of Heather's friends who detested her, the desperate parents who were too broken up to care about her, the steadfast, adoring boyfriend who'd maybe take a nanosecond from his grieving to curse her name. It was the right thing for Gaia to do. The fact that she dreaded it so much only made it seem more necessary.

Gaia emerged from the elevator and hesitated in front of the nurses' station.

"You're a friend of Heather Gannis?" the orange-haired nurse asked without even looking up from her computer.

"I—"

"Waiting room on your left," the nurse said, still not looking up.

Gaia loitered another moment, feeling wrong about going to the waiting room under false pretenses. But what was she going to do, pour out her heart to the overburdened nurse? Like she'd care that Gaia dumped coffee on Heather or that Heather bitched her out at a party?

"Okay," Gaia said, as meekly as she'd ever said anything. "Thanks."

Walk. Walk. Walk, she ordered herself.

Okay, there they were, spilling out into the hallway. The Friends. When they saw her, would they make a scene right there in the waiting room? Throw stones? Burn her at the stake?

The first murderous glance came from Tina herself. Many others followed as Gaia attempted to slip past the too full room. The murmur of hushed conversation stopped.

Tina gaped at her but was apparently so appalled, she couldn't speak. Instead the good-looking boy who'd been with Tina last night, the old suede-jacketed star of Gaia's cafe fantasy, stepped in.

"Why are you here?" he demanded.

Why was she here? That was a good question.

Because it was the last place on earth she wanted to be?

Because self-flagellation was the only thing that felt right?

Gaia's real answer made her sound like a kiss-ass, so she didn't want to say it out loud: She was here because she wanted and needed to apologize to Heather, even if Heather couldn't hear. Gaia didn't want to pander to the crowd, and she wasn't looking for social resurrection. She was perfectly happy being a pariah. That was as comfortable to her as a pair of old shoes.

So, as often happened, she said nothing. She continued on her way down the hall without a particular plan in mind.

The second room on the right, through a wide-open doorway, was Heather's. Gaia drew in a sharp breath and quickly averted her eyes. She hadn't meant to go right there exactly. She hadn't imagined how Heather would look, frail as a bird, hooked up by scores of tubes to machines that dripped and machines that bleeped, shorn of the self-consciously cool clothing and the beauty that made it so much easier for Gaia to ridicule her. Gaia suddenly felt like throwing up.

There was something much, much worse than your enemy receiving praise, fame, and riches and living happily ever after with an exceptionally handsome guy: your enemy getting slashed in the park after you hoped it would happen.

Her eyes swept into the room again. There, as expected, she saw the dark head of The Boyfriend, bowed over Heather's prone, still body. Maybe he was crying.

Oh, shit. Shit. Shit. Gaia had no right to be there. What had she been thinking?

It was some selfish hope for exoneration that brought her, nothing nobler than that. Now what? She'd walk herself to the end of the hall. She'd wait a minute or two. She'd walk herself back out to the reception area, maybe find a waiting room on another floor, keep her own private vigil for a few hours—or days, if necessary—until things settled down. And then, as politely as possible, she'd apologize to Heather's parents and ask if she might have permission to apologize to Heather. They'd think she was a complete freak, but that hardly mattered, did it?

Gaia trudged to the end of the hall. On her way back she cast one last look in Heather's room. Quiet though she was, The Boyfriend chose that very moment to look up.

Gaia's eyes stuck to his, and she couldn't move them.

Her body reacted before her mind. Her head swam. The Coke she'd had for lunch climbed up her esophagus. All oxygen departed her lungs.

It was him. He was it.

It, him, he was Heather's boyfriend.

The evil, ugly monster with the matted, stinking hair and the razor-blade fangs moved up from her stomach and took a chomp at her heart.

Gaia staggered toward the elevator so he wouldn't see her when her knees gave out.

IN RETROSPECT, IT WOULD HAVE BEEN

A Salted Slug

so much better if Sam had stayed where he was.

Instead, for no good reason, he allowed his unfaithful legs to carry him from Heather's side, where he belonged, down the hall and after *the girl*.

It was impossible for him to explain why. He didn't decide to do it. His body was just suddenly up and moving. It was like when the doctor thwacked your knee. You didn't *decide* to kick your foot.

"Wait," he said as she fled from him just as she had a few days before.

Heather's sisters and a crowd of friends blocked the hallway, impeding the girl's progress. She dodged and wove like a running back facing a defensive line.

"Leaving already, Gaia?" he overheard Carrie Longman say in an unmistakably hostile voice.

The girl broke through the line and made for the elevator bank. Sam followed her there along with a lot of whispers and nasty looks. It honestly did not occur to him that *the girl* was the girl Carrie had been addressing until he was facing her, just two feet away from her, in front of the elevators.

His thoughts were covered in molasses. They moved achingly slowly with big gaps between them.

The girl Carrie had been addressing was called Gaia. . . .

This girl he was now gaping at was called Gaia. . . .

This girl was *the girl*. . . .

The girl was Gaia. . . .

Gaia was the one who had . . .

"Y-You're Gaia," he said to her.

She was silent for a long time, just staring. Her eyes were too much for him.

"You're The Boyfriend," she said slowly.

It sounded like a felony, like an atrocity, the way she said it.

"Sam. My name is Sam."

"Oh." Her face was strangely open, her eyes a whirlpool.

He was scared to let himself read them this time. He was scared of getting sucked in.

"I—you—w-w-we—," he stammered. What exactly did he want to say?

He could see from the panel above the nearest elevator that it was climbing toward them. 3 . . . 4 . . . 5 . . .

"You're the Gaia who saw the guy with the knife in the park last night," he blurted out in a disorganized rush. "You're the one who didn't warn her."

The girl's face was a little too white for a person with a beating heart. Her hands trembled at her sides. She nodded.

"W-Why? I don't understand. Do you dislike her that much?"

"I—I guess I do."

Silence. 6 . . . 7 . . .

He needed to pull himself out of this trance, to get a little distance. He needed to remember who needed defending here. He looked away from her, summoning his shield of righteous indignation. "What is wrong with you? Are you some kind of monster?" He hated the way his voice sounded.

She took so long to respond, it was punishing. Those wide, boundless eyes pinned him to his spot with a look that made him feel horrible, like a salted slug.

"You're not what I thought," she said finally.

Why should *he* feel horrible? *He* hadn't done anything wrong.

The elevator arrived on eight. The doors opened with glacial slowness.

Suddenly he hated her. It was only partly rational, partly fair. She was the source of all the problems, of Heather's condition, of the shameful, disloyal thoughts that had invaded his brain. Now in her face, in her eyes, he saw none of the tenderness or the possibilities he saw before.

"I hate you," he said, amazed as the babyish words emerged from his own mouth.

She stepped into the elevator. "I hate you, too."

He watched her face until the doors closed.

Unbidden, that stupid saying entered his mind: that one about hate not being the opposite of love.

Cold Coffee

"WHO PICKED CJ OUT OF THE lineup?" the older woman asked, leaning over the table that divided them, resting her chin in her palm.

Marco could see down her lavender blouse to the tops of her breasts spilling out of a white bra with lace edges. He wanted to kiss her and touch her so bad. She always wanted to talk first. That was the way most girls were, in his experience. So his mouth went one way and his mind another.

"Nobody knows for sure. Some guys think it was that blond girl—that, uh, friend of yours. A couple of them saw her in the park last night before that other girl . . . you know." He didn't feel like going any deeper into this particular subject. He wanted to talk about how good her shiny red hair looked all loose like that and the dream of his she'd starred in last night.

She crossed her legs under the table, and her knee brushed his. "I heard on the news that the girl who was slashed—they didn't release her name—is out of a coma and expected to make a full recovery," she said.

"Yeah? That's good news for CJ. They'll stick him with assault instead of murder. He never meant to hurt her so bad."

"CJ's in custody? Nobody came up with bail?" she asked.

He pressed his shin against hers. "Nah. It was like a hundred grand or something. His mother lives in Miami. She doesn't even know about it."

"So maybe you'll need to take over in his absence?"

Marco lifted his shoulders so they looked extra big. "Yeah, that's the plan. Tarick, you know, Marty's older brother, wants me to, uh, take care of this old Jew foreigner in the park, this crazy guy who sits over by the chess tables."

She nodded and sipped her coffee.

Marco looked down at his own coffee. He'd hardly touched it. He'd only ordered it because it seemed `more mature than a Coke`. The coffee was cold now, and an iridescent grease slick quivered on the top. Everything in this diner was greasy, but the tables in back were private.

Why was she so fascinated by this stuff? Nothing seemed to shock her or upset her. Was she a writer for a magazine or something? Even though she was older, she was so freakin' sexy, he didn't care much as long as she changed the names and all that.

"Why the old guy?" she asked.

Marco shrugged. "'Cause he's there. He's kind of a joke in the park. This loser kid who wants to be part of things—Renny is his name—he loves this old guy. Marty and them think it would be funny."

"Are you going to do it?"

Marco smiled in a way he thought was both tough and mysterious. "I'll see."

She didn't smile back. "Do you want something else?" she asked. "A Coke?"

He couldn't wait anymore. He stood and grabbed her hand. "I want to get out of here."

She remained seated. "I want to finish my coffee."

1 poppy-seed bagel with cream cheese

1 large coffee with milk and 2 sugars

3 Wint-O-Green Life Savers

When I was twelve, my mind's eye would sometimes flash on ex-cruciating images from the night I lost my mother. They destroyed me, but I couldn't stop. The worst thing you can do in that situation is order your mind *not* to think of something. You know, the old "don't think of an ele-phant" problem. So I invented these tactics for distraction.

The first line of defense was to think about kids at school. Not my friends, exactly, because I didn't have many of those, but the people I fantasized about being friends with. I'd weave these scenes filled with cute dialogue about the fun we'd all have palling around together.

The second line of defense was imagining a boy to fall in love

with. What would he look like?
What kinds of things would he say
to me? Would it be love at first
sight, or would it take me a few
minutes to overwhelm him with my
charm?

If those two didn't work, I
exiled my mind to listing
European capitals, which my dad
made me memorize when I was
three.

And finally, if my mind offered absolutely no place to
hide, if thinking at all was
sheer torment, I would distract
it by cataloging what I'd eaten
the day before.

Tonight, lying on the floor of
my room, the first three attempts
led to:

1. Heather
2. Sam
3. Belgrade

I skipped directly to yesterday's breakfast.

Sam was watching
the place across
the park where
Gaia's back had
been minutes
before.

the

pretty

one

"I don't know,"
he said
absently. "I
got distracted,
I guess."

HEATHER WAS GOING TO BE OKAY.

Heather was expected to make a full recovery.

Gaia was so happy, she felt like telling the man behind the sandwich counter at Balducci's.

"Roast beef?" he asked her.

"Yes," she said. "On that." She pointed to an extravagant-looking roll.

It was all over school today, all anybody was talking about. That and the part Gaia played in the catastrophe. The way the rumor mill was spinning, Gaia expected she would be charged with the slashing herself before the end of the day.

And that was, admittedly, part of the reason why it was 11:45 A.M. and Gaia was buying a sandwich rather than listening to her imbecilic math so-called teacher botch an elementary explanation of sine and cosine.

She paid for the nine-dollar sandwich and headed down Sixth Avenue, swinging the green-and-white bag. Zolov would eat like a king today. She imagined his face when she surprised him at the unusual hour.

Cutting was a serious offense, as she'd been told a few thousand times. Ooooh. She pictured the vice principal calling George at work. Or, God forbid, Ella.

She almost skidded to a stop at a pay phone at the corner of West Eighth. She plunked in her quarter and dialed George's work number. "George Niven, please."

George's voice came on a few seconds later. "This is George Niven."

"Hi, George, it's Gaia. How's it going?"

"Just fine, Gaia. Just fine." He sounded surprised and pleased. "You sound like you're . . . uh . . ."

"I'm actually calling from a pay phone, because I left school early, because I wasn't feeling well."

"I'm sorry to hear that." His voice was filled with such genuine concern, she felt a little bad. "Did you speak to—"

"It's nothing serious. It's . . . well, you know, it's *that* time of the month, and I get these really bad cramps sometimes." Gaia knew there was no faster way to get a man off the phone than to bring up her period.

"Right, right. Of course. Understood." She'd never heard him talk so fast.

Poor George. It was hard enough having a girl in your house, let alone one who arrived fully formed at the age of seventeen.

"So, would you just give them a call and let them know what's up?" she asked.

George was clearly so traumatized, he didn't argue. "Yes. I'll give them a call at the . . . uh, office there. You, uh, just let Ella know. She'll take care of you. There's, uh, there's no better sick nurse than Ella."

Gaia almost laughed at that one. Ella's skirts were too tight to sit at a bedside, and she probably couldn't distinguish aspirin from arsenic. God help George. Love was more than blind. It was deaf and dumb, too. It was catatonic. It was vegetative.

Sixth Avenue passed her by in a stimulating buzz. The buses, the baby strollers, the three-man Peruvian band that played on the corner, the delis overflowing with fruit and flowers, the guy selling dirt-cheap tube socks, underpants, and secondhand books from a card table set up by the curb.

The world was fresher and a lot more spacious when you were supposed to be in school. Kind of like a public pool during adult swim.

She rounded the corner of West Fourth in eager anticipation. Maybe today she would buy a bag of those sugary roasted nuts. The exquisite smell was already reaching her nostrils. Yes, today would be the day.

She breezed into the park, actually appreciating the sunshine for once. It made the place seem so different from the malicious gang nest where Heather had been slashed. She saw Zolov's hunched, familiar back and almost ran for him.

Then she stopped short. She dropped the bag and watched the silver-foil-covered sandwich roll over hexagonal gray stones. She put her hand to her heart.

He was there. The Boyfriend. Sam. Whatever.

He was sitting directly across from *her* friend, concentrating on the chessboard. How dare he? Was he trying to hustle poor old Zolov? Couldn't he see the old man had nothing to lose besides his terrible coat and his Power Ranger? Shouldn't he be in school or something?

She hoped the old man would summon up all his skill and beat the crap out of him.

The Boyfriend, Sam, whatever, looked scruffier today. The cuffs of his flannel shirt weren't buttoned, nor were they rolled up. His hair was sticking up a little in back, and his eyes looked tired. Probably from staying up all those hours worrying about Heather.

Blah. *Blah.* The thought made her sick.

Gaia grabbed the sandwich and stuffed it back in the bag. Now what? She didn't want to see him or talk to him, but she didn't want to flee like a little mouse, either.

Of course he had to look up right then. Right then, as she clutched her pathetic green-and-white bag, paralyzed with uncertainty, eyes round and startled.

Why did he have this effect on her? Why? Had she some intuitive knowledge, the day they played chess, that he was Heather's boyfriend? Did she recognize he represented the best possible way to torment herself?

She couldn't be having these alien feelings about Heather's boyfriend. It was too cruel a coincidence. Was somebody up there having a belly laugh at her expense?

Her mind flashed back to their last encounter in the hospital, and she wanted to groan out loud. She felt her cheeks turning warm.

No doubt about it. She was a femme fatale. A romantic heroine for the ages. A heartbreaker. A female

James Bond. A role model for girls everywhere.

Of the two boys Gaia had ever met in her *entire life* who could have possibly ever maybe meant something important to her (and coincidentally, the only two who had ever beaten her in chess—Stephen from around the corner being the first), she'd told them both she hated them. She was two for two.

No wonder she'd never kissed anybody. "I hate you" wasn't exactly come-hither. It wasn't a big turn-on to most guys. Not ones who belonged on this side of prison, anyway.

Maybe she could sell a book touting her romantic advice. *Gaia's Rules*. Not only should you not call the sucker back; go ahead and tell him you hate him.

And as a follow-up she could publish her popularity secrets. Okay, it was time to go somewhere else. Time to let up on the mean-yet-indifferent laser beams she was directing from her eyes.

She wheeled around, sandwich bag in hand, and walked toward the fountain. It was a beautiful, warm day. Why didn't she just go to the fountain? That was a normal thing to do.

The benches were filled with mothers of babies, nannies, college students, people who didn't have jobs. There, directly in front of her, bathed in the buttery shade of a yellow umbrella, stood the pushcart filled with nuts so sugary and delicious, the smell alone could make you hallucinate.

And she was going to buy a bag. So what if her stomach felt like it had been stapled shut?

"One bag, please," she said to the cart's proprietor as he stirred the caramelized mass. She thrust two dollars in his hand, and he gave her the warm, paper pouch filled with sticky nuts. The smell was a living thing. She put one in her mouth. She chewed. She tried another.

She kept chewing as she walked herself from the fountain to the dog run near the perimeter of the park, feeling her hopes deflate as the grease from the nuts soaked through the paper to her fingers.

Sugar-roasted nuts, as it turned out, could be added to the list that included vanilla extract and bread and meeting a guy you could fall in love with— things that smelled a lot better than they tasted.

"CHECKMATE."

Six Minutes and a Pawn

Sam glanced up in surprise. Zolov wasn't looking at him with his usual winking smile of triumph. He was looking at him with pity.

He had lost? Already? How could that be?

Of course, he always lost to Zolov. In spite of his

insanity, Zolov was a truly great player. In his day the old guy had beaten or drawn many of the greatest chess players in the world. But usually Sam and Zolov fought their way through long, dramatic battles, masterful exchanges of material. Today it was `six minutes and a pawn`.

"Vhat happened to you?" Zolov asked.

Sam was watching the place across the park where Gaia's back had been minutes before. "I don't know," he said absently. "I got distracted, I guess."

"By zat geerl?"

Sam couldn't breathe. He was choking. Was it possible to choke to death on your own saliva? "W-Who?"

"Za preetty vun. She's smart, too, you know."

"I—uh—I don't know who you mean."

Zolov was now smiling. "I teenk you do."

Sam almost bit his tongue in annoyance. After two years of listening to Zolov theorize about the young man who sold sodas by the fountain (World War I Polish spy called Tuber), the social worker from the homeless coalition (malevolent alien from a whole other solar system), the old man picked `quite a moment to be perceptive`.

"I gotta go," Sam said, standing. "Good game," he lied, handing Zolov a five. "I'll see you Thursday."

"Sam?"

Sam turned around in amazement. Zolov called

him "boy" and "keed" and "you," but he never called him "Sam."

"Yeah?"

"You go get zat geerl and tell heer I vant my sand-veech."

"No way," Sam muttered to himself. No way was he ever going anyplace near that kind of trouble again.

As a child, I was a disaster. I had a terrible stammer, which made me shy and pitifully awkward. My teeth pointed in every direction, and my hair was so thick, it lay in a stack on my head.

It started early. I was a maladjusted baby. You may think all babies are at least a little bit cute, but I wasn't. I didn't walk till after I was two. I don't think I learned to talk at all until I was four years old.

My stammer was triggered by everything but by nervousness most of all, and I was always nervous. It was your classic catch-22: My nervousness made me stammer, and the more I stammered, the more nervous I got. I even stammered in my thoughts.

I was badly isolated. I spent all my time either on the computer or playing chess. Or playing chess on the computer. I started playing in chess tournaments when I was about six. Even

SAM

among chess geeks I was considered untouchable. Stop by a chess tournament sometime, and you will see how truly scary that is.

I have an older brother to remind me of all this, in case I ever forget.

When I was twelve, my parents started to worry about me in earnest. I suspect they were embarrassed to take me anyplace. I had a crash course in speech therapy. Several, to be honest. A vengeful orthodontist installed an aircraft carrier worth of metal in my mouth. My mom dragged me to a haircutter who cost about a thousand dollars. She outfitted me at the Gap.

By the time I returned to school for seventh grade, I was unrecognizable. I actually considered changing my name and just starting from scratch.

So I guess you could say life as I know it began when I was twelve. I was born that first day of junior high.

I'm fine now. Even good, according to a lot of people. I know how to dress. I know how to speak. And even so, I'm still good at chess.

I masquerade as one of the blessed. One of the normal, effortless joiners who believe, without thinking about it too deeply, that the world exists for people like us. It's a lie, of course. I come from the other side. I know what it's like over there.

There are still vestiges of dorkdom in me. (See my use of the word *vestiges*, for example.) They pop up all the time. They remind me that if I were born in another age, say, prehistory—before braces and speech therapy—I would be the dorkiest caveman who ever lived. And the person I was probably meant to be.

Her gaze swept
over Sam's
still body,
and she had an
almost **melting**
overwhelming
need to go **away**
to him, to
kneel over him
and make sure he
was breathing.

SHE WASN'T *THAT* PRETTY. OKAY,

First and Second Punches

she was that pretty. But not pretty like Heather—the kind of pretty that everybody noticed right away. Gaia's face, devoid of makeup or any expression meant to please, was unfortunately more mesmerizing to Sam every time he saw it. God, and those eyes. They haunted him. He couldn't get a fix on them—one time they were the endless azure of a summer sky, another time the blue-violet of early evening, and still another the indescribable color of a typhoon.

He turned up LaGuardia. It was almost eight-thirty in the evening, and he wanted to get to the hospital to see Heather before visiting hours were up. He'd cut through the park. Just a corner of it.

But it wasn't just the way Gaia looked. Was it because she was so unbelievably good at chess? Granted, that had really thrown him. But that couldn't explain it fully, either.

He had every reason to dislike her. He *did* dislike her. No decent person would have treated Heather the way Gaia had. For a while he'd tried convincing himself that he was thinking about her so much because he disliked her, but it wasn't working anymore.

Sam was a rational person. Overly rational,

if you listened to Heather, or his mother, or most of his friends. He wasn't romantic. He wasn't poetic. He wasn't nostalgic. He wasn't obsessive—until this week, anyway. What was wrong with him? What were the chances that she, Gaia, had thought about him even a minute for each hour he'd thought of her?

He was a rational person. He would figure this out, and maybe then he could make it go away, he assured himself as he glanced toward the chess tables, squinting through the darkness to see that none of the few shadowy figures was hers.

He didn't see her, but he did see something strange. He moved closer.

He first recognized the hunched shape of Zolov swaying to get to his feet. Another figure was hovering, bearing down on the old man. He heard a groan, first quiet, then it grew loud and terrifying. Sam was running before he was able to process what was happening.

"Zolov!" he shouted.

The old man was waving his arms, trying to defend himself from the attack. He shouted hoarsely in a language Sam didn't understand.

It was a young man, Sam realized as he raced toward them, and he had a razor blade.

"Get away from him!" Sam shouted.

The young man turned his head and locked eyes with Sam for a millionth of a second. He was young, dark haired, intense, pumped up on adrenaline or something else. Sam hated him. What kind of monster would attack a fragile, crazy old man? Sam watched in horror as he threw Zolov to the ground.

Zolov cried out. Sam saw blood on the old man's face, flooding the crags and wrinkles. His heart was seized with panic. He threw himself at the attacker and shoved him as hard as he could. Thoughts were only fragments moving through his mind at uneven speeds. The attacker lost his balance, but only for a moment. He steadied himself and came at Sam.

There was a fist, really big. Sam heard an awful-sounding crack, then saw the orange insides of his eyelids. He blinked his eyes open. He was still on his feet. His cheekbone was blazing with pain. One eye was pounding, already swelling with blood.

The fist was coming again, but time was Oslow now. Slow enough for Sam to dodge the fist and to remember that he had never been in a fight before, that he was out of his league. He willed his hand to clench. He trained his good eye on the guy's mouth. He swung as hard as he could.

His knuckles connected to soft flesh. The guy grunted. Sam felt a surge of energy so strong, it seemed to erase his memory, to blow out his consciousness. He swung again without thinking. He caught an ear this time, hard. The guy staggered to one side, caught his balance. He didn't come back at Sam, as Sam was expecting. Instead he stepped backward, putting several more feet between them.

"You're dead," he hissed at Sam through blubbery, swollen lips. "I'm going to kill you." And then he ran off.

Sam was almost instantly kneeling at Zolov's side. The old man was groaning softly. Sam took his shirt and gently wiped away blood so he could determine the seriousness of the wound. It appeared to be shallow and less than two inches in length but bleeding heavily. Zolov's eyes fluttered open, then shut again. His breath was short and raspy. Sam was suddenly terrified the old man's heart was going to stop. He hated to leave him, but he needed to get help.

"Zolov," he whispered, cradling his head. "You're gonna be okay, but I need to call an ambulance. I'll be back as fast as I can." He laid the gray, frizzled head on the soft ground. He stood looking at him for another moment before he took off at a sprint for the public pay phone.

AS SOON AS GAIA HEARD THE NOISE

Another Mistake

the fine, light hair on her arms prickled and her skin was covered with bumps. She had the feeling sometimes that when she sensed danger, her vision and her hearing became almost supernaturally acute. She could almost feel her muscles feasting on oxygen, preparing for action. She knew the muffled cries and moans were Zolov's well before she actually saw him.

Zolov's attacker broke away as Gaia flew to the old man's side. She put her arms around the frail shoulders, examining the wound on his face. There was a certain amount of blood, but it was already thickening around the slash. That was a good sign. She clutched him gently. "You're going to be fine," she promised him, not wanting to leave him in his disoriented state.

But she had to because, amazingly, the demon who had attacked the old man was still within sight. Gaia ran like hell. In the darkness she saw nothing more than his silhouette.

The attacker sprinted toward the south edge of the park. Gaia flew after him, her rage undergoing nuclear fission as her feet pounded the pavement. What kind of monster would attack a helpless old man?

He was fast, but she was faster. She literally launched herself from the ground and tackled him from behind. He shouted in surprise. They rolled together across a grassy patch, limbs tangling. Strong arms circled her hips, pulling her down. They tumbled again before she managed to pin him under her. She secured his torso between her knees and shoved his head to the ground. Her hands were tightening around his neck before she looked him in the face.

She closed her eyes in disbelief. When she opened them again, her heart changed places with her stomach.

It was Sam.

She was so astounded, she let go of him, and in an instant he'd flipped her over. Now he was kneeling over her, pressing her shoulders into the ground with his hands.

"*Gaia*, what do you think you're *doing?*" he bellowed at her.

She saw clearly now that one of his eyes was purple and almost swollen shut. Her mind was whizzing, trying to make sense of it.

"Zolov is hurt," Sam yelled only inches from her ear. "He was slashed. I need to call for help!"

Her ears rang painfully. "Y-You," she choked out. "I thought you—"

"You thought I what? I slashed him? Are you insane?" Sam's eyes—or the one that was still open, anyway—were wild with adrenaline. Her waist was gripped too tightly between his knees. He was digging the heels of his hands into her chest.

In a lightning-quick move she managed to get one hand around each of his arms and pulled them out from under him. His weight collapsed on top of her, and she quickly flipped him over again. She drove her knee into his abdomen and held him steady with her forearms. "Then who did it?" she demanded.

He stared at her with a mixture of anger and disbelief. "Some asshole who's going to get away if you don't *get the hell off me!*" He wrapped his arms around her back in a bear hug and tried to roll her again, but this time she wasn't budging.

He was holding her so tight, her face was buried in his neck. "Fine," she said as well as she could, considering her lips were pressed against his skin. "Let me go, and I'll let you go." But neither of them moved.

"Fine. You let go first," he demanded in her hair. His voice was strained by the presence of her knee in his stomach.

Gingerly, slowly, she let up the pressure from her knee.

"Whoa!" she called out as he threw her off him, fast and surprisingly hard. Her butt landed on the pavement. "Ouch," she complained.

She was mad. She couldn't help herself. As soon as he was on his feet she sprang to hers and shoved him. He reeled backward a couple of steps, then leaped at her and shoved her right back.

Her eyes widened in disbelief. As soon as she caught her balance, she stormed at him. He was a lot taller than she, so she had to jump to jab her shoulder into his solar plexus.

"Uff!" he grunted. She was satisfied to see she'd

nearly knocked the wind out of him. She put two hands on his stomach and pushed him to the ground.

With admirable speed he rolled toward her and hugged her ankles. "Oh!" she shouted in surprise as he pulled her legs out from under her. She fell directly on top of him.

In anger and confusion she grabbed the first thing she could—his hair, as it turned out. He grabbed hers right back. She was lying on top of him, one arm around his neck. His legs were clasped around hers, his arm circling her waist.

Where had her great fighting prowess gone? She'd been baffled, confused, angered by this guy who wasn't extraordinarily skilled or trained. And now she'd been reduced to pulling hair?

"There he is!" a voice shouted.

From their tangle on the grass they both looked up, mute.

Sharp Edges

"OH, SHIT," SAM MUMBLED, STILL clutching Gaia as the guy who had attacked Zolov came near, flanked by two guys on each side. The guy's lips were grossly misshapen, and he looked mad enough to dismember, if not kill.

Suddenly Sam found himself holding Gaia even tighter, but strangely, his motive had transformed. He no longer wanted to pull her limb from limb; now he felt an urgent need to protect her.

There were five of them. Count them, five. Three of them were big. Two of them looked young—in their middle teens, maybe, and not totally filled out. For a moment he buried his eyes in Gaia's soft, pale hair.

If it weren't so surreal and horrendous, he would have laughed. In the last five minutes he'd thrown the first and second punches of his life, found himself wrestling on the ground with the object of his infatuation—not only brilliant at chess but a match for Hulk Hogan. Now he was holding her in his arms and smelling her hair as he faced imminent death at the hands of five angry gang members while his ancient friend and mentor was possibly bleeding to death.

"Get off your girlfriend and stand up," the slasher demanded roughly.

Somehow it didn't seem necessary to point out that Gaia was not his girlfriend. They sorted out their limbs and both stood up. They exchanged a look, filled with things he couldn't decipher. Amazing how quickly your enemy seemed like your friend when faced with a worse enemy.

"Jesus, it's *her*," one of the guys said.

Sam looked at Gaia again. He couldn't guess what that meant. "Leave her alone," he barked at them, stepping forward. He suddenly felt like he was playing a role in a movie, portraying a character who said and did things he never would. Best to keep pretending because reality—namely five guys (and possibly one girl) who wanted to kill him—was hard to take.

"Gaia, go," he said in a low voice. "I'll be okay." Ha! Had his character really just said that? She was standing so close, he could still feel the warmth of her body. It was intoxicating—really not what he needed at the moment.

The guy, the swollen-lipped slasher, was only a few feet away now, bouncing a little on the balls of his feet. His friends had circled Sam and Gaia. Two of them wore floppy hoods, covering their shaved heads and keeping their faces in shadow. Another had a Doo-Rag pulled low over his forehead. As he looked at them Sam was weirdly calm and disconnected. He was resigned to getting beat up. He felt more scared about what they might do to Gaia.

"Let her go," Sam said.

The guy's smile was grotesque with the swollen lip pulling in odd directions. "My bud CJ thinks she did him wrong."

One of the hooded guys came forward and grabbed Gaia by the shoulders. He dragged her several yards from Sam, pinning her arms to her sides in a bear hug.

The horror was now dawning on Sam. He felt bile rising in his throat. Anger mixed with fear to make desperation. Gaia's eyes were huge and luminous.

He went after the guy who held her. Fast, without letting himself think too much, he hauled off and punched the guy, catching his jawbone so hard, his knuckles blazed. Gaia slipped quickly out of the guy's grip.

Get away, he urged her silently. Run away and get—

He'd grabbed her waist and was about to physically shove her when a slamming blow to the back of his head shattered his mind. He spun around and got a sharp kick in the stomach. He was lying on the ground now, disoriented by the number of arms and feet and faces spinning against a sapphire sky. A kick landed on his chest and took his breath away.

He saw Gaia's face over him, glowing white like an angel's. Broken thoughts and feelings lay in pieces, with edges sharp enough to cut. He reached for her. He wanted to tell her something, but he couldn't fit the aching, full-hearted feelings into words. The last thing he saw from the corner of his eye was a Timberland coming at the side of his head. After that, thankfully, he saw and felt nothing.

Sleeping Beauty

GAIA WASN'T AFRAID. SHE WAS never afraid. But she felt the abstract terror of a world without Sam, without the idea or the possibility of Sam, and she didn't want to live there. It felt so dark and arid that it would surely dry up all of her senses and parch her last blossom of hope.

Her rage exploded, less controlled, more intense than ever before. The five of them became an indistinguishable mass to her, without human features. She took them on as one multilimbed creature. Her adrenaline carried her, so she didn't have to think or count or predict.

She took one of them out with her fist. Clean, just like that. Another one required a combination of kicks to finish him off. In the process she took a sharp jab in the ribs and another guy's fist caught her in the forehead as she tried to duck. She could feel the blood gathering at the wound. The red drips were a nuisance in her eyes, but she was too far gone to feel pain.

Two of the guys bobbed in her peripheral vision. The third she had head-on in her sights. She planted a kick in that vulnerable place in his neck just as another one slammed her from the side. Another down, she registered as she tried to find her balance. Then

171

came another slam from the side. The blood stung her eyes and tinctured her mouth with its coppery flavor. Head wounds bled too much. It was a shame. She might not have enough time.

Two weaving heads, eight thrashing limbs. It was an ugly but simpler creature that remained.

Her gaze swept over Sam's still body, and she had an almost overwhelming need to go to him, to kneel over him and make sure he was breathing.

Bam! A blow to her stomach sent her sprawling on the ground. *Focus, Gaia,* she urged herself. She had to focus as hard as she possibly could to get them through this. Loss of blood made her hazy and faint.

Another guy came rushing toward her at an angle she could use. She caught his momentum and threw him over her head. He rolled twice. It gave her enough time to get back to her feet. But just as she did the other one smashed her from behind and sent her back to the pavement. As she raised her head, she saw a pale, scared face peering from a stand of trees. She knew the face. He took a few steps forward.

"Renny, you little shit, get over here!" the bigger of the guys bellowed.

Renny was frozen, except for his face, which quivered like a squirrel's.

Suddenly Gaia felt her arms wrenched roughly behind her back. The two of them were holding her. She tried to jab her way free with her elbow, but she couldn't move it.

"Come on, little boy, here's your big chance!" the other guy called.

Gaia didn't feel like writhing to get out of their grip. It was a waste of time. The blood was leaving her head and making her feel tired. She wished she could just pass out and be done with it.

"Renny! Step up, man. You in or out?"

Renny took another step forward. He looked terrified at the sight of Gaia, no doubt something right out of a horror movie with all that blood on her face and shirt.

Suddenly Gaia saw the dull glint of steel. She thought she was imagining it at first. But even the idea was enough to clear her foggy head.

Yes, it was real. She could see it clearly now. The fat-lipped guy was pushing a gun, a .38-caliber pistol, into Renny's hand. Where had it come from? Why hadn't she been paying better attention? "Finish her off, Renny. Do it now!"

Gaia's adrenaline level notched up. Her body was on full alert, but her mind had entered that dreamlike state, wondering numbly, philosophically, whether this was the end of her life. There were few physical brawls she couldn't find her way out of, but a gun changed everything. It empowered the cowardly and rendered skill, bravery, and character useless.

That was why Gaia, though she was trained to be an exceptional markswoman, never used one. She'd rather lose on her terms than win on those. Now the gun was in Renny's hand. Shaky, but pointing directly at her. He wasn't looking anywhere near her eyes.

Oh, this was hard to take. Was little Renny, her favorite chess whiz, really going to sink a bullet into her? It seemed like a very bad life where that would happen. If he was going to, she hoped he would get on with it because she didn't feel like sticking around much longer to watch.

Renny looked like he was going to puke. His eyes were glazing over, and his skin was the color of iceberg lettuce. He came up so close, she could hear his breath. She was staring down the barrel of the gun. She pulled her eyes back to Renny's.

Look at me, she demanded of him silently. Look at me! *Look at me!* If he was going to do this, let him do it for real. Let him know the full meaning of popping that trigger.

Don't be a coward, Renny. Look at me!

At last he did. His eyes lighted on hers. He hesitated only a moment. Then he turned and ran like hell. Gaia heard the gun clattering on the pavement.

Good boy, Renny, she told him silently as he sprinted for the streetlights.

"Freakin' coward," one of the guys muttered.

It gave Gaia the burst she needed. She slammed her heel as hard as she could into one guy's shin. When he let her go to clutch his leg, she wrenched herself free from the other guy and followed up with a searing blow to the side of the injured guy's head. Then another rapid jab to his abdomen. He crumpled, gasping for breath.

She lunged for the gun, grabbing it from the ground. Without a pause she hauled off and threw it. It traced a high arc through the sky. She didn't have time to watch where it landed.

She faced the last one now. He was familiar to her from another time, but her head was too blurry to cobble together a memory. His lips were swollen, and his jacket was speckled with blood, probably hers. Gray spots grew and multiplied, clouding her vision. She heard the punch to her shoulder before she felt it. She stepped back and shook her head in the hope of clearing it. She came forward and cracked her fist across his nose. His fist landed hard on her cheekbone. She reeled back, losing her footing, almost falling directly onto Sam.

On your feet, girl, she begged herself. But then she heard something. It was faint but approaching fast and sounded to her more beautiful than a Mozart symphony. The guy heard it, too. He stopped. Listened. He gave her a last look before he ran.

Bless you, Renny, she thought as she fell back against Sam, listening to the siren coming near.

She turned as gingerly as she could. She put her hand on Sam's chest. He was breathing. He definitely was. She put her hand gently on his cheek, then skimmed her fingers over his battered eye. She smoothed his hair back from his beautiful forehead. She hadn't touched another human being like this in almost five years. Transfixed, she ran her trembling hand from the cool softness of his upper cheek to the masculine stubble of his chin. His perfect skin was broken in several places. What had she done to him?

And almost more disturbing, what had he done to her?

Tears spilled from her eyes and mixed with the blood drying on her face. A drop of the pink moisture landed on his forehead. And another. It blended with the beads of sweat on his brow.

She felt like she was entering a trance as she lowered her face toward his. She touched her lips against his with exquisite gentleness, slowly deepening the kiss as she surrendered her heart.

She heard voices coming near. She lifted her head. Sam's eyes fluttered open and then closed again.

She could die now. She laid her head on his chest and melted away.

To: L
From: ELJ
Date: October 2
File: 776244
Subject: Gaia Moore
Last Seen: Washington Square Park, New York City, 8:37 P.M.

Update: Subject hospitalized after prolonged fight with several gang members and a man identified as Sam Moon, age 20, sophomore at NYU. Three gang members arrested at the scene, two others fled. Old man known as Zolov was taken to the hospital and treated for a surface wound to the face. Subject received surface wound to the head, resulting in considerable loss of blood. Multiple contusions. Expected discharge 10/3.

To: ELJ
From: L
Date: October 2
File: 776244
Subject: Gaia Moore

Unacceptable. Subject was not to be injured
under any circumstances. Contact me immediately for new placement.

When he was
near her,
his own mind
betrayed
him. **dangerous**
The smartest
hope
thing he
could do was
stay away
from her
permanently.

"IT'S SO TRENDY, ALMOST BLEEDING

to death. All the cool girls are doing it."

Gaia didn't open her eyes. Instead she considered the voice, felt the calloused hand wrapped around hers. She meant to smile, but it came out wobbly. "Hi, Ed," she said.

Boy Flowers

When she opened her eyes, she saw a small bundle of orange carnations perched in a Snapple bottle on the bedside table. "Those are such boy flowers," she noted in a weak, slightly raspy voice.

"What do you mean?"

"Only a boy would buy dyed carnations," she explained. "Girls buy less obvious stuff, like tulips and irises."

"Are you saying you don't like them?"

"No, I do like them. I accept that you are a boy. I'm happy that you are a boy."

Ed looked happy that he was a boy, too.

"So who did you beat up this time?" he asked.

"That sounded like a question," she said.

"Oh, yeah. This is like reverse *Jeopardy*. Um . . . let's see. . . . You beat up ten guys, each four times your size, and one poor bastard got in a lucky punch."

She nodded. "Pretty much. Only multiply the equation by one-half."

"Only five guys." He shook his head. "You're losing your edge."

Gaia studied his face thoughtfully. "I guess you could say it was six guys—only one was kind of a mistake."

"A mistake."

"I got in a fight by accident with Sam—Heather's boyfriend."

"Wow, you really do get around."

"I didn't mean to. I thought he'd slashed Zolov, the old guy who plays chess in the park. But it turned out Sam was only trying to help."

"I see. But you discovered that *after* you knocked his head off." He made an obvious effort not to let the end of his sentence bend into a question.

"Sort of," she admitted.

"Mmmm. Maybe you'll find an excuse to beat up Heather's parents next."

"Ha-ha-ha."

Gaia closed her eyes. Her right cheekbone was throbbing, the cut on her forehead stung, and her stomach muscles ached. She was suddenly too tired to think.

"Hey, Ed," she finally said.

"Yup."

"Thank you for trying to be my friend."

"Am I succeeding? Uh . . . I mean . . ." He cleared his throat. "I am succeeding." He said it in a deep, smooth voice, like a news anchor.

She laughed. "Annoyingly well."

He squeezed her hand. "I'm glad."

She moved her toes under the stiff sheets. "Is Heather still in the hospital?" she asked.

Ed nodded. "Two doors down."

"You're joking."

"No, they moved her out of the ICU. She's going home tomorrow, just like you. Maybe you two can have a joint party."

Gaia sighed. "I still need to apologize to her."

"I don't see why."

"For almost getting her killed," Gaia said.

"But that wasn't your fault."

"Yes, it was."

"It wasn't."

"Was."

"Wasn't."

"Was."

"Wasn't."

"Was."

Ed let out his breath in frustration. "Gaia."

"What?"

"You have got to get over yourself."

"What do you mean?"

"Not everything bad that happens has to be about you."

For no reason that she could understand, tears flooded Gaia's eyes. Something big grew in her throat that prevented her from swallowing. Ed was getting close to a place that hurt, and she wanted him to go away. She tipped back her head so the tears wouldn't spill over her bottom lids. Thank the Lord for water cohesion.

Ed watched her carefully. His expression was gentle but serious. "You're tough as hell, Gaia, but you're not a god. You're made of the same stuff as the rest of us."

"Ed?" she asked in a thick voice. "Would you leave now? I think I can only handle having a friend in five-minute bursts."

ZOLOV WAS IN ROOM 502. HEATHER

Remember Heather

was now in room 724, and Gaia was in room 728. Sam had been released from the emergency room last night after being examined and bandaged. He had slept—or at least lain—in his own bed most of last night. Today he made his rotations like a physician. Like a disoriented, exhausted, overwrought, inept physician who hadn't actually gone to medical school.

He had no idea what happened last night. It was a complete mystery why he wasn't dead and who'd fought off the gang. One of the policemen thought it was Renny, the kid who'd called 911, but that didn't make much sense. One of the paramedics jokingly suggested it was Superman.

Sam had this strange, hazy memory of Gaia . . . but no. That was obviously a fitful hallucination—a product of his own deranged fantasy life.

Zolov's slashing wound was minor, but he was so old, the doctor on call wanted to observe him for another twenty-four hours. Zolov seemed to Sam in happy spirits and was very fond of the hospital food. He'd already discovered an orderly who loved to play chess.

Heather lay in the bed only a foot away from him, almost good as new and being released the following afternoon.

Gaia, he hadn't actually spoken to. He'd only prowled around the door to her room like a cat burglar, wanting to catch a glimpse of her but feeling too weird to actually enter.

"So Carrie told me that Miles and them are all coming over tomorrow night. It was supposed to be a surprise, but . . . you know."

Sam didn't know, but he nodded, anyway. Heather had been chatting gaily at him for almost an hour. She was propped up in her bed, surrounded by at least a billion flowers, wearing her own pink linen robe. The bouquet he'd carefully chosen was hidden behind two veritable towers of greenery and a gargantuan basket of fruit. Nurses and doctors and scores and scores of visitors slipped in and out, attending to her as if she were a reigning queen. Her face was flushed and lovely.

"And you'll be there, right?"

Sam glanced up. He'd forgotten to listen to the first part of the question. He nodded again.

"Great. I mean, my mom is going to, like, shit if I'm not in bed by ten. But it will be fun, anyway."

Heather didn't know Gaia was just down the hall. She'd accepted his explanation for his swollen purple eye with a minimum of questions. She'd cooed about how brave he was and how he'd avenged her, which wasn't true, of course, but whatever.

". . . Don't you think?" She was looking at him expectantly after a long soliloquy on something or other.

Sam nodded, grateful Heather only asked yes or no questions and rhetorical ones at that.

"I figure we can just order more if we run out," Heather continued.

How had Heather managed to turn a hospital stay into such a social whirlwind? he wondered as two more random friends waved at her from the doorway. "We'll come back," one of them whispered loudly in a we're-cool-to-the-fact-that-your-boyfriend-is-here kind of way.

"Right," he said absently.

185

He was thinking about whether or not the door to room 728 would be fully open and what he might say if he did venture into room 728. And then he felt ashamed. What kind of asshole obsessed about a troubling near stranger when his girlfriend was in the hospital?

He was considering this when Heather's face changed distinctly. He turned to see why. He clamped his jaw down so hard, he nearly crushed his back teeth.

"Um, hello?" It was Gaia hovering at the door. Her face was tentative. He'd never seen her hair down before. It was a pale, beautiful yellow, and there was lots of it—it fell below her shoulders. Her few freckles stood out in the fluorescent light.

Heather's expression turned from surprised to pinched and angry. "What are you doing here?"

"I—I—um, actually spent the night down the hall because—"

Heather shook her head in disbelief. "I swear to God, it's like you're stalking me."

Gaia looked desperately uncomfortable as her gaze shifted from Heather to Sam and then back again. Her skin looked so pale, it was almost translucent. She tugged and fidgeted with her grayish purple hospital gown. "I don't know if you heard, but I . . . there was . . . this fight last night and . . ."

"Do I care?" Heather's voice was so harsh, Sam winced inwardly.

"No, it's just . . ." Gaia sighed and started over. "It doesn't matter. I just wanted to tell you that I'm very sorry for not warning you about the guy with the knife in the park. It was a bad and dishonorable thing to do, and I don't need you to say it's okay or anything. I'm not looking to be friends. But what I did was wrong, and I'm very sorry for it."

Sam's heart moved up through his chest and into his throat as he watched Gaia. He saw something in her eyes (when he let himself) that was so profoundly vulnerable and scarred that her defiance only made it more moving and distressing to him. Was he the only one who saw it? Was he imagining it? He found himself hoping with unfamiliar passion that Heather would be kind to her. Gaia's speech was met with at least a minute of silence.

"Are you done?" Heather finally asked.

Sam's heart dislocated his tonsils. He couldn't swallow. He was supposed to be on Heather's side. She was his girlfriend, and furthermore, she was the one who'd been wronged. But he struggled against the impulse to put his arms around Gaia and tell Heather to go to hell.

Gaia nodded.

"Then please go away," Heather said. She was capable of causing hypothermia when she felt like it.

Gaia left just as Heather's mom arrived in the

doorway. Sam practically leaped to his feet. "Heather, your mom probably wants some time with you," he mumbled, needing to get out of that room if he was ever going to breathe again. "Hey, Mrs. Gannis," he said politely, bolting past her.

He paused for a moment or two before following Gaia into her room. Although it was only a matter of thirty feet from Heather's, it belonged to a different universe. Aside from a pitiful clump of bright orange flowers in a sticky-looking glass bottle, it was colorless, empty, quiet. Gaia was sitting with her arms around her knees on the radiator under the window, `staring out at the rain.`

"Gaia?" he said.

She turned around. She had those eyes again. "Hi."

She looked like a waif in her hospital gown. Her feet were bare, her ankles surprisingly delicate. Her toenails were mostly covered in chipped brown polish. She had such a big presence, he'd never realized how slight she could appear.

It was too quiet. He needed to say something to her, but the feelings stirring in his core weren't getting anywhere near his mouth. He found his legs taking steps that brought him close to her.

"How are you doing?" she asked softly, filling a tiny part of the silence.

"Oh, fine," he said, as if that were a surprising question. "What about you?"

"Fine. I'm going home tomorrow."

"I'm glad."

He shifted his weight from one foot to the other. "So, where are your folks?"

Her pupils seemed to dilate, but she didn't look away. "I don't have any."

Sam wanted to slit his throat. And yet somehow the information didn't completely surprise him. "I'm so sorry. I didn't mean—"

"That's okay," she said quickly. "How could you have known?"

"I—I didn't . . . I—I just . . ." His voice petered out. So much for the speech therapist.

"Sam," she said.

His name sounded different than it ever had before. "Yes?"

"I am very, very sorry for attacking you last night. I wish I had it to do over."

For some odd reason, he found himself smiling a little. That was the one thing in his life he would have left just the same. "No, no. It wasn't your fault. I'm the one who's sorry . . . for . . . for everything."

"I seem to have a lot to apologize for," she said quietly, studying her fingernails. Her hands were exceptionally graceful, although her nails were bitten down to the quick.

"Some people do, and they say nothing," he murmured. He hoped she would know what he meant.

She nodded.

"Gaia, do you have any idea what happened last night?"

She tilted her head. "What do you mean?"

"I mean, somebody beat up those guys and . . . saved my skin. Maybe yours, too. Do you have any idea who it was or how it happened?"

Her eyes didn't move from his. She was looking for something from him as intently as he was from her. "Probably no more than you," she said equivocally.

He took a deep breath. "I have these strange fragments of memories, but . . . well . . ." He found his cheeks warming at the images in his mind. "But they don't make sense."

Gaia shrugged. "Oh."

"I mean, you didn't . . ." His voice was obviously beseeching, but he couldn't supply the rest of the question.

She wasn't going to help him.

"Maybe it will come back to one of us," he said lamely.

"Maybe."

He stuck his hands in his pants pockets. "Did you see Zolov today?"

Gaia smiled. "Yeah. He's happy. He keeps asking for more pudding."

Sam smiled, too. Suddenly he wanted to stay here and smile at her for the rest of his life.

"Yeah," he repeated stupidly.

She lifted up her arm to brush a strand of hair from her face and as she did revealed a deep, prune-colored bruise on the tender underside of her arm. "Oh," he said out loud, his breath catching. Suddenly he wasn't just close to her but nearly touching her. Two of his fingers hovered around her elbow.

She lifted her arm again and glanced at the bruise, wondering at his reaction. "This?" She turned out her arm and offered it to him.

For some reason the dark, angry bruise on her soft, sweet skin pained him beyond words. It was a helpless spot, even on Gaia's body. She has no parents, he found himself thinking disconnectedly. She has a terrible bruise on that hidden, sad part of her arm and she has no parents.

Without thinking properly, he let his fingertips land on her skin just above the inside of her elbow. Gaia looked down at them, but she didn't flinch. Together they watched his fingers slowly graze the damaged spot so gently, he wasn't sure whether he felt her skin or simply her warmth.

The warmth radiated up into his face, now bent over her. He was hypnotized by that passage of skin. He inhaled her subtle fragrance—a faint but tantalizing mixture of chamomile and Chap Stick and caramel and faded laundry detergent.

Was he breathing? Was his heart still beating?

"It's nothing much," she said in something just above a whisper. "You should see the ones on my stomach."

Oh, God. The mere thought of her stomach was a mistake.

"And this," she said. She lifted a curtain of gold hair to show a nasty bruise on her hairline just above her ear.

Now his hand was on her hair. He'd first realized it last night, that her hair was magical stuff. It was weightless and sparkled with strangely mutable color—as if it were shot through with sunlight.

His eyes were on her wound, then suddenly his lips. It had nothing to do with thinking. If it had anything to do with thinking, he never would have done it. Because he was a cautious, rational person. Everyone said so.

His lips touched her hairline so tenderly. She breathed into him, letting her head, her body relax against him. She let out a tiny sound. A hum, not a word.

He'd found his purpose with her, in that touch of his lips, in those few seconds. Without caution or anything related to reason, he knew (he didn't know how he knew) that he had a unique power. He alone had it. Did she know? Did she care? Would she hate him for it? Or would she, could she, love him?

As his lips moved with exquisite gentleness from

the bruise in her hairline to the bandaged cut over her left eyebrow, he knew that he somehow possessed the power to kiss her and make her better. It was a puzzling, inexplicable kind of certainty that came only in dreams. It was an idea so complex and fragile that if he even blinked, he feared he would lose it.

Let me show you, he thought as his lips moved toward hers. Let me show you what I can do.

She was staring up at him in wonder. Her fingers had wrapped around his. Her breath was slow and just barely audible. Her lips were parted in a question. Her blue-violet eyes opened into a billion possible worlds.

"There you are!" The booming words cut through the spell with the force of an ax.

The pretty, plump nurse who'd spoken them was carrying only a paper cup and some pills. "There you are!" she said again, this time clearly to him. Her voice was so loud, it was disorienting. Sam wished he had a remote control to pause her or at the very least turn down the volume.

"You're *Heather's boyfriend, right?*"

Could they hear her all the way uptown? he wondered absently.

"She's *looking for you*—asking *everybody* where *you went.*"

Could they hear her in Harlem? In Connecticut? At the North Pole?

Sam had traveled deep into a netherworld, and it

was hard coming back. He looked at Gaia, but her face was turned to the window.

"Gaia?"

When she turned back to him, her face was different.

"Yeah?"

"I'll see you later?"

"Sure, maybe," she said.

Her eyes were no longer the color of the clear night sky soaring up into a universe of stars and moons and planets and galaxies. They were iced over. Shut.

"Hey, Sam," she called as he walked toward the door.

He felt something dangerous as he turned to her.

"You and Heather make a great couple," she said. Her voice was as frigid as her expression.

All hope and warmth drained away. He blinked.

"I'm not sure how to take that," he said.

She shook her head. "It doesn't matter."

Sam's sore muscles tightened. He pulled his eyes from her face and forced the fuzzy clouds in his mind apart, letting in the cold light of reason.

He was awake. He was fully awake, and the dream was gone. Now he could remember that he disliked Gaia. Even hated her. She was trouble. Within a week of meeting her he'd been beaten to a pulp and two people he really cared about were in the hospital. Gaia was angry and dangerous. When he was near her, his own mind betrayed him. The smartest thing he could do was stay away from her permanently.

The smartest and most rational thing he could do was to get himself back to Heather's room and remember why he loved her.

2 KRISPY KREME DOUGHNUTS

Distraction à la Gaia

1 Granny Smith apple
1 large coffee with milk and 3 sugars
5 roasted nuts

He refused
to look up
and pay her
face any
attention **and**
at all
until **finally**...
he felt the
metal barrel
against his
temple.

SHE WAS SO ANGRY, SHE'D PICKED a fight with George. She was so angry, she was wearing her highest heels. Even her aqua miniskirt wasn't helping her mood.

Good-bye, Marco

Marco put his hands on her hips and pushed her against the wall.

The only thing the stupid, vain kid had going for him was his looks, and now he was monstrous with his swollen nose and misshapen lips.

"Come on, darling," she whispered to him. "We need some privacy." She removed his hands and used them to lead him down the narrow hall of the Gramercy Inn to room 402, their very own love nest.

Once he was in the room, she plucked the Do Not Disturb sign off the inside doorknob and hung it on the outside. She closed the door hard and locked it. She clattered the key down on the glass-topped bureau.

He was already pulling his cotton T-shirt over his head. She saw deep bruises on his ribs and shoulder. Slob that he was, he threw the shirt on the ground and came toward her with those inexhaustible hands.

"Darling," she cooed, "you know I need to talk to you. I asked you not to hurt my friend, and now I've learned she's in the hospital."

Marco, as usual, was in no mood for talking.

"Mmmm," he said, burying his face in her neck.

This had been fun two days ago. Today it wasn't.

"Marco, did you hear me?"

He had the unbelievable gall to throw her on the bed. She took her handbag with her. As he kissed her, she fumbled with the latch and opened it.

"Marco, I asked you a question."

His hands were gliding under her shirt. They were cold today.

He refused to look up and pay her face any attention at all until he felt the `metal barrel against his temple`. His eyes grew round, and his lips opened. He spluttered but couldn't find words.

Ella gave him another few seconds to fully appreciate her change of mood before she pulled the trigger and sent a silent bullet deep into his head.

She untangled herself from him and deposited the gun into her slim, square bag. She straightened her clothes and glanced in the mirror. Her lipstick was still perfect. She smiled wide. None on her teeth.

This interlude had done nothing to `quell her anger`. But now it was three o'clock, and Gaia, the true source of her temper, would be home from the hospital. Ella slung her bag over her shoulder, enjoying the weight of the gun, and strode to the door without a backward glance.

She was so tired of that girl.

LOST

To Christopher Grassi

I used to worry that I was stupid. In spite of all the high test scores, the genius parents, and all the mythology (you know, stuff like walking at two months and communicating in sign language at eight months), whenever I made a mistake, like following Loki's purposely misleading clues or inviting some drug addicted Goth girl to stay with me, only to have her boyfriend rob me blind and beat me, I worried that deep down, I was actually a half-wit.

But I'm not going to do that this time. I'm not going to let myself go down that road again. Even though I let myself believe the impossible, I'm not going to allow my long-held suspicion that I'm secretly a moron rise to the surface.

Even though I let myself believe at precisely the moment I should have doubted. Even though the formula of "I believe my life can be good!" equals "It's only going to get worse" has already been proven to me over and over, I'm not going to attribute my missing all the obvious signs to a lack of intelligence.

Granted, not *everything* was right with the world. My mother was still dead. Sam was still dead. And George and Ella and Mary. And Heather Gannis was blind, thanks to me. There was still a lot that would never be right. Never could be. But there was so much that *was* right, it was almost possible to forget the rest. For one moment everything was fine.

Loki was as good as dead.

I knew once and for all and with absolute certainty who my father was.

He was safe and sound and living within the prescribed physical proximity necessary to carry out the fatherly role.

He had Natasha.

I had Ed.

And while there were still a million unanswered questions, I had all the time in the world to ask them. My father had all the time in the world to answer them. Everything was fine. Everything was sweet. Everything was actually. . . . cozy. I was ready to move on to a new life. A life where I would come home from school to my father and his live-in girlfriend and her daughter, who had become almost like a sister (or at the very least she'd become like the daughter of a father's live-in girlfriend who I could cheerfully tolerate on a continual basis). A life without neck strain from constantly checking over my shoulder. A life where I would have birthdays and family vacations and maybe even a pet.

A life that resembled that of a normal girl.

I let myself believe that this was possible. That it was, in fact, already happening.

But I'm not going to fret over the stupidity of believing. Wouldn't that just be a waste of psychic energy? Another excuse to

engage in an endless cycle of
negativity? Isn't that what
experts in the field of human
behavior would say?

I'm quite sure it is. I'm
quite sure that whether or not
they've appeared on *Oprah*, and
regardless of whether their TVQ
is high enough to secure their
own spin-off programs, experts in
the field of human behavior would
agree that my will to believe was
not a sign of stupidity.

Experts would agree that my
will to believe was a sign of
insanity.

Everything had **unnatural** come to a **twist** Very Brady Standstill.

THE RED AND BLUE LIGHTS FLASHED

Another Living Gaia Nightmare

at Gaia Moore as she chased them up the slick pavement of Third Avenue. Her breathing was steady and controlled, her focus unwavering. For once she was content to be living on the dull, lifeless Upper East Side. It made the running so much easier than it would have been in almost any other neighborhood of Manhattan, and most of the four outer boroughs. It made it possible to ambulance-chase without losing sight of those lights. Without having to hurdle winos and sidestep theater geeks and bum-rush tourists. In fact, at this time of night the streets were actually deserted. The froufrou ice-cream shop owners had gone home to their froufrou families, and the rest of the population were either crammed into the multiplex or some third-rate comedy club where out-of-work actors shared their witty observations and prayed for laughter.

It made it easier to concentrate on the running. And concentrating on the running kept her from thinking about the person in the back of the ambulance. The fact that he was unconscious. The fact that she had only had him for such a very short time before tragedy struck. Again.

Gaia was accustomed to running. She normally loved it—the sensation of her long blond hair whipping back from her face, the burning in her thighs as they worked, the efficient pounding of her heart, the sweat forming on her palms inside her clenched fists. And it wasn't an abnormal thing for her to be doing, even dressed as she was in combat boots and faded gray cords and her only nice black sweater. This could just be any other night for Gaia Moore. Except for one thing.

She wasn't chasing some thug or rapist or drug dealer or even one of her evil-ass uncle's henchmen. And she wasn't running away from a gun or a knife or a flamethrower or a needle. She hardly ever ran when faced with any of those weapons, anyway. No. She was running because her father was in an ambulance that the idiot EMTs wouldn't let her ride in.

This was new.

Also new was the fact that someone was running alongside her. Keeping pace. Sweating profusely, but keeping pace. Ed Fargo. The love of her life. The guy who had been sucked into yet another living Gaia nightmare.

"Hey, Gaia, want me to carry you?" Ed joked. The mere thought of it was absurd. He'd only recently started walking again, and he was panting so heavily, he could barely get the words out. At this point he could no more take on the added weight of a stick of gum than make good on that offer.

But that was what Gaia loved about him. His ability to make fun of his very manliness just to get a laugh out of her. He was the perfect boyfriend—the perfect addition to the picture-perfect life that had started to take form around Gaia only moments before, until everything had come to a Very Brady Standstill. Gaia had been sitting at a dinner table—a real dinner table with food on actual platters and plates, drinks in actual glasses, and a tablecloth on the actual table. With her were her father and Ed, the people she loved, and Natasha and Tatiana, the people she could see herself loving. It had been like a family. It had been like a dream. And now it was obliterated.

Gaia spotted the blue-and-white sign for the hospital up ahead, and the ambulance darted around the corner, heading for the emergency entrance.

"Good," Gaia said, her adrenaline spiking and forcing her to run even faster. "We're almost—"

Suddenly Gaia hit something hard. Something hard on the inside but somehow soft on the outside. She hit it at such speed that she went bouncing backward and landed on her butt, her tailbone practically meeting up with her skull.

"Watch it, bitch!" someone shouted.

Gaia shook her head. She saw Ed skid to a stop a few feet ahead, just now getting control of his momentum. Then she noticed the feet. The black-booted

Shaq-size feet that were attached to a proportionally sized man who was leering down at her from above. He had three gold teeth and a matching gold necklace. He cracked his already battered and torn knuckles and made a clicking sound in the back of his throat.

Great, Gaia thought. *The Upper East Side picked the perfect time to go and get a personality.* This guy definitely did not belong here among the socialites and the privileged. And he was definitely itching for trouble. Little did he know that this was the very wrong night and he had decided to interfere with the very wrong girl.

"Hello, sweetheart," he said as Gaia rose to her feet.

His breath smelled like tuna fish and tequila. There was some sort of festering sore on his chin. Gaia drew herself up to her full height, her fists automatically clenching at her sides. He still towered above her.

"Excuse me," Gaia said, swallowing the urge to toss this guy head over heels onto his back. She started past him, but his meaty hand landed on her shoulder.

"Where do you think you're going, little lady?" he said, his hot breath hitting the back of her head as he tightened his grip.

Gaia froze. Ed looked at her, resignation crossing his face. He knew her. He knew what she was going to have to do. Gaia looked back at him calmly.

"I think you should go ahead," she said firmly.

But before Ed could move, the behemoth grabbed

him in a choke hold with one arm. "Not so fast, buddy. You'll just have to stay here and watch while me and your girl have some fun." Behemoth leaned over as if he were going to caress Gaia's cheek for added effect, but she was way too fast for him. She intercepted his reach and grabbed his arm, twisting it behind his back and setting Ed free.

"Run," Gaia commanded, trying to convey her desperation with her eyes and not her voice. "I need you to look out for my dad." And without giving Behemoth the satisfaction of a second glance, Ed bolted. It took a brave and noble guy to stand up and possibly take a beating for the girl he loved, but it took an even braver and nobler guy to walk away and let the girl he loved take care of the dirty work for him.

Behemoth was still sporting an expression of shock at the girl half his size who was able to take him on, when Gaia grabbed his arm even tighter, twisted it until she heard a crack, and shoved him across the sidewalk. He fell like a nice-size tree, face first, and just lay there for a moment, baffled. Then Gaia grabbed the wounded arm again and yanked at it, causing an extra shout of pain for good measure. She was actually glad there was no one around to witness the tussle—Gaia had no time for any knights in shining armor jumping in and trying to protect her.

"I think you need to find a new pastime," Gaia said, wondering how many girls he'd already assaulted using his I'm-a-sudden-wall-on-the-sidewalk maneuver. "Somewhere other than here."

"All right! Let go!" Behemoth shouted. He was near tears. Pathetic. Gaia didn't know why she was wasting her time with him. She released his arm and took a step back, but the second she glanced away, he flipped over and used his good arm to snag her around the knees. It wasn't smooth, but it was effective. Gaia went down, and before she could think, the huge guy had all four of her limbs pinned to the sidewalk under his considerable weight.

"I'll take you right here if I have to," he grunted, spittle hitting Gaia in the face as she struggled. He was too big and awkward to be a good fighter, but if he managed to stay on top of her like this, she had no chance. She felt like someone had dropped a building on her.

But then he released one hand to go for her zipper and made the mistake of bending his head closer to hers as he maneuvered. Gaia pulled back as far as she could and hit him with a nasty head-butt. There was a resounding crack, and the guy reeled back, bringing both hands to his forehead. As Gaia struggled up, he managed to reach out and backhand her, sending her sprawling on her side.

She got to her knees and leered at him, irritated that

11

he was bothering to fight back. Gaia had somewhere to be, after all. Her father was lying just a block from here, being poked and prodded and tested and hopefully saved. She didn't have time to mess around with this guy.

Behemoth lunged at Gaia, and she quickly ducked away, but she took a boot to the chin and felt something in her neck snap. She rolled to her feet and took her fighting stance as the guy stood up as well. He looked mighty pissed. Blood dripped from his mouth as he curled his upper lip. There was a gaping hole where one of the gold teeth used to be.

"You're gonna pay for that," he said.

Then he came at her with some serious punches, a few of which he landed, most of which she blocked. He was strong but slow, and as Gaia feinted and ducked and weaved, she scanned her immediate surroundings, trying to see a few moves ahead. Trying to figure out a way to knock him out. Put him out of commission. Because he clearly wasn't a person who was going to run from a girl.

Finally he threw a punch that caught air and nearly knocked himself off his feet. Gaia seized the moment. She leapt up onto the stoop behind him and jumped onto his back, wrapping her forearm around his neck. He flailed and struggled but wasn't flexible enough to reach around and haul her off him. Gaia gripped him tighter and tighter as he staggered, clenching her teeth and holding her breath as she pushed *his* breath out of him. At last Behemoth took a lumbering step, then another, then fell to his knees. Gaia's feet hit the ground.

She released him, and he slumped forward onto the sidewalk. Dead asleep.

Gaia's faced twisted into an unconscious smirk. The big badass was sleeping like a baby. He actually looked kind of funny lying there all passed out. Then her vision clouded and her head went groggy, and she realized that she was about to do the same.

Dammit! No! Not now! she thought, staggering in the direction of the hospital. She couldn't have a post-fight breakdown. Not when her father needed her. But the more steps she took, the deeper the fog grew, and Gaia was just able to duck behind a row of garbage cans for cover before she hit the deck.

ED STRODE INTO THE HOSPITAL

Choking Himself Purple

emergency room, shoulders back, exuding a sense of purpose. He tried not to think of the size of the guy he'd just left his girlfriend with. He tried not to dwell on his wounded pride. Gaia could take care of the thug. And while she was doing that, Ed would make

13

sure he took care of Gaia. And that meant looking after her dad.

"I'm looking for Tom Moore," Ed said firmly as he stopped in front of the desk in the ER. "He was just brought in."

The young nurse turned her tired brown eyes to the computer screen and tucked a wayward curl behind her ear before she started tapping at the keyboard. Someone very nearby let out a bloodcurdling scream that made Ed jump, and a baby in the corner answered with a screech that could have shattered glass. Two men near the coffee-vending machine yelled at each other in Arabic, one of them clutching an arm that was so broken, Ed could see its `unnat-ural twist` from across the room.

He swallowed hard and returned his attention to the nurse. Oh, how he hated hospitals.

"Are you family?" she asked in a bored way as she watched the screen. Apparently she was immune to the billion distractions around her.

"Yes," Ed said without missing a beat. "I'm his son." He'd seen enough movies to know that this was the only correct answer to this question. In fact, he always wondered why people didn't always say yes. It wasn't like the hospital personnel ever bothered to check ID. This particular nurse was so detached that Ed could have been a squat Asian woman and she would have believed he was Tom Moore's son.

"Okay, Mr. Moore," the nurse said, addressing Ed. "Your dad is being checked over in exam room three just back there." She pointed over her shoulder without looking away from the computer.

Mr. Moore. He liked the sound of that. Even though if he and Gaia got married, he wouldn't change *his* name, it kind of made him feel like—

Okay, Fargo. Focus.

"Thanks," Ed said, glancing up at the light blue curtain drawn over an open door. He had taken one step in the direction of the curtain, when Tatiana and her mother came bursting through the electrical sliding doors on the other side of the room.

"Ed!" Tatiana shouted. She jogged across the room, her mother close behind. Her blond hair was uncharacteristically mussed, and she had a panicked air about her as she ran right into his arms. She was obviously upset. They all were. They'd just witnessed one of the most important people in their lives choking himself purple, and there was nothing any of them had been able to do about it.

Ed gave Tatiana a quick squeeze, and then she pulled back, her blue eyes flicking left and right. "Where is Gaia?" she asked, adjusting the strap of her shoulder bag.

"She got sidetracked," Ed replied.

"Sidetracked? How? Her father is in the hospital!" Tatiana's mother, Natasha, cried, throwing her hands up. Her face was red, and her eyes were swimming in unshed tears. Natasha was clearly on the verge.

Ed reached out and put both hands on the older woman's shoulders. "She'll be here," he said firmly, looking into her eyes. He and Natasha had recently spent a full night together waiting for Gaia, and Natasha hadn't been shy about the fact that she had no patience with Gaia's behavior. But this time it was different. This time he knew for sure she was coming. Gaia wouldn't let anything get in the way of being here for her father.

Not even the truck man I left her with, Ed thought, indulging in a wave of nervous uncertainty. He glanced at the glass doors. Where exactly was she?

Natasha took a deep breath. "Where is Tom?" she asked, glancing toward the nurse at the desk, who was now dealing with the arguing Arab men, about as interested in their plight as she had been in Ed. Natasha twisted her one silver ring around and around and around, like she was trying to unscrew her finger from her hand. "Did they tell you anything?"

"He's in one of the exam rooms," Ed said calmly. Someone around here had to be calm. Suddenly Ed felt like the solid, responsible, in-charge manly man. He stood a little straighter.

"We will go see him," Natasha said, starting past Ed.

"Hold on," he said, stepping in front of her so quickly, her head hit his raised arm. "I think maybe I should go back there alone."

Natasha's face scrunched up and hardened all at once, and for a moment Ed thought she was going to go into a full rage right there in the middle of the emergency room. This was exactly why he didn't think she should go back there. She was in no state to be dealing with doctors and nurses.

"You don't tell me what to do!" she said. "I need to see him." She turned a deeper shade of red than he'd ever seen on a person. Realizing suddenly that he might have just overstepped his bounds, Ed looked to Tatiana for help. She caught his eye and then stepped up behind her mother, wrapping her slim fingers around her mother's arms.

"Ed is right," she said. "You can't go back there like this. First we'll sit and calm down, then we'll be able to see Tom."

Natasha seemed to instantly deflate as she allowed Tatiana to lead her over to one of the chairs along the wall. All in all, Ed thought, he'd handled himself pretty well so far. He'd established himself as Tom's son and defused a potentially volatile situation with Natasha. Gaia would be proud.

Now all he needed was to find good news behind that curtain. That was what Gaia really needed.

Please just let it for once be good news. . . .

HE WAS ABLE TO HEAR EVERYTHING.

Compulsively Shined Shoes

After months of being trapped in this cold, white cell, he had trained himself to hear it all. Every turn of a key in a lock. Every click of a door. Every footstep. Every word. Every sneeze. Sometimes he even heard a breath. With nothing to see, nothing to smell, nothing to feel, his hearing had become honed. Like that of a bat. Or a mouse. Or the lab rat he was.

There was something going on. New sounds. New words. New tones. Things were starting to fall apart; that much was clear. He could tell from the high pitch in his captors' voices. He could tell from the running. The quick clip-clip of their compulsively shined shoes.

He pressed his fingertips and palms up against the glass that closed him off from the sparkling white hall beyond. From the gleaming tile. From the one tiny crack in the plaster on the far wall of the hallway that he'd studied so hard and for so long that it had started to appear in his dreams. It was the only thing of discord in this regimented, sterile place. Or at least until now.

Footsteps came. Rapidly. His heart hit his throat,

and he pressed his cheek against the glass, waiting. Suddenly a guard ran by, left to right down the hall, zipping past his eyes in a blur of color. So close, yet so untouchable.

More voices.

"What are you going to do with them? You can't move them! We have strict orders to—"

"The orders don't matter anymore! We have to contain this!"

A third voice. A scared voice. Possibly the voice of 501, the guard with the twitchy eye. "I don't even care now! Just let them go! If the cops come here and find this place—"

Let them go! the prisoner thought, pressing his face so hard into the glass, it hurt. *Yes! Let them go!*

"NO! We have our orders!"

"Aren't you listening to me? Loki's not coming back! He's as good as dead! I say we save ourselves!"

There was a loud clatter. A punch landed. A jaw cracked. A body hit the floor. The prisoner had a sinking feeling that the silenced one was the one who would have helped him. He swallowed hard. If Loki were as good as dead, wasn't he as well? Would the morons out there even bother to continue to feed him? Would he rot away in this white room for the rest of his numbered days?

The moment he stepped back from the glass, 457 appeared at the side of his cell. This was the round-jawed, pudgy yet strong Hispanic guard who brought the prisoner his shots. Who held him down while 492 and 501 administered the serums. The numbers were embroidered in gold thread along their black collars. They were the only names he'd ever known his captors by.

He narrowed his eyes as 457 hit whatever it was at the side of his cell that made the glass slide up silently and out of sight. Guard 457 drew his gun from his holster and leveled it at the prisoner's heart.

"What's going on?" the prisoner asked calmly.

"I'm moving you," 457 said. "One false move and I have no problem taking you out."

The prisoner looked at 457 and waited. "What, no handcuffs?" he asked, arching his eyebrows.

"Don't get funny with me. I don't need 'em. I got this." The guard lifted the gun half an inch. "Now move out into the hall and make a right. I'll be right behind you, and there's nowhere to go but straight, so don't try running."

His pulse was racing like a Thoroughbred's. Was this actually happening? Was he going to move outside these four walls? He tentatively stepped past 457, never taking his eyes off the gun until he was in the hall. It was colder out here. The air was crisper. Sweeter. It was a whole new smell, and his nostrils actually prickled. He almost closed his eyes to savor it but stopped himself. Better to stay alert. Take it all in. Find some way to escape.

"Move it," 457 ordered.

He walked down the hall, past the other cells. Some were empty. One held a girl, a redhead, who cowered in a corner, rocking back and forth. One held an older man, stooped and tired. He looked up as they passed, his blue eyes hopeful.

Why were these people here? What was their offense? Was it merely loving someone, too? Was that all they had done?

The hallway opened onto a larger room where 501 was just struggling to his feet. A bruise was already forming on his left cheek.

"I thought I put you down," 457 said to the smaller man, still keeping his gun trained on the prisoner.

Guard 501 looked the prisoner over. His eye twitched once. "Just let them go," he said again. "If we get caught, we're taking the fall. Remy and them have already split, you know."

The prisoner looked at 457, who betrayed himself by flinching at this last news. But then his grip tightened on the gun. "We can't let them go," he said. "We have orders."

"Fine," 501 said. Then, faster than the prisoner ever would have thought possible, 501 ripped his gun from his holster and blasted a shot, sending 457 reeling backward.

The prisoner stood there for a moment, stunned and free, as 457's gun clattered to the floor. The wound was in his shoulder, but it was bleeding like a geyser. He didn't even shout out. He simply looked surprised.

"Well?" 501 said, the twitch wild now. "Run, you idiot!"

That was all he needed. The prisoner took off through a door at the far end of the room. There was another hallway, and a guard came running toward him from the other end. He raised his arms and ran, ready to give the man a swift elbow to the jaw if he tried to stop him, but the guard just ran right past him as if he weren't even there.

The next door opened up onto a brightly lit room that was three stories high and made almost entirely of glass. He blinked against the harshness of the light, almost appalled by it. Until he realized it was sunlight. Until he realized that those spindly things on the other side of the glass were trees.

Salivating now, he careened toward the exit door, across a marble floor dotted with black speckles and trimmed with gold. Every second he expected someone to jump out and tackle him to that floor. Every moment he expected to hear a shot ring out or a voice call for him to stop. But nothing came. There was no one. And in moments he was tasting fresh air.

Outside, he found himself feeling almost drunk. There were birds. There was wind. There was grass and asphalt. A fast-food wrapper skittered across the pathway in front of him, its bright red color one of the most beautiful things he'd ever seen.

A slam sounded from the compound behind him, and he realized that he wasn't yet free. He wasn't yet safe. He ran toward the woods that bordered the building. Ran until the branches ripped through the soles of his soft slippers. He spotted a large rock and collapsed behind it, pressing his back up against its cool, uneven surface.

His breath was harsh and ragged. He hadn't had this much exercise in months, and it made his heart pound dangerously. He sat for a moment and waited, gasping as quietly as possible. Listening. Waiting for the army that he was sure would be sent after him. They couldn't really all be gone. Most of them had to be there still. And when they realized what 501 had done, they would deal with him and come after the refugee.

He waited. He waited until his breathing normalized. Until his nose stopped running. Until his fingers were so cold, he could barely curl them.

No one was coming. Maybe no one even realized he was gone yet.

He stood and started to run again, cutting through the woods, just hoping he was going the right way. All he needed was a road. That, at least, would be a start. He almost laughed when he heard traffic up ahead. He was on his way. He was on his way back to her.

From: X22
To: Y

Subject is en route to hospital after minor delay caused by the girl. Nothing to be concerned about. Everything has gone as planned.

From: Y
To: X22

Do not let the subject out of your sight. The girl cannot get in the way again. I need not remind you of the importance of this operation. I will accept no mistakes.

All that
was left
of him
was a
bloodstain
and a
gold tooth
on the
sidewalk.

**fresh
cut**

ICU, ICU, ICU. . . INTENSIVE CARE

unit. This is definitely not good, Gaia thought as she bounced up and down on the balls of her feet, watching the little numbers on the elevator wall light up.

Lobotomy

The nurse and the guy in the wheelchair behind her were watching closely as Gaia willed the elevator to move faster. She didn't blame them for staring. After all, she did have a fresh cut on her cheek, and she did smell like garbage, and she did look like she'd just woken up on the street, totally strung out. Add to that the fact that the nurse downstairs had told her her father was still unconscious and in *intensive care,* and Gaia was sure she was coming off as pretty damn scary.

Finally the bell above her dinged, the doors rattled open, and Gaia stepped out of the elevator and almost directly into the arms of a waiting Ed Fargo.

"Hey," she said, reveling in his closeness and the safety of his embrace. "How'd you know it was me?"

"They called up from downstairs and told the nurse my sister was on her way up," Ed said, pulling back and cupping her face with both hands. His eyes crinkled at the corners, and her heart gave a pleasant little flop. "Hey, sis," he said.

"Okay, now I definitely need therapy," Gaia said, managing to crack a smile.

Ed turned her face slightly and winced when he saw the cut down her cheek. "Ooh," he said. "Are you all right?"

"You should see the other guy," Gaia joked. She hadn't, in fact, seen him again. When she'd finally come to, Behemoth had been gone. All that was left of him was a bloodstain and a gold tooth on the sidewalk.

Ed tenderly kissed the spot just above the top of the cut, and Gaia sighed at the tingling sensation in her skin. She knew it was probably the last good thing she'd feel for quite a while.

Gaia turned and looked around the ICU unit. It was made up of a circle of rooms surrounding a circular desk, at which sat three nurses who were sipping coffee and gabbing happily, like the people in the rooms around them weren't all at death's door, including her father. That was what the ICU was, after all—the last stop before going over to the other side.

Natasha and Tatiana stood next to a room on the far side of the unit, their heads bent close together as they spoke urgently. The curtain was drawn over the door next to them, and Gaia could see the shadows of figures moving around inside.

Her father was in that room. Prone. Unconscious. How could this be happening?

Gaia took a deep breath and leaned her side into

Ed. For some reason, she wasn't quite ready to approach that room. "Is he. . . ?"

"He's stable, but he hasn't woken up yet," Ed replied, wrapping his arm around her. "They have a couple of specialists in there now."

"Specialists?" Gaia asked, tilting her head up to look at him. She didn't like the sound of that.

"Neurologists, I think," Ed replied.

"I don't understand this," Gaia said, allowing herself an unusual amount of vulnerability. "He choked, the EMT guy gave him the Heimlich. . . . He should be fine. Why is he unconscious?"

"I don't know," Ed replied, hugging her a bit closer. "But I'm sure they'll figure it out."

Yeah, right, Gaia thought. *The brilliant doctors will figure it all out.* Why did she have a hard time believing that? Maybe because no one she knew had ever gone into a hospital and come out the better for it. Maybe because it was impossible, in her life, for things to improve. Everything always just got worse and worse until it seemed like she'd hit rock bottom. But then—surprise!—somehow she always managed to blast through that bottom rock and burrow a little deeper.

"Come on," Ed said, giving her a nudge. "Let's go wait with Tatiana and her mom."

Gaia allowed Ed to lead her around the ICU desk and over to the wall where Tatiana and Natasha were standing. The nurses fell silent as they walked by, gawking at Gaia's injury and shooting each other glances. Already Gaia hated the ICU. It was bright, it smelled of ammonia, and it was way too clean. In her battered, dirty, broken state, she stood out like a clown at a funeral.

"Gaia?" Natasha questioned as she and Ed approached. The older woman was clearly thrown off by Gaia's mangled appearance.

"Hi," Tatiana said, glancing at Gaia's cut. "What happened?"

"Nothing unusual," Gaia replied, lifting one shoulder. "For me, anyway."

Tatiana smiled her understanding smile, and Gaia was grateful that there would be no more questions. They had more important things to focus on.

"What's going on?" Gaia asked. Ed still had his arm around her, and she didn't move away. She felt like she kind of needed it there right now. She could hear low voices on the other side of the curtain. Two men whispering as they checked monitors, made notes, decided her father's fate.

"There is a Dr. Galvin and a Dr. Simbuka examining your father," Natasha said, her hands clasping her elbows tightly. "They said they will be out shortly."

The voices suddenly grew the tiniest bit louder, and Gaia saw two pairs of highly shined shoes at the bottom of the curtain. Her heart leapt with hope, and she chided herself for it. It wasn't as if they were going to have good news. That couldn't possibly happen.

The curtain snapped aside, and a tall man with sandy blond hair and the whitest teeth Gaia had ever seen stepped out of the room. He wore a pristine white coat and a tie with little yellow flowers all over it. It was all a bit too Mr. Rogers for Gaia. He moved aside, and a much smaller, much pudgier, much younger man with dark skin and a short ponytail stepped out after him.

"Mr. Moore?" the taller man asked, looking at Ed.

Ed took a moment to snap to at the sound of his newly adopted name. "Uh. . . yeah. This is my. . . other sister, Gaia," he said, loosening his grip on her slightly.

Other sister? Gaia thought. Then she saw Tatiana out of the corner of her eye and realized that they'd all appropriated Tom as family so that they could be here. So that the doctors would talk with them. *Smart move.*

"Gaia, this is Dr. Galvin and Dr. Simbuka," Ed said. They each reached out to shake hands with her in turn. Gaia touched them each briefly, then pulled her arms back in to hug herself.

"How's my dad?" Gaia asked. "Is he awake?" She hated the childish, hopeful sound of her voice.

"I'm afraid not," Dr. Galvin replied. He looked down at his chart, stalling for time. Gaia knew that he didn't have anything written there that he couldn't just rattle off. There was something he had to tell them that he didn't know how to tell them. Or didn't want to.

"What is it?" Gaia asked, her concern and impatience getting the better of her.

"Well, your father's vital stats are all good," Dr. Galvin said. "His heartbeat is a bit slow, but his brain waves are strong—"

"His brain waves?" Natasha blurted, disturbed.

"Yes," Dr. Simbuka put in, leaning forward slightly to see Natasha past Dr. Galvin. "It's a routine test for an unconscious patient. And like Dr. Galvin said, they're strong, so that's a good sign."

Unreal, Gaia thought, glancing up at Ed. *There's an actual good sign.*

"But still, I think we're going to need to call in a specialist," Dr. Galvin said, making a quick note on the chart.

"Wait, I thought you were a specialist," Ed said.

"I am, son, but we're going to need a pathologist. You see, with vitals like these, there doesn't seem to be any real cause for your father to be unconscious," Dr. Galvin explained. "Your father's condition is highly irregular."

Figures, Gaia thought as his words sank in. When was anything in her life ever regular? Couldn't a person just eat dinner with his family and get through it without a major medical emergency? Nope. Not in her particularly freakish brand of existence.

"What does this mean?" Natasha asked, reaching out for Tatiana's hand. Her daughter gripped her fingers tightly. "Will he be all right?"

"Unfortunately we're going to have to wait for the pathologist's opinion. We'll run some more blood tests, and we'll do another EEG in the morning to see if anything has changed," Dr. Galvin said as Dr. Simbuka cleared his throat uncomfortably behind him. "I suggest you go home and get some rest. Hopefully we'll have some answers by tomorrow."

Rest. *Yeah, right.* Like that was going to happen.

"Oh, no," Gaia said. "I am not leaving this hospital."

Ed reached for her, but she'd stepped away from him. Although moments ago she seemed to need his touch, now the thought of touching anyone was repelling. She knew it was childish, but she hadn't heard what she wanted to hear. She hadn't heard that her father was going to be just fine. Instead she'd heard that his fancy Manhattan round-the-clock team of specialists knew little more than the janitor mopping down the ladies' room. And now they wanted her to *leave* him here? Alone? No. She would not be calmed down. Not even by Ed.

"Gaia," he said soothingly.

Gaia's shoulders tensed. "I'm sorry, but there's no

way I'm leaving here tonight," she said, gripping herself even more tightly.

She had to be here to keep an eye on things, or who knew what they would do to her father? By tomorrow he could have a lobotomy, amnesia; he could be paralyzed. Gaia had been handed over to Loki and his men by a bunch of hospital personnel who hadn't even bothered to check and see if she was a *patient* at their hospital.

"Gaia, come on," Ed said, touching her shoulder from behind. "The last thing you need right now is to be up all night."

Gaia sighed and let her shoulders slump slightly. She knew he meant well, but he couldn't possibly understand how she felt at that moment. With every fiber of her being she knew that if she stepped one foot outside this hospital, her father was going to get worse. This was her life. It was the only way things ever went down. At least if she stayed here, she would feel like she had a modicum of control.

"Please, Ms. Moore," Dr. Galvin said. "We'll take good care of your father."

"I'm not going," Gaia said more firmly this time, looking up into the man's kind, clear blue eyes. Then she turned and looked at Ed, willing him to just hurry up and agree with her. She couldn't take much more of this standoff. She was teetering on the edge of some serious misery, and the last thing she wanted to do right now was fight with anyone. Least of all him. "I'll stay in the waiting room, but I am not leaving this hospital."

Ed sighed, resigned, and the doctors seemed to read him perfectly. Ed knew there was no point in arguing with her, and they decided to take his cue. Dr. Galvin looked at Gaia and shrugged. "Suit yourself," he said. "But I really don't see the point."

Of course you don't, Gaia thought. *You've probably never been kidnapped right out of a hospital bed.*

"Well, I'm going to go home to see if I can try to distract myself. Maybe get some studying done," Tatiana said. She crossed over to Gaia and gave her a quick but firm hug. "You call me if anything changes, okay?" she said, smiling reassuringly.

"I will," Gaia said, grateful at the very least to have people around her who cared for her. Who cared for her father. For once she didn't have to deal with everything alone, which was comforting.

Tatiana turned and gave her mother a nice, long hug, whispered something in her ear, and walked off toward the elevators. Gaia couldn't help but notice the doctors watching her appreciatively as she sauntered away.

"I'll stay," Ed said, slipping his hand into Gaia's. "For a while, anyway."

"Thanks," Gaia said, her heart warming pleasantly as she gave his hand a squeeze. "Are you sure?"

"Come on," Ed said, tugging on her arm. "Let's go see what they have in the vending machines. I bet a sugar rush would cheer you up right now."

Gaia rolled her eyes but cracked a small smile. What would she do without Ed Fargo? Probably curl up in a ball in the corner and slowly lose it. She looked at Natasha as she took one step away from her father's room.

"Keep an eye on the door," she mouthed. Even though Loki had been neutralized, there was still a slight chance that his men could be a threat to her father. They were, after all, still out there, and one of their main purposes in life was to kill Tom Moore. Gaia didn't want anyone or anything interfering with her father's recovery. If there was even going to be one.

Natasha nodded, understanding. "I'm just going to talk to the doctors a bit more," she said.

Gaia cast one last look at the door that led to her father, then allowed herself to be pulled toward the hallway. *He's going to wake up,* she told herself. *This is just a run-of-the-mill hospital visit. At this time tomorrow, you'll all be laughing about this.*

Unfortunately she had a hard time believing any of it.

I never really thought that I could be anything to Gaia. I mean, I hoped, I daydreamed, I obsessed—but who ever really thought it would work? Look at her, for God's sake! She's a ninja without subtitles. She's Buffy without the styling gel. Who does she need? No one. What does she need from me? Nothing. What good could an average guy with nothing but a skateboard and a dream be to her? None.

But things are different now. I always knew Gaia had a vulnerable side. Obviously I knew. I've been her friend from the beginning. I've been there for my share of breakdowns. But I could never really help her. I couldn't protect her from the people that wanted to hurt her. I couldn't help her when Sam died because, let's be honest here, there were some selfish motivations.

But now. . . now she's letting me in. This I can help her with. I know about hospitals and injury and sickness and family crises. These are things I've endured. These are things I've weathered. These are things I've conquered.

These are things I can help her through and protect her from, at least somewhat.

And it's nice to be there for her. To have her lean on me. It's nice, for once, to be the protector.

The
fugitive
almost
swallowed **jagged**
his **unchewed**
heart
whole. **pieces**

THE MOON HUNG LOW IN THE SKY AS

Beef Jerky

he staggered from the woods toward the garish lights of the Mobil station. He'd lain low in the forest for hours, his heart seizing at every rustle of the wind, his breath catching at every snapping twig and hooting owl. Finally, when he couldn't take it anymore, the paranoia, the cold—and sugar, he needed sugar—he decided the coast was clear. Or at least clear enough to begin the next leg of his journey.

He shuffled over to the side of the building and leaned back against the chipping paint on the concrete wall, his knees trembling with fatigue. There was only one car at the pump—a Jaguar—and it was just pulling away. He knew that if he was to have any chance of getting back to the city, he was going to have to hitch a ride. He also knew that no one in their right mind would pick up a guy who was walking around in the middle of the night in ripped slippers and a white jumpsuit. He wasn't sure he'd want to ride in the car of the person who *would* pick him up.

Peeking around the side of the building, he gazed through the smudgy windows of the minimart that made up half the gas station. There were racks full of food—pink cakes wrapped in cellophane, red-and-white packages of beef jerky, row after row of candy bars. His stomach growled painfully, and he clenched his hand over it, feeling hollow. He had no money, and he wasn't going to steal. At least, he wasn't going to steal something big. But in a life-or-death situation, it couldn't really be considered stealing, could it? A pack of gum was all he needed. Five sticks of Juicy Fruit packed enough sugar to stand between him and diabetic shock. All he had to do was slip the glossy yellow package in his pocket without the clerk noticing. It seemed easy enough. But as he planned his next move, the sound of an approaching car threw him off track. This could be his getaway.

He slipped farther back along the wall, out of sight, and said a little prayer. Let it stop. Let it be a van or a truck he could sneak into. The engine grew louder and louder and the little bell dinged, indicating the presence of a new vehicle in the gas station lot. He glanced around the corner again when the engine died and saw a man twice his size and twice his age, with a scruffy brown beard, groan his way out of a red pickup truck. He wore a hat with an American flag on the front and the slogan These Colors Don't Run.

He was instantly liked.

The bearded driver loped into the minimart and appeared moments later with a hubcap attached to a key. He walked around the other side of the gas station, scratching lazily at his beard, and the fugitive took his chance. He glanced into the minimart to find the proprietor drooling over a porn magazine, then ran for the truck. It seemed to take forever just to cross the lot, and he felt so exposed, he could have been naked. But soon he was tucked cozily between the metal bed of the truck and the canvas cover overhead. There were a few bags around him, but he fit quite nicely if he curled into a fetal position.

Now all he had to do was hope that the bearded man was heading for New York. The last thing he needed was to end up in the middle of rural Connecticut. Or worse—a New Jersey mall town.

A few moments passed in agonizing doubt. Was he doing the right thing? Should he just call the police? What if he was caught? Where was this guy, anyway? How the hell long did he need to take a whiz? The fugitive almost climbed out of the truck a dozen times. Then he heard the door of the minimart open and knew the bearded man was returning the bathroom key. There was no going back now. If he tried to climb out of his hiding place, he'd be caught for sure.

Suddenly another car approached, pulled into the lot just behind the bed of the truck, and stopped but was left idling. The fugitive almost swallowed his heart whole. A sizzle of fear ran up his spine, over his skull, and through his chest, settling over his stomach like a frigid wet blanket. He slipped his fingers between two of the snaps on the canvas cover and popped them free so that he could see out.

The car was a black sedan. No plates. The driver opened the door and climbed out. The fugitive stopped breathing. It was 422—the most ruthless of the guards. The one who had beaten him down in the early days— back when he still had fight in him. Guard 422 was impossibly tall, pushing seven feet, and had the shoulders of an NFL linebacker. His cold, dead eyes gazed around the parking lot, slipped right over the fugitive, whose heart stopped cold for a moment, then kept moving.

The fugitive glanced at the sedan's passenger seat, and he could just make out the profile of 457, whose right arm was in a sling.

Moving as little as possible, the fugitive lowered the canvas cover and curled up again, his lower back tightening, his eyes squeezing shut. So they had come for him after all. He was done for, and he knew it. It didn't take a Mensa man to think to look in the back of a pickup truck.

The door to the minimart opened and closed, and the fugitive started to pray again. He'd never been so religious in his life as he'd become in the last few hours. Once more the door opened and shut. Footsteps approached, crunching over silt and asphalt. He held his breath, he squeezed into an even tighter ball, he pressed his lips together.

Any second the canvas cover was going to be ripped free. Any second he was going to feel 422's ironlike hand on his throat. Any second he was going to feel what it was like to die.

The door to the cab opened, and the truck sagged just a bit to the side as the driver climbed in, then righted itself again. The door slammed. The engine started. The muted sound of country music filled the air. And then the truck was off.

The fugitive waited a good ten minutes before he was able to unclench himself. When he did, he checked behind the truck and saw nothing but the dark road, stretching out for miles behind him. He was safe. He finally started to breathe.

That was when his stomach seemed to realize the coast was clear. It let out the loudest growl he'd ever heard it make and left behind a painful emptiness. He pressed his hand against his gut.

There has to be food in here somewhere, he thought, pulling a duffel bag toward him. He found the zipper and yanked it open, catching it twice on the nylon material. It was a clumsy, blind search in the dark. His hand traveled over balled-up shirts, socks, bottles of shaving cream and shampoo. He ran his hand along the bottom, then shoved the bag aside and groped blindly for the next—a backpack stuffed with magazines, a carton of cigarettes, lighters, and what felt distinctly like a candy bar in a plastic bag. Mouth watering, he pulled the bag free and opened it. Two Snickers bars—just what the doctor ordered.

He shoved an entire bar down his throat, nearly choking himself in the process, the unchewed nuts scratching his throat. All he wanted was to down the second one as well, but he knew he had to hoard it. There was no way to know where his next meal would be coming from. And he was dying for a drink. Just one drop of water to cool his gummy tongue. But another wild search yielded nothing. He took a deep breath and held his knees to his chest, listening to the sound of the road rushing by beneath him.

Just don't think about it, he willed himself. *Don't think about water or liquids or wetness.* He could do it. He'd mastered the theory of mind over matter. All he had to do was think of her. Focus on her and everything else faded away. Besides, soon enough he would have all the water he wanted. All the food he wanted. All the comfort he wanted.

Soon enough he would be home.

ED AWOKE TO A FUZZY GRAY ROOM

Primal-Guy Urges

full of unfamiliar shapes and the smell of lemon-scented cleaner and rubber. The first thing he registered was that Gaia was asleep in his arms. Actually, that Gaia was asleep half on top of him. Her right leg was over his belly with her calf hooked down his side, her right arm was flung across his chest, and her cheek rested in the nook of his arm. He squeezed his eyes shut and opened them again, careful not to move any other muscles.

"Paging Dr. Chang! Doctor Chang, please come to emergency," a throaty voice called out over a PA system. The microphone crackled once before cutting out.

Suddenly Ed remembered.

They were in a hospital room down the hall from the ICU. They had slipped in here last night after the stiff couches in the waiting room had twisted the muscles in their necks beyond repair. Ed moved his head slowly to one side, looking for a clock of some sort, and felt the pang in his tendons. He had no idea how long he and Gaia had been asleep, but the sun was trying to push its way through the blinds over the skinny window on the far wall. He was surprised no one had found them here yet.

Carefully Ed lifted his arm from around Gaia's shoulders and checked his watch. 7:32. If they didn't get a move on, they were going to be late for school.

Gaia sighed in her sleep and shifted slightly, pressing her thigh and cheek deeper into Ed's body. He smiled and curled his arm around her again. Screw school. He could stay here like this with her all day. He loved the coziness of it all, cuddling up here in this single bed with her, seeing her in an almost vulnerable state. He was actually impressed that she *let* him see her like this—all cute and helpless and sweet.

She blinked a few times and opened her eyes, the characteristic morning confusion creasing her features. Then she looked up at Ed, cocking her head slightly, and met his gaze. His heart wasn't ready for the thump she caused.

"Hey," she said, reaching up and clumsily pushing her hair away from her face.

"Morning," he replied.

She sighed contentedly and moved her cheek back to his chest. "Mmmm. Your heart's pounding." God, she was adorable in the morning. Before she remembered to put on the armor.

"Gee, I can't imagine why," Ed said wryly. It wasn't the only part of his body that was reacting to this romantic moment. But he had to ignore his `primal-guy urges`. It wasn't going to take long for Gaia to remember where they were and why. It wasn't the time for. . . anything else.

He kissed the top of her head.

"I like waking up with you," Gaia said simply, then let out a huge yawn, tucking her hand around him and behind his back.

"It doesn't suck," Ed replied with a chuckle. "We should do it more often. . . you know. . . when all this is over."

Gaia took in a deep breath and turned to him fully,

her chin pressing into his breastbone. "Right. When all this is over. I was trying not to think about that."

"Sorry," Ed said with an apologetic frown. "We don't have to think about it. We can think about other things. Happy things like. . . TiVo. . . or. . . Popsicles. . . or. . . Winnie-the-Pooh."

"Winnie-the-Pooh?" Gaia asked, her forehead wrinkling.

"I've always found him a little disturbing," Ed said. "It just kind of grosses me out that he wears a top with no bottom. Know what I mean?" he asked, not really waiting for an answer.

"And besides, what the hell's a 'Pooh'?" he continued, still not coming up for air. "They call him Winnie-*the*-Pooh, as if everybody knows what a Pooh is. But really, now, do *you* have any idea what a Pooh is?"

Ed looked at Gaia like he expected a definitive answer to his well-thought-out, much-pondered questions. But all he got was a nice, long kiss, for which he was totally unprepared.

His heart flip-flopped around in his chest until she shifted. He started to pull away, thinking she would do the same. But she didn't. She pressed her whole body into his and parted his lips with her tongue. Ed's breath caught, and he pushed his hands into her hair, cupping the back of her head and pulling her even closer.

Her hand slid across his chest, and she touched his cheek with her fingertips. The tenderness of the gesture

47

gave him chills. Ed had no idea where this sudden urge for intimacy had come from—especially considering that her father was practically comatose down the hall—but he didn't care. He decided to just go with it.

He pulled the hem of her T-shirt from the back of her cords and pressed his hands into her bare back, half expecting her to stop him. But she didn't even flinch. He smiled amid all the kissing. There was nothing on this earth like Gaia skin.

When they finally parted a few minutes later, his lips were raw, his pulse was racing, and Gaia had a pleasant and beautiful flush across her cheeks. She lay back next to him in the crook of his arm, and they both stared at the ceiling, catching their breath. Her sweater was on the floor, and her T-shirt was half untucked. His hair was sticking out in twenty directions.

"What was that all about?" Ed asked finally.

"I had to shut you up somehow," Gaia replied.

Ed laughed and rested his arm across his forehead. Yep. He could get used to waking up like that. As long as it wasn't in a hospital.

"I should go check on my dad," Gaia said, sitting up suddenly and throwing her legs over the side of the bed.

"Want me to come?" Ed asked, propping himself up on his elbows.

"No, it's okay," Gaia said. She shoved her feet into her boots and snatched up her sweater. "You go to school. Hopefully I'll see you later."

"Hey, I was going to go see Heather after school today. You want to come?" Ed asked.

"I don't know. . . . I'll probably be here," Gaia said, looking up at him as she crouched on the floor to tie her boot.

"Well, we could come by here and then go there," Ed said as he hopped down from the bed. "She's starting at her new school tomorrow, remember? I know she could use some moral support."

"Right," Gaia said. She stood up and smoothed her hair back behind her ears, a few wrinkles forming at the top of her nose. "I'd forgotten about that. Okay, I'm there." She grabbed his arm and twisted it to see his watch. "Damn. I gotta go," she said again. She started toward the door, but Ed quickly grasped her wrist, stopping her.

"Hey," he said, wrapping his arms around her waist. "Everything is going to be fine."

A shadow of doubt crossed her face, and she glanced away. Ed swallowed hard when she looked back at him with uncertainty.

"Everything's going to be fine. . . and I love you," he said, feeling like he was jumping off a cliff without a bungee. It wasn't that it hadn't been said before; it was that it hadn't been said back all that many times. He knew she felt it; she just had a hard time saying it. So telling her always seemed like a bit of a risk.

Gaia kissed him quickly, then hugged him tight. "I

49

love you, too," she said over his shoulder. He smiled, and then she was gone.

GAIA KNEW SOMETHING WAS WRONG

the moment she stepped into the ICU. One of the nurses from the night before was still on duty, and after glancing at Gaia, she cast a nervous look toward the side of the room. Gaia followed her eyes and saw Natasha sitting in a metal chair, bent over at the waist, sobbing quietly.

Karmic Twin Thing

"What?" Gaia said, not moving. "What happened?"

Natasha's head popped up. There were fresh streams of wet tears down both cheeks and light smudges of makeup beneath her eyes. Her hair had been pulled back in a ponytail, but frazzled wisps stuck out in all directions. She was wearing the same clothes she'd had on the night before.

"What is it?" Gaia said. The sound of her own voice irritated her. There was no fear there, no uncertainty. She sounded dead. And in a way, in that moment, she supposed she was dead inside. Because she knew what she was about to hear.

"It's your father," Natasha said, sniffling and standing up.

Kind of figured that one out, Gaia thought, the sarcasm her last private defense.

Natasha pushed her hands across her cheeks, wiping away the tears. "He fell into a... a... a coma a couple of hours ago."

With that, Natasha collapsed into her chair once again, crying like a child lost on the street. Gaia's hands curled into fists at her sides, her jagged, bitten nails cutting into her palms. This couldn't be happening. It was all wrong. How could he be in a coma? What had gone wrong in his brain last night and *why*? How could choking... *briefly*... cause a coma?

But Gaia wasn't surprised. Not really. Not on any sane level. After all, she'd known something like this would happen. Bad to worse. What else was new? She should have stopped the EMTs before they ever put him in the ambulance. Could have, really, if she'd tried. This was all her fault. Hospitals were no place for sick people. Not in her world, anyway.

Why did this have to happen? Why now?

Swallowing back a sizable lump that had sprouted up in her throat, Gaia crossed the ICU and walked right into room 419. Her father looked like a wax statue. He lay flat on his back, his face turned toward the ceiling, his eyes closed. His chest rose and fell at a regular pace. His hands lay flat at his sides. There were wires

51

connected by tape to his temples, and one of his fingers was clamped in a sensor attached to a machine that beeped away near the wall. His skin was pale and pasty. She walked over to him, reached out her hand, and touched his cheek. It was like ice.

If it weren't for his chest moving, she would have been sure he was dead.

Hot, angry tears sprang to Gaia's eyes as she stared at him. She knew she should have stayed in this room. Should have killed anyone who tried to make her move. They had done something to him, and now it was too late. There was nothing she could do to snap him out of it.

Gaia picked up her father's lifeless hand and squeezed it, then leaned down to his ear. "I'm so sorry, Dad," she whispered. "I'm so... so... sorry."

What she would have done for one of those TV moments. For him to suddenly squeeze her hand, brought back to life by the simple sound of her voice. But the machines continued to beep, and her father continued to lie still.

Gaia dropped her father's hand, kissed his cold, shiny forehead, and turned and walked slowly from the room. She crossed over to Natasha and plopped into the chair next to hers, slumping down until her butt was almost hanging off the edge of the seat. It was unreal, actually. Loki was in a coma, and now Tom was in a coma. Had his men come to even the score—keep them on a level playing field? Or was something else tying these two men together? Some kind of karmic twin thing?

"What did the doctors say?" Gaia asked blankly.

"Nothing," Natasha replied, her voice cracking. "No one will tell me anything."

Typical, Gaia thought. What was it with doctors, anyway? Did they want to keep families in the dark about their loved ones' conditions, or was it that they never really knew as much as they wanted people to think they knew? At that moment Gaia felt that it had to be the latter. Everyone around her was clueless. No one would be able to help her dad.

"What am I going to do?" Natasha said suddenly— quietly.

"Huh?" Gaia blurted, the whole not-thinking-before-she-spoke thing coming into play.

"Tom and I were finally free," Natasha continued, sniffling. She crumpled up a battered tissue, the veins on the backs of her hands seeming to pop out, blue and ugly. "We were finally going to have a normal life. And now. . . now. . ."

I know the feeling, Gaia thought.

"I just don't understand," Natasha said. "How could this have happened? There was no warning. . . ."

She trailed off again. Gaia reached up awkwardly and patted Natasha's hand. Then she felt the inappropriateness of the gesture and pulled away. Mothering was not in Gaia's nature, and the last thing she'd ever thought she'd have to do at a time like this was comfort someone else. Besides, sitting around and feeling sorry for themselves wasn't going to help anyone. It certainly wouldn't help her father. She was sure he would tell her exactly that, if he could.

I have to get out of here.

Gaia stood up quickly, and Natasha sat up straight, pulling in a shaky breath. "Where are you going?" she asked, holding a wrinkled tissue to her face.

"I don't know, somewhere. . . school, maybe," Gaia said. She was itching to move. Itching to put her mind on something else, in any way possible.

Natasha smiled wanly. "That is what your father would want," she said. "They are going to take him for a CAT scan in a little while. I will call the school if anything changes."

"Thanks," Gaia said, shoving her hands in her back pockets. She looked at her father's room and tried to hope. She tried to form some sort of coherent wish to send out there to the Fates, but her mind was a blank. There was no longer any will to hope within her. She turned and bolted for the stairs.

To: Y
From: X22

    Subject is down and prepped for removal.
Agents from C team are in place. Await further
instructions for extraction.

From: Y
To: X22

    D team will contact you with the particulars
for your journey. Proceed with caution. The girl
is smarter than she looks.

None of this makes sense. I need to know what is going on with Tom. I cannot stand being in the dark like this. I cannot tolerate the ignorance I am forced to bear. I always know. I always know what is happening. That is my job. That is who I am.

But no one is able to tell me. Or perhaps they are able, but they are simply choosing to keep me uninformed. I don't even know that. I don't even know if I am being lied to, if facts are being withheld.

Why have I been shut out? What went wrong? What did I do wrong?

The feet of
a dead body
lying next
to a
black **fighting**
sedan,
its door **back**
still
yawning
open.

HE DIDN'T KNOW HE'D DOZED OFF

until he was jolted awake by the sound of squealing tires. Less than a second later he was thrown against the bags to his left as the truck was hit and careened off the road. The noise was deafening, the crushing, the scraping. The fugitive braced himself for whatever was to come. Would the truck roll? Would it hit something else? Would it explode? And how the hell had he picked the one getaway vehicle that was destined to get into an accident?

Grand Theft Auto

There were shouts. The wheels bumped over the rough crease on the blacktop that separated the highway from the shoulder before the driver jerked the wheel and found the lane again.

The fugitive's muscles relaxed a bit. Okay. It was over. He was fine. But he barely had time to breathe before the truck was slammed once more.

His eyes searched the haziness wildly, helplessly. This was no accident. Someone was purposely hitting the truck. Someone was trying to kill them. Or at least drive them off the road. He couldn't move. Couldn't even sit up. Couldn't do anything to help the poor, innocent driver he'd sucked into his nightmare. For one fleeting instant he envisioned himself popping down the tailgate and tumbling out the back of the truck onto the road, but survival instinct prevented him from doing that. That would mean certain death.

Suddenly the truck jerked left and hit the car that had started this `monster truck rally`. He was flung across the bed, into the wall on the other side. His head hit hard, and he bit his lip against the pain. The driver guy was fighting back, that much was clear. He knew he'd liked that guy for a reason.

There were more shouts, unintelligible. He brought his hand to the back of his head, and it came back with a trace of blood, but not too much. He would live. For now.

The engine roared angrily as the truck sped up, lurching forward and flying down the highway. The rancid stench of exhaust filled his nostrils. For a moment he thought the truck driver had lost their pursuers, but soon they were bumped again, this time from behind. Finally, it seemed, the truck driver had reached his limit. With a grand screeching of tires that sent the smell of burning rubber into the air and sent the fugitive flying forward this time, the truck came to a stop.

This is it. This is where I die, he thought, hating himself for the way he was just cowering there. Just hiding. Waiting for it to happen. But he didn't know what else to do except hope for a miracle.

The door to the truck creaked open and slammed, shaking the walls around him.

"What the hell are you—"

Instantly a shot was fired. Very nearby. He waited to hear the sound of the truck driver's body hit the ground. He didn't.

"That was a warning, friend," a gruff voice called out. It sounded comfortable. Not alarmed.

Another shot, from the other direction. Less loud.

Instantly a third. From the same gun as the first, that was certain.

He couldn't take it anymore. He had to see what was going on. And if that meant facing the consequences, so be it. But he wasn't going to let the truck driver die if he could help it. The death would be on his own head, and that was something he was sure he couldn't live with.

He popped open the tailgate ot the truck bed, and the early morning sunlight surprised him. He crawled out awkwardly, his back and knees protesting in pain as he straightened up for the first time in hours. The first thing he saw was the truck driver, standing with his back to the fugitive, a shotgun poised to fire, smoke rising from its barrel. Then he saw feet. The feet of a dead body lying next to a black sedan, its door still yawning open. A handgun lay a few feet away. Then he saw 457, good arm raised in surrender, at the exact same moment 457 saw him.

The truck driver turned around at 457's surprised

eyes, and when he saw the fugitive standing behind him in all his white-jumpsuited glory, he nearly dropped his gun.

"Now where the hell did you come from?" he said.

At that moment 457 ran toward them.

"Look out!" the fugitive called. But it was too late. Guard 457 bent at the waist and barreled right into the truck driver, bringing him down with the sheer force of the speed he'd built up. He tackled him to the ground, sending the shotgun skittering off across the deserted highway, where it came to rest right next to the concrete divider.

The fugitive acted before thinking. He jumped right over the scuffling men, hurdled the prone body of 422, and sat down behind the wheel of the sedan. His foot was to the floor on top of the gas pedal before he'd even closed the door. At the sound of the car peeling out, both 457 and the truck driver `stopped midpummel` and looked up in shock. The guard made a feeble attempt to run after him but stopped before he got very far. In the rearview mirror the fugitive saw him turn back to the truck driver just before he crested a hill and could see no more.

So much for calling attention to himself. He'd just committed grand theft auto after causing a shoot-out on the highway. But there was nothing he could do about that now. All he could do was hope that he hadn't just cost an innocent man his life.

THE AIR OUTSIDE WAS WARM, PUNC-

tuated only by the occasional chilled breeze. Most people would have said that the promise of summer was in the air. Would have noticed the buds flowering on the trees that ran down the center of Park Avenue, dividing the north-

Grungy Sweater

moving traffic from the south. Most people would have noted that the messengers were wearing shorts now and that the sidewalk cafés were brimming with girls in sundresses.

All Gaia saw was the sidewalk. The concrete moving under her feet. The cracks in the cement. She had decided to walk to school. It was a seriously long walk, and she knew it would make her late, but she needed to walk. She normally wouldn't even have considered going to school at all. Would have wandered the streets all day, expending her angry energy, her pent-up frustration, her need to kick a little ass.

But now there was a reason to go to school. There was something there that might actually make her feel better. There was Ed. And it would probably be smarter to go talk to Ed than to find a fight in Union Square Park. Or Central Park. Or Bryant Park. Or Washington Square Park. Whatever park her feet might have otherwise brought her to.

Every time Gaia did look up, the world around her

seemed to mock her—seemed to know exactly what to do to drive her personally to the brink. The man emerging from McDonald's, holding the hand of his tiny daughter, who was looking up at him with unabashed love. The perky, grinning faces on the posters in the windows of the many, many Gaps she had to pass on her way downtown. The laughter of a group of kids her age, hovering on a corner, sucking on lollipops, out on some kind of happy-go-lucky field trip. She glared at the girls in their private-school skirts with their highlighted hair and their two-thousand-dollar smiles and hated them instantly.

That would never be her. She would never be that carefree.

By the time Gaia got to school, she felt like kicking down the door. Maybe this hadn't been the best idea after all. But she still wanted to see Ed. She just wanted to hold his hand. She needed to so much, she could practically taste it. And besides, if this whole school thing didn't work out, she could always bail. She could always find some thug to beat up if she needed to.

The halls were deserted, and Gaia drew herself up straight, feeling almost liberated as she walked to class. Like she was getting away with something by being out in the hall alone. And if anyone asked her what she was doing out without a pass, she would tell them to screw off. Her father was in a coma. At the very least that fact should earn her a get-out-of-detention-free card.

The second Gaia opened the door to enter her English classroom, the bell pealed out and chairs scraped back away from desks. Her teacher, Mr. Conroy, looked up in surprise when he saw her standing in the open doorway.

"Oops," Gaia said flatly. "Too late."

Then the students started filing toward her, and Gaia stepped back to let them pass and to wait for Tatiana.

"Gaia!" Tatiana said when she emerged from the classroom. With her perfectly mussed bun and her crisp white shirt over low-slung jeans, she scanned Gaia from head to toe. Apparently she didn't like what she saw. "You look awful," she said, her eyes flicking back over Gaia's grungy sweater.

"My dad's in a coma," Gaia said.

"What?" Tatiana blurted, paling. She looked confused, shocked, dismayed. "How?"

"Who knows?" Gaia said, starting down the hallway toward the stairwell and their next class. Locker doors slammed, a couple made out against the wall, some kid farted to impress his friends. Life was going on.

"It's not like the doctors even know," Gaia added. "They never know anything."

Tatiana's perfect brows knit, and she looked at some spot ahead of her on the floor as they walked. Like concentrating on that spot was going to clear things up for her.

"And my mother. . . ?"

"She's there. She's trying to get some answers," Gaia said, shoving open the wooden door in front of her with the heel of her hand, making a satisfying bang. *Good freakin' luck.*

"Did they let you see him?" Tatiana asked over the din in the stairwell, glancing over her shoulder as she ascended to the third floor. "How did he look?"

Gaia waited until they were in the hall again to answer.

"He looked awful," she said, flicking a chunk of hair away from her face. "Maybe it runs in the family."

Tatiana's eyes were full of sympathy, and Gaia had to look away. The last thing she wanted right now was to indulge in any mushy sentiment. Maintaining the emotionless wall around her was the only thing keeping her from breaking down. And breaking down was not an option.

"Anyway, they took him for a CAT scan, and they said the results would take a while," Gaia continued, sidestepping a couple of guys who were chasing each other down the hall. "I just had to get out of there. . . you know?"

"Well, we'll call my mom's cell at lunch and see how he's doing, okay?" Tatiana said, pausing outside their history classroom. She fixed her big blue eyes on Gaia's face, and once again Gaia had to avert her gaze. As close as she and Tatiana had become while their parents were gone, she still wasn't used to this. She wasn't used to having anyone around to reassure her. It made her feel pressure to say more. And really, what else was there to say? She felt angry, she felt confused, she felt guilty, she felt sad. She had no idea what was going on with her father. Was any of this really groundbreaking territory?

"We should go in," Gaia said, arching her back to slip through the space between Tatiana and the open door. As she headed for her regular seat in the far back corner of the room, Gaia passed between Trish and Sarah, two FOHs, who were giggling and whispering as always. One was wearing a brown top and a turquoise skirt, and the other was wearing a turquoise top and a brown skirt. They both drew back their heads in an exaggerated fashion when Gaia walked by, as if her very presence offended them. Which it probably did. But after shooting the obligatory eye daggers at her back, they promptly returned to their conversation.

If communication of such little substance could actually be *called* conversation.

"Omigod! He's in your *music* class?" Trish exclaimed, her well-lined eyes wide. "Does he *sing*?"

"I don't know," Sarah replied as she absently unwrapped a piece of gum and handed it to her friend. "But he played a little guitar. It was so hot."

Gaia's top lip curled up in a sneer. Who the hell were they talking about?

."Well. All I know is, we needed some new blood around here," Trish said, popping the gum into her mouth. "Our class is *devoid* of interesting prospects."

Oh, so there was a new guy. That explained the FOHs' sudden transformation from Manhattan snobs to Valley girls. Probably another `rich, preppy snob` who would just suck all the oxygen out of the halls with his inflated ego. Gaia stared at Mrs. Backer as she wrote a list of significant dates from World War II on the board. Maybe the lecture, at least, would get her mind off things. Of all the females in the class-room, the elderly, graying, rolled-panty-hose teacher was probably the only one Gaia could relate to. At least she occasionally had something interesting to say.

"Ooh! There he is!" Trish whispered.

Gaia glanced at the door. The guy who walked in did not disappoint her preconceived notions. He was tall and suspiciously tan for this time of year (points deducted) and broad enough to nearly fill the door-way. He wore a gray New York Yankees jersey (Gaia's team, via Ed, of course—points added for that) over a white T-shirt and a pair of jeans—clearly brand-new (points deducted). His hair was dark and slightly lacquered (points deducted), but even from the other side of the room Gaia could tell that his eyes were light. Almost `impossibly light` (a point or two added).

He stepped into the room and looked around with

his chin lifted and an air of confidence about him as if he owned the place. On his first day.

Gaia hated him.

"Oh, hello," Mrs. Backer said, noticing the visitor. She slapped her hands together to clear the chalk and brought one hand to her chest. "I'm Mrs. Backer. And you are?"

"Mr. Montone," he said with a hint of sarcasm, handing her his transfer slip.

"Well, nice to meet you, Mr. Montone," Mrs. Backer said, glancing over the tiny piece of pink paper and then handing it back. "Take any empty seat."

His eyes fell on the open desk next to Gaia's, and she squeezed her own eyes shut briefly. Perfect. Now she was going to have to spend this whole godforsaken period sitting next to this guy, who would definitely prove to be wearing an entire bottle of Drakkar Noir.

Slowly and confidently he strode down the aisle, passing by Trish, who blushed crimson when his leg brushed her toe. When he reached his desk, the new guy paused and glanced at Gaia. His eyebrows raised, and an expression of disgust crossed his features. Not that Gaia was surprised. She was used to this exact sneer. (More points deducted for lack of originality.)

He slid into the seat slowly, pressing his forearms into the desk, which caused his arm muscles to flex slightly, a calculated maneuver. (Major points deducted.) Gaia got a look at the back of his shirt and the number 2 embroidered onto it. two. Derek Jeter's number. It figured he'd have that pretty boy's jersey. (Jeter *was* the best in the business, at least according to Ed, so she couldn't deduct points for that, much as she wanted to.)

Much to her chagrin, she had to admit she'd been wrong about the cologne. The new guy's cologne actually smelled quite good. Something from the CK family, perhaps.

Trish and Sarah were whispering like crazy now, casting very unsubtle looks toward the back of the room. Finally Sarah got up with her history book, straightened her skirt, and walked to the front of the room, then down Trish's aisle. When she was a couple of feet from the new guy's desk, she stopped, holding her book with both hands, looking like an eager eight-year-old about to give her first oral report.

"Um, Jake?" she said, shaking back her brown hair. "I'm Sarah? From your music class?"

"Yeah?" Jake said, leaning back in his seat and looking at Sarah's legs.

"I thought you might wanna share my book?" Sarah said hopefully. "You know, until you get your own?"

"Yeah. Thanks," Jake said.

Sarah grinned and slipped into the seat at Jake's other side, then slid the desk and chair closer to his so that he could see her book. Gaia suddenly felt the need for a long, hot shower. Jake. *Ugh*. Even the name was bad.

ED WATCHED THE VOLLEYBALL AS IT

arced slowly back and forth over the net, hit by students who were not remotely interested in displaying any kind of athletic prowess. It popped up and over, up and over,

Gym Class Bloodletting

the *bump-thwack, bump-thwack* creating a mesmerizing rhythm. He watched it because he needed something to focus on while he tried to figure out what to say. What was he supposed to say to his girlfriend about the fact that her long-lost father was lying comatose in a hospital?

Hey! Don't worry! He'll snap out of it! Not likely.

He looked at Gaia. At her hard-yet-beautiful profile as she stared at the cinder-block wall across the gym from the bleachers. He was out of conversation starters—he'd already tried to get her to talk about what she was feeling, but she hadn't bitten. She wasn't one for opening up. While most of the girls in his class would have found a pity-me rant quite cathartic, it just wasn't Gaia's style. There would be no heart-to-hearts. At least not yet. Maybe later, when everything had had time to sink in. And when she was ready to talk, he would be more than ready to listen.

But that still left the problem of what to do now. His heart was breaking for her, but he knew he couldn't say that. She'd probably hurl. Or look at him with that Gaia sneer. Or possibly even punch him for the crime of first-degree sappiness.

Ed was about ready to resort to knock-knock jokes when he noticed Gaia straightening to attention. Tatiana had just walked out of the locker room on the other side of the gym and was now sliding along the wall toward them, maneuvering around the volleyball game. She looked up at Gaia, her expression disturbed and wary. Ed felt his mouth go dry. Neither he nor Gaia spoke as Tatiana climbed the bleachers and sat down on the step in front of them, turning to her side with her feet up so they could talk.

"I just got off the phone with my mother," she said, wrapping her arms around her knees.

"What is it?" Gaia asked, the tension already high in her voice.

"Nothing," Tatiana replied. "Nothing's changed. But the doctor said that the longer that nothing changes. . ."

She trailed off and Gaia's jaw clenched shut, the muscles in the side of her face working.

"She sounds very upset," Tatiana continued, resting her chin on her knee and staring off into space. "It must be very serious."

Ed swallowed hard when he caught the shift in Gaia's expression. Caught her eyes going dead. He took her hand.

"We know it's serious," Gaia said. "Trust me."

"It's just. . . my poor mother. She was so happy. . . ," Tatiana continued.

Gaia and Ed turned to each other in disbelief. Did Tatiana really just say what Ed thought she had said?

"What are we going to do?" Tatiana asked, her wide eyes watery as she gazed up at Gaia.

At least she used the word we *this time*, thought Ed.

"It's gonna be all right. I don't know how, exactly, but it will," Ed said, looking from Gaia to Tatiana and back again. He wondered how long Gaia would allow Tatiana to get away with her insensitive behavior.

"I hope you're right," Tatiana said with a sigh. Ed wanted to reach out and shake her. He understood that she was upset for her mother, but it was Gaia's dad who was in a coma. Wasn't it blatantly obvious that they should *both* be comforting *her*?

"Why don't we change the subject?" Ed said loudly, forcing a grin. Gaia squeezed his hand in approval and loosened her grip a bit.

"I'm in," she said, looking out across the gym again. Tatiana shot him a confused, somewhat irritated glare, her forehead creasing just slightly. Like, how dare he interrupt her? Well, Ed dared because he loved Gaia. And because Tatiana was behaving with an odd lack of sensitivity to the situation. And because he wasn't particularly in the mood to witness a gym class bloodletting.

"Do you still want to go to Heather's this afternoon?" Ed asked Gaia, wrapping his other hand around the top of hers. "It might be good for you to focus on something else for a little while."

Gaia took a deep breath and blew it out through her nose. "Yeah, I guess we could still do that," she said, dropping her feet heavily from the bleacher step she was sitting on down to the next step. "I just want to check on my dad first."

"Sounds like a plan," Ed said.

"Tatiana! You haven't played yet! Get down here and sub in!" the gym teacher, Mrs. Argeski, shouted out from the court below. She reached down with her wrinkled hand and itched the badass scar on her leg that had been the inspiration of urban legends among the student body for years.

"But Mrs. A.—," Tatiana began.

Don't argue, just do what the woman says, Ed silently commanded. He couldn't wait for Tatiana to step away.

Mrs. Argeski crossed her arms over her nonchest, and her beady blue eyes focused on Tatiana, her mouth set in a grim line. Ed could practically feel the chill in the air. Mrs. Argeski was a person one didn't argue with.

Tatiana rolled her eyes and finally shoved herself away from the bleachers. Ed was relieved. Tatiana was only exacerbating the already uncomfortable situation. The moment she was gone, Ed shifted his weight toward Gaia, turned his knees toward her, and squeezed her hand once more.

"Can you believe her?" he asked quietly, glad to have Gaia to himself again.

"I know. I mean I always knew she was self-centered, but that was ridiculous." And with that, Gaia turned her head toward the court as if to signify that the subject was closed. Ed was amazed at Gaia's ability to keep things to herself. He could never do it. But if Gaia was finished talking about Tatiana, then so was he. Besides, dropping the whole Tatiana issue freed Ed up to lavish all his attention on Gaia and do everything to help alleviate her stress—like offer to make a junk-food run.

"Is there anything you need? Ring-Dings, Yoo-Hoo. . . Krispy Kreme, maybe?"

Gaia smiled weakly. "Thanks, I'm good," she said. She lifted their entwined hands between them. "This is kind of nice."

Ed blushed slightly. "It is, isn't it?"

"We almost look like a real couple," Gaia said.

"You mean the kind that sits really close together

in the cafeteria and feeds each other french fries and makes everyone around them vomit?" Ed asked.

"Not that kind," Gaia replied, her eyes dancing again.

"How about matching T-shirts?" Ed suggested, arching his eyebrows.

"No," she replied.

"ID bracelets?"

"No way."

"Can I get a tattoo of your name on my—"

"No!"

Gaia laughed. And when she laughed, her whole face changed. She lit up. She became even more beautiful. Ed's heart grew warm and tingly just watching her until she came down into a simple smile.

"Are we the kind of couple that kisses in gym class?" he asked, sliding in closer to her.

Gaia looked down at his lips, the smile pulling at the corners of her mouth. "Maybe. . ."

Ed's pulse pounded in his ears as he leaned in toward her. Forget about jokes. Public displays of affection were a much more effective distraction from grief. But just as his lips were about to touch hers, the bleachers around them started to shake. Someone heavy was loping his or her way toward them from above.

"I hear you can fight."

Ed pulled back to see a seriously big guy with seriously greasy hair plop down at Gaia's other side. His bare knees were covered with dark hair, and his calf muscles bulged as he rested his pristine Nikes on the step in front of them. He cracked his knuckles as he looked Gaia over from head to foot.

Ed felt his face flush crimson as Gaia dropped his hand and turned toward the new guy. The oily loser from hell. Who was this person? Where had he descended from? And why did Ed feel like his hand was a lot emptier than it was?

"So?" the guy said to the silent Gaia. "Can you?"

"Fight?" Gaia asked. There was already a challenge in her voice. A cockiness. She already knew she was going to beat the crap out of this guy. But who the hell was he? And where did he get off sitting down next to Ed's girlfriend as if he weren't even there?

"I only ask because I'm a black belt and I'm bored," the guy said, tilting his head quickly to the side in something like a shrug of the skull.

"And this has what to do with me?" Gaia asked.

Nothing, Ed told her telepathically. *This guy and his belt have nothing to do with you. Doesn't he recognize a good canoodle when he sees it?*

"I want you to show me what you got," the guy said, lacing his fingers together. He turned his hands inside out and stretched his arms forward, then looked at the mat in the far corner of the room. His eyes turned playful, challenging. Even— *gulp*—flirtatious?

Ed reached out for Gaia's hand and caught air. She

was already standing. She was already on her way down the bleachers, heading for the mat. She was already flexing her fingers.

Ed looked down at his hands and sighed, trying to ignore the hollowing out of his heart. So much for distraction by smooching. Instead it looked like there *was* going to be a little bloodletting in gym class.

I didn't want to kick Jake's ass. Not particularly. At that moment I really wanted to kill Tatiana. So much for the sister figure thing. Although I suppose sisters occasionally want to kill each other.

But seriously—where does she get off treating my father's coma like it's her personal tragedy? Sure, her mom is close to my dad, but he's *my* father. It makes me sick just thinking about it, but if I got into it with Ed, I'd end up venting all my anger on him. And he doesn't deserve that.

But Jake's different. I have no problem venting my anger on him. Sometimes you just have to kick a little ass. And luckily for me, Jake offered himself up. It was a prime opportunity to vent all the repressed anger I had been on the verge of spewing all day.

Plus there was the added bonus of wiping that cocky grin off his smugly tan face.

the air

parting

around his

fists

as **cathartic**

he threw

swift punch **growl**

after swift

punch

GAIA NOTICED THE CURIOUS STARES

of her classmates as Jake followed her along the wall,
over to the wrestling mat in
the corner of the gym. It
was the girls, mostly. Probably
wondering why the hot new
commodity was even both-
ering to talk to Gaia Moore
of all people. Just wait until
they saw what she was about

Old-fashioned Throw Down

to do to him. He probably wouldn't be so revered once
he'd been put down by a girl. Once he had a shiner the
size of her fist. And maybe a couple of other bruises for
good measure.

She could already feel the adrenaline pumping
through her veins the moment her foot touched the
squishy, rubbery surface of the mat. She curled her
fingers and clenched them, then uncurled them again.
When she turned around, she expected to be looking
right into those light blue eyes with their teasing glint.
Instead she was looking at the top of Jake's head. He
was sitting on the edge of the mat.

"What are you doing?" she asked.

He yanked at the laces on his Nikes. "No shoes," he
replied.

"Uh-uh," Gaia said. "Nope. I fight shoes on."

This was not going to be a karate match. This was

going to be a good old-fashioned throw down.

Jake slowly grinned and retied his laces. "All right."

He stood up, and when he faced her, Gaia had to admit—to herself—that his size really was impressive. The muscles in his arms were healthy and defined, and his shoulders dwarfed her. Still, she wasn't afraid. Not Gaia. She was actually a little excited.

"Begin," Jake said.

He moved his left leg back in one smooth, almost graceful motion and raised his fists. This guy was by the book. Gaia took her stance as well, her nylon gym shorts swishing as the legs rubbed together, and she and Jake started to circle the mat. Gaia kept her attention on his fists and his eyes all at once. Most fighters told you what they were about to do with their eyes. But just in case Jake had a poker face, it was a good policy to watch the fists as well.

She was not going to make the first move.

Jake blinked, and Gaia's arms moved up just slightly to block the first punch, aimed at her face. Then the second, aimed at her gut. It was a split-second combination but no problem for Gaia. Jake took a little hop back, then quickly tried another combo—two quick jabs, both blocked. Gaia was impressed. Usually people didn't attack that quickly and in such fast succession. Jake wasn't interested in feeling her out. He wanted to show her he was ready.

"Come on," he taunted, hands raised. "Are you gonna hit me or what?"

81

Gaia threw a right hook at his face, which he swiftly ducked, then an uppercut, which he swiftly dodged. Her third punch caught nothing but the tip of his ear. Jake dipped his head, swung up again, and smiled.

"Not bad for a chick," he said, the grin widening.

Gaia flattened him with one crack kick to the face.

Jake lay on the ground for an instant, stunned, and a few people over in the bleachers cheered. Gaia looked up and saw some of the guys clapping and hooting around Ed, who sat sullen and staring. His face was slowly turning purple. Apparently this whole fight scenario didn't exactly sit right with him.

"Okay, that's it," Jake said, pushing himself to his feet.

Unfortunately Gaia didn't have time to ponder Ed's feelings. When she looked at Jake again, he was clearly pissed off. His brows were low over his eyes, and his face had darkened with a humiliated flush. She could see his biceps bulging under his T-shirt sleeves. Gaia smiled. This was getting good.

He was fast. Too fast for a guy his size. Gaia could almost hear the air parting around his fists as he threw swift punch after swift punch. Her responses were there, but she found herself actually *thinking* about the fight. Thinking about her next move and his and how to counter it. She never had to think in a fight. It was always on instinct.

Suddenly Jake backhanded her across the jaw, and she crashed to the ground, rolling onto her side. She had never seen it coming. It felt like the bottom half of her face had disconnected from the top. Her hand instinctively went to her jaw as if she were trying to hold the thing on as a red-hot flash of pain crossed her vision. She looked up at him, unable for the moment to mask her surprise.

"You done?" he asked, stepping over her and looking down at her with a cocky little smile. She could tell what he was thinking—too easy.

"Not likely," Gaia replied. Now she really, *really* hated him. She pushed herself to her knees and glared up at his smirk. "Just getting started."

"Oh, yeah?" Jake replied, unconvinced. He put out his hands, palms up, and waggled his fingers at her. "Bring it on," he said, bending slightly at the knee.

Gaia glanced around and saw that a little audience was forming around the mat. The volleyball game had stopped, and even Mrs. Argeski was watching them with interest. Probably psyched that after all this time someone was actually working up a sweat in her class.

Gaia stood and jabbed a kick right to his face, which released a satisfying grunt of surprise. He was knocked slightly off balance, so she quickly swung a left, but he turned away from it and her arm kept moving, taking her around with it. Meanwhile Jake reeled back and sidearmed her right in the jaw. Again. Gaia's head snapped back from the force of it, but this time she managed to stay on her feet.

Not for long.

Grinning, Jake punched her hard in the gut and Gaia doubled over, feeling like her stomach was about to come out her back. As if his knuckles had left an imprint on her skin. She coughed, struggling for breath, and as Jake grabbed her by the back of the neck and yanked her up again, one thought crossed her reeling mind.

These are not karate moves. He's street fighting me. He's a street fighter.

Jake shoved her forward again, trying to toss her to the floor, but she turned right and spun out of it, her arms flailing for balance. She gasped for air and hunted for a focus point as the room spun around her. Before it ever had time to come to a stop, Jake kicked her right in the face, and she hit the floor on her hands and knees.

What was going on here?

Still dizzy, Gaia got right up but kept her head down and rushed him, intending to basically tackle him to the ground and get this over with, but he grabbed her around the waist and suddenly she was upside down, soaring through the air with a damn good view of the raftered ceiling above. Jake tossed her like a bag of laundry over his shoulder and she landed on her back behind him, looking up at the staring faces of her classmates. The somewhat-embarrassed-for-her faces of her classmates.

God, she was hitting the floor a lot here. There was a chance, even, that she might not be winning this fight. Not acceptable.

Gaia rolled over onto her stomach and got to her feet again. She swung a right with every ounce of her strength, but Jake dodged and it just glanced off his cheek. He responded with a nasty uppercut, and Gaia's head snapped back again, her nose jabbing up into her skull.

She saw spots. She couldn't think. Blood seeped from her nose. She had to get it together before Mrs. Argeski figured out what was going on. Gaia quickly wiped the blood off her nose with the sleeve of her shirt, then folded back the fabric to hide the stain. Then, as a preemptive strike, she caught Argeski's eye, put on a goofy face, and pointed to Jake while flexing her muscle, as if to show how much fun she was having "toying with the new guy." Jake picked up on Gaia's charade and added his own little touch of authenticity by turning to Argeski and pretending to bite his nails in fear. Their performance did the trick—Argeski smiled and left them to their own devices. They were quite the little improv team, Jake and Gaia. But the moment Argeski was out of sight, it was back to business.

Jake took a fierce swing at Gaia. There was no way for her to block what was coming before it came. All she could think was, *Who is this guy? Where the hell did he come from?* He hit her blind side with a left hook, then swung back and backhanded her with his right. She was on her knees again, and she was definitely losing. Right here in front of everyone. All she'd wanted to do was vent everything out of her system and instead she was getting everything *beaten* out of her system.

"I should've figured," Jake said from somewhere above her as she stared at the ground, trying to get her bearings. Blood spotted the mat in front of her, and she sniffled. Her nose was entirely clogged.

"What was I thinking? You're just a chick," he added with a laugh.

Gaia's throbbing fingers curled into fists. Her eyes narrowed and her jaw clenched, sending out electric shocks of pain. It only made her angrier.

"Now you done it," one of the guys in the audience said.

Gaia stood up, sprang into the air from her right leg, and landed on her left while kicking up with her right. Her foot whacked right into his jaw and kept going, cracking his head back. He staggered, surprised, and she pummeled his stomach with a left, right, left, right, left, right until he was backed up against the wall. Then she threw a right jab so hard, she came up off her feet from the force of it. He tried to counter with a right, but she ducked it. She grabbed the front of his shirt and pulled him past her, shoving him to the floor. Then she grabbed his shoulders, yanked him up again, shoved him away from her, and jabbed a kick right into his chest.

Jake leaned back into the wall, choking for air. Gaia turned her back to him, grabbed both his arms and flipped him over her head onto his back.

Gaia was beyond ready to finish this. Jake was just too good, and this was the first moment she had him where she wanted him. The only people who fought like he did—the only people who made her think and pause and reel—were Loki's men. Was it possible that Jake was one of them? Had he been sent to her school to keep an eye on her, maybe to even kill her right here in gym class?

Jake sprang from his back and threw himself to his feet, and Gaia jumped back just in time as a roundhouse kick swung past her face, his foot so close, she could see the lines in the bottom of his sneaker. The force of throwing the kick and hitting nothing kept Jake spinning, and when he was turned away from her, Gaia jabbed a kick into the small of his back. His knees hit the floor, but then he quickly swept out his leg and took Gaia off her feet. She hit the ground on her butt—hard—and Jake was instantly on top of her, trying to pin her down.

God, he was strong. His hands pinned her wrists as he tried to flatten her legs with his knees. Gaia flailed in an attempt to at least get her legs free and suddenly realized that he was going to win. After all this, he was going to pin her. She was not going to wipe the cocky grin from his face; she was only going to make it cockier.

And he was laughing. In her face. He was already laughing.

Gaia let out a loud, `cathartic growl`, and somehow she managed to free her right leg. She crossed it over her left under his torso and swung it up, with all the strength she had in her, to meet his side. Jake was thrown off of her to the right and lay on his back. Gaia pushed off the ground with her hands, landed on her feet, and shoved her boot into his neck just as he was trying to get up. He struggled, but she only pressed harder. When Jake finally started to choke, Mrs. Argeski stepped in.

"All right, Ms. Moore, that's enough," she said, walking over to stand next to Jake's prone body. "I think you win," she said with a satisfied smile.

Gaia had to concentrate to make her foot move. Part of her wanted to snap the guy's neck. But when he got up, rubbing at his raw, red skin and looking every bit the confused, upset, humiliated teenage boy, she knew that Loki hadn't sent him. He was too authentic to be a spy. He was just a damn fine fighter.

As the class erupted into applause, Jake turned to Gaia, snapped his legs together, and executed a little bow. Gaia rolled her eyes. *What does he think he is, some kind of martial arts gentleman?*

She pulled her arm across her face, and the blood from her nose left a long red streak on her skin. Mrs. Argeski appeared with a wad of towel and pressed it into Gaia's face, sending a fresh sliver of pain through her skull.

"Keep your head back," Argeski warned.

"Gaia, are you all right?" Ed's voice asked from somewhere at her side.

But Gaia couldn't answer. Her vision started to cloud over, and she realized she only had moments. Moments before the postfight blackout she always suffered rendered her unconscious. That couldn't happen in front of all these people. They couldn't see her weakness. Jake couldn't see her weakness.

She turned and busted through the crowd, staggering for the locker room. She shoved through the door and into one of the shower stalls, where she was able to just pull the curtain closed before darkness consumed her.

"GREAT GIRL YOU GOT THERE, FARGO," Rob Jeffers said with a laugh, slapping Ed on the back as the crowd around the wrestling mat started to disperse. "She's gotta be a wild thing in bed. I bet she likes it freaky."

"Rob, you don't even know what *it* is," Ed shot back.

"Oh! Snap!" Javon Benton called out, covering his mouth in glee as Rob turned ten shades of red.

Ed slipped away from them and headed for the

bleachers, fighting to keep his face from betraying his irritation. In these situations it was always best to play along to cover his true feelings. In this case, embarrassment, resignation, jealousy. Who was this cover boy who had just rearranged his girlfriend's face? And was it just him, or had she seemed to enjoy it?

All around him his classmates were talking.

"Did you see the way she—"

"God, he was all *over* her—"

". . . bet he copped a feel at some point. Who wouldn't?"

Ed was definitely going to throw up.

"Still, man," Javon remarked, shaking his head as he and Rob fell into step with Ed. He put his hand on Ed's shoulder companionably. "It can't be easy to watch your woman get all hot and bothered over the new guy."

"Funny, all I saw was her kicking the ass of the new guy," Ed replied.

"And that doesn't bother you?" Rob asked, grabbing his book bag off the bleachers.

Yes. "Why should it?"

Javon and Rob exchanged a look. "All I'm saying is, maybe you should find yourself a woman who's actually a woman," Javon said, slapping hands with Rob over his cleverness.

"Hmmm. . . Maybe that's exactly what I need," Ed said, rubbing his chin with mock thoughtfulness. "Now, tell me, where did you get *your* blow-up doll again?"

The mocking smile fell right off Javon's face. "Dude, that's not right," he said coldly. He turned and shuffled off toward the locker room with Rob trailing behind. "My boy's lookin' for a smack down," Javon muttered under his breath, his head hanging sheepishly.

Feeling like he'd just emerged from a battle of his own, Ed lowered himself onto the bottom step of the bleachers. Sometimes being the comeback kid took a lot out of him. Especially when he was inclined to agree with his tormentors.

He pushed his hands into his hair at his temples and rested his elbows on his knees, his heart heavy. He was going to wallow in it for a while. Wallow in the mental image of Gaia pinned to the floor with that guy hovering over her. That hungry look on his over-sized face.

Ed also hadn't missed Gaia's intrigue when she'd realized what a worthy opponent Jake was. He'd seen her smile. He'd seen that little spark in her eyes. Jake had challenged her. For a girl who loved to fight as much as Gaia did, that had to be a turn-on.

"Mr. Fargo, you might want to get changed before the bell rings," Mrs. Argeski said. "I'm sure your next teacher won't appreciate you showing up in those shorts."

Ed looked at her, confused. He hadn't even realized she was standing there, yet she was only about a foot away, her hands on her tiny hips.

"Yeah, sorry," Ed said. He clomped up a few bleacher

steps, grabbed his backpack, and then started back down.

"Snap out of it," he said to himself under his breath as he trudged across the gym. "You and Gaia are together now. Stop being an insecure baby."

Besides, Jake was so not Gaia's type. Okay, he was good looking. Ed hadn't missed the way every single girl in class had looked him over appreciatively and whispered and giggled as Gaia led him to the wrestling mat. He did have a certain dark, brooding, Affleck-esque quality. And for some reason the phrase "hunka hunka burning love" kept popping into his mind. (He definitely had to stop watching eighties sitcom reruns.)

But look at the two people Gaia had liked since she moved to the city. Sam Moon. Tall, preppy, scruffy, WASPy, smart. A chess master. Not a kung fu fighter. Not remotely.

And him. Ed Fargo. An ex-skate rat who'd been in a wheelchair up until a few weeks ago and had no proven fighting skills. And yeah, he had somewhat rugged good looks if he did say so himself, but he wasn't a big, beefy, slick meathead. He wasn't a broad-shouldered Greek or Italian or whatever god.

No, Jake wasn't Gaia's type. Ed was her type. Her only type. Ed had absolutely nothing and no one to worry about.

She would
gladly
meet him
anywhere
and **bloodshot**
promptly
hand him
his spleen.

HE SLUNK THROUGH THE LOCKER

room, flinching at every shout that echoed from the gym, every imagined creak of a door. Guiltily he yanked on lock after lock, cringing at the noise he was making, but none of them gave. These kids were too paranoid. Too untrusting. But considering what he was trying to do, they clearly had the right to be.

Somewhere Here

His brilliant plan for the acquisition of some normal clothing had tanked. He was at a loss. He came to the last row of lockers, ready to give up, and then he saw it. A large laundry bin with a handwritten sign taped to the wall above it.

Lost and Found.

He practically dove into the bin, pulling out a pair of shorts too small for a twelve-year-old, a T-shirt that looked like it had been used to clean up vomit, and a Lakers sweatshirt that had been cut down into a tank top. He tossed these items aside and kept fishing until he finally came out with a workable ensemble. He stripped out of his coveralls and shoved them into the nearest garbage can, then pulled on his new clothes and stepped in front of the mirror.

He looked ridiculous. He wore a pair of huge sweatpants he'd had to roll at the ankles, an ill-fitting

Creed T-shirt, and a zip-front sweatshirt with a broken zipper. The sneakers on his feet didn't match. One was a black high-top, the other a white tennis shoe. But it was the best the lost and found had to offer. Besides, his clothing didn't matter. He was here. He was finally here.

Suddenly the door to the locker room swung open, and his heart hit his throat. He glanced around wildly and jumped into the nearest shower stall, pulling the sheer plastic curtain closed and backing up until he hit the far wall.

"Man, can you believe that bitch?" some guy said. "That girl is wack!"

"Yeah, she's psycho, all right. I bet she could beat the living crap outta you, though, Gordo," another voice answered.

"Please. She stepped up to me, she'd be down for the count before you can say jailbait, my friend."

This earned some laughter. The fugitive closed his eyes and felt his whole body warm. They were talking about her. They had to be. There wasn't another girl in the Village School who could beat the living crap out of anyone, he was certain. Half of him wanted to fight them for what they were saying about her, and the other half wanted to kiss them for confirming that she was here. She was okay. She was alive.

"Whatever, brotha. That new guy is ripped, man. If she can take him, she can whip your sorry ass."

The door opened again.

"Hold up, hold up. Here he is," one of the guys whispered. A momentary hush fell, and then the talk started up again. Forced. Paranoid.

"So, G., you study for that Spanish test?"

The fugitive tuned them out after that. He waited patiently, barely breathing, until all the locker doors had slammed, all the laughing and gabbing had died away. He waited until he heard the bell ring. Then he waited some more.

By the time he emerged from the locker room, the halls were empty and silent, save for the occasional muffled, droning teacher's voice coming through closed doors. As he moved along the wall, every inch of his body tingled with anticipation. His fingertips, his nose, his stomach.

She was here somewhere. Somewhere within these walls. And even though it wasn't safe to be here, even though they'd undoubtedly look for him here, he couldn't make himself leave. He just wanted to see her. That was all he wanted in the world.

Still, he forced his feet to move toward the front door. They were out there somewhere. They were still after him. If they found him here, who knew what they would do to him.

He paused at the end of the hallway that led to the stairs that led to the door that led to the street and the crowds and anonymity. It couldn't be that much longer until the bell rang. She was here somewhere. Somewhere here.

A door slam reverberated through the halls and shook him out of his trance. Enough was enough. He had to move. He turned and ran down the steps as quickly as his tired legs would move. He would see her soon enough. All he had to do was stay alive long enough for that to happen. She would come to him.

AFTER SITTING THROUGH AN ENTIRE

Smelly Rag

boring, rudimentary math class smelling herself, Gaia decided it was time to find a new shirt. She'd shed her sweater earlier, but she hadn't changed out of the already rank T-shirt underneath. And after that sweat-inducing fight with Jake, she was now worthy of New Jersey's most pungent trash heap. Besides, it was practically covered in blood. She shoved through the masses of moving students to get to her locker, ignoring their wrinkling noses and looks of disdain, just hoping she'd stuffed something semiclean in there at some point during the year.

Gaia spun her lock distractedly, thinking of Jake and the fight and his moves. If he weren't such a flaming egomaniac, she would have asked him how he'd tossed her so easily over his shoulder. It was pretty intense and wholly unexpected. It had to have something to do with the grip. . . . But she would never give him the satisfaction. Almost losing to him had been bad enough. Gaia yanked at her locker door, and it didn't give. She scoffed at herself and started her combination over again, this time actually concentrating.

When she popped open the door seconds later, a small piece of white paper, folded into a tight square, fell out and hit the floor at her feet. It had slid from the top of the pile of crap that started at the floor of her locker and came up to almost waist height. Gaia looked at the little square, surprised, then glanced around before stooping to pick it up. The last thing she wanted was for one of the FOHs or one of the jocks to notice that she had a secret note in her locker. She would be old and gray before she'd ever hear the end of it. If, of course, she lived that long.

It's probably from Ed, Gaia told herself as she unfolded the page. It was really kind of cool the way he managed to make her feel special without going for all the flowers and candy that most idiot guys went for. Not that anyone had ever done that for Gaia, but she'd heard about it somewhere.

As soon as she saw the writing, however, she knew it wasn't from Ed. In big, awkward block letters it read simply, *Meet me at the Seventy-second Street entrance to the West Side Highway. Make sure you're not followed.*

Okay. What the hell was this about?

Gaia looked around cautiously, searching for anything odd, out of the ordinary. Anyone who didn't belong. A few freshmen girls exchanged notes down the hall, and the guy who'd had the locker next to hers all year was chatting up some chick right next to her. People moved along the hallway in both directions, shouting and laughing and pushing each other around. The same old same old. Gaia's brow furrowed as she read the note again, but there wasn't much to read into it. It was a pretty straightforward demand. But who had sent it? Loki? Was he out of the coma already? Had he already come back?

Gaia folded the note up into a square even tinier than before and shoved it into the back pocket of her cords. If it *was* from Loki, she would gladly meet him anywhere and promptly hand him his spleen.

She yanked an oversized black T-shirt out of the bottom of her locker and pulled it over her head. Then she reached up under it and easily ripped the thin material of the gray one underneath. She pulled the smelly rag out of the bottom of the black tee and balled it up. *Might as well be semiclean if I'm seeing my uncle today.*

Of course, she knew that this meeting could definitely be a trap, but she didn't care in the slightest. She was bored and stir-crazy sitting in her classes, and besides, she had nothing to lose. And if Loki or his men were waiting for her on the corner of Seventy-second and the West Side Highway, then maybe she could find out what was going on with her father. Find out who was actually behind all this.

Gaia slammed her locker door and headed for the street.

THE LADIES AT THE DOG RUN KEPT

shooting him looks. He wasn't used to looks like these—paranoid, a bit disturbed. He was used to looks of appreciation. Looks of admiration. He'd never had much of an ego, but he knew that he was pleasing to the female eye— and in the Village to many a male eye.

Ramrod Straigh

But these women were a little afraid of him. And why not? He was dressed like a degenerate who fished his clothes out of a Dumpster, and he probably looked like a druggie. He hadn't eaten since he'd downed the truck driver's Snickers bar early that morning, and he was definitely weakening. He was probably pale and dirty and sweaty and bloodshot. He knew he should turn away and let the women watch their frolicking dogs in peace, but he couldn't do it. It was too soothing, watching the little beagle and the golden retriever cavorting with each other, sniffing each other, letting out the occasional playful bark. It was too normal. He couldn't tear himself away.

God, he loved the city. There were so many people, so much life. So many cars and bikes and buses and dogs and pigeons and vendors and horses and skateboards and Rollerblades and babies. This was a place where he could get lost. This was a place they'd never find him.

Out of nowhere an arm circled him from behind and dragged him back, scaring his optimism right out of him. He kicked out his legs as he was yanked away from the fence. He tried to turn his head, but his assailant's head was right behind his, blocking his movement.

"Hey! What the. . . Help!" he shouted, struggling to no avail, his pulse pounding in his ears. His fingers gripped the forearm that held him, trying to tear it away, but it was too strong. No. This wasn't happening. Not when he was so close. Not when she was on her way to him.

"Help! Do something!" he shouted in vain.

He looked at the women, his eyes wild, but the older one put her hand on the younger one's back and moved her away slightly, checking over her shoulder in fear. They weren't going to help. How could they? He was going to have to help himself.

He pulled his right arm forward and brought his elbow back as hard as he could into the stomach of the man who held him. The guy let out an, "Oooof!" and released the fugitive. He spun around and looked right into the beady eyes of 457.

The truck driver, he thought instantly. *The truck driver is dead.*

But apparently he'd done his damage before he went. The guard's left eye was ballooned shut by a purple bruise. A fresh cut ran down the right side of his jaw, and his lip had puffed up to twice its normal size. He looked like a reject from the set of a monster movie.

"Didn't think you'd be seeing me again, did you?" 457 said with an awkward sneer, straightening himself up. He really was immense. Impressively intimidating, even with the sling, even with the pummeled face. And he'd killed a man this morning. An innocent man who'd done nothing wrong except leave his truck in a gas station parking lot.

The fugitive swallowed back a thick chunk of sorrowful guilt and jumped back as 457 lunged at him. Before he could even give it a second thought, the fugitive turned and started to run.

It was drizzling, and there weren't that many people loitering around Riverside Park, with the chill in the air and the wind and the wetness. His legs carried him with great speed down the sidewalk and over the awkwardly spaced stairs that led to the water. He could hear 457 grunting as he sprinted after him. All the fugitive knew was that he had to get away. He had to lose this guy somehow, or he was done for.

That and the fact that his legs were working surprisingly well under the circumstances.

He came around a blind bend, blocked by a large bush, and almost ran headlong into a `scrawny man on a racing bike`. The fugitive dodged with millimeters to spare and kept right on running even as the biker spouted epithets. Seconds later he heard a cacophonous crash and knew that 457 had collided with the biker. He didn't look back. He merely hoped that it would take a while for the two men to extricate themselves from each other.

The fugitive ran until his lungs felt like they would explode. He ran until sweat stung his eyes. He ran until his thigh muscles quivered like Jell-O and the soles of his feet cried out in pain. When he finally stopped, doubling over and gasping for breath, he was just feet from the water, separated only by a low fence and a slight drop-off. The river's ripples lapped peacefully at the shore below him as his breathing started to slow. A woman jogged by him, `ramrod straight,` listening to her Walkman in her perfectly coordinated running outfit. She didn't even give him a second glance.

When he finally stood up again, he looked around—listened—but there was no trace of 457. What was he supposed to do now? He was dozens of blocks from his meeting point, but he couldn't go back. The guard might be waiting for him. He could be hiding anywhere.

He took a deep breath, his lungs protesting in pain, and let the drizzle bat away at his face for a moment, cooling him as he thought things through to their logical conclusion. And the logical conclusion was this: He *had* to go back. All that mattered was seeing her. Making things right. It was all that had mattered for so, so long.

Ever so slowly the fugitive started to move, his legs shaking beneath him. He retraced his steps along the jogging path, pausing at every blind corner, peeking around every bush, every parked car, sure that at any moment he was going to be ambushed. But each cautious peek yielded nothing. Had 457 actually bugged out? Had he finally given up? Nah. Not possible. Maybe something had happened to him. This was, after all, New York. Perhaps the guy on the bike had beaten the crap out of him and left him for dead.

Stranger things had happened.

By the time the fugitive arrived again at the tip of Riverside Park, at the corner of Seventy-second and the West Side Highway or Joe DiMaggio Highway or whatever the hell they'd renamed it in his absence, he was feeling quite comfortable. Whatever had happened to 457, he didn't care. All that mattered was that the guy was clearly gone.

Somehow, miraculously, the fugitive was finally safe.

A homeless man sat on the step that surrounded the monument at the entrance to the park. The fugitive sat next to him to wait, suddenly exhausted beyond belief, sighing a relieved sigh. Any second she would be here, and nothing else would matter.

That was when he felt the hard, cold barrel of a gun against the back of his head. He stopped breathing.

"You know, kid, I was going to bring you back, but I've changed my mind," 457's gruff voice growled. "I think I'm just gonna kill you."

He said a prayer, ruminated for a moment on the tragedy of how close he'd come, and closed his eyes. He was too exhausted to fight anymore. His arms weighed four thousand pounds apiece, his legs even more. He wondered, in a detached way, if he would even hear the firing of the gun before he died.

Then the strangest thing happened. The homeless man's arm shot out and whacked the gun right out of 457's hand. It went tumbling end over end, arcing slowly through the air, and landed on the other side of the dog run fence, where the golden retriever promptly picked it up in his mouth and ran.

For a split second everyone froze in place, stunned. The homeless man, with his toothless mouth hanging open. The fugitive, with his life still flashing before his eyes. The guard, who looked like he was about to shake apart with fury. The two female dog owners, who seemed about ready to move out of New York.

"You idiot!" 457 shouted.

"Serves you right for mugging a homeless kid," the homeless man said.

The guard let out a guttural roar and tackled the fugitive from behind, sending him to the ground. His face scraped against the brick surface of the park's entryway and he skidded along, wincing in pain. Then 457 flipped him over and straddled him, pinning his head to the ground with his forearm to the neck. The pain was excruciating. The fugitive couldn't move, he couldn't breathe. He could feel the wind on his face, but the air was gone.

"I don't need a gun to finish you," 457 spat, saliva spattering against the fugitive's face, hitting him in the eye.

The world started to swim before his eyes, and suddenly he knew he was going to die. Before he saw her again. He'd failed. He'd failed. He'd failed. His arms reached up, but it was no use. It was almost over. The blackness was coming on.

Soon it would all be over.

Meat Grinder

AS GAIA SPEED-WALKED DOWN Seventy-second Street, heading for Riverside Drive, one huge droplet of rain smacked right into her forehead. Then she felt nothing for thirty seconds. Then another one hit her shoulder. The wind on Seventy-second Street was fierce, and that morning's summerlike conditions were rapidly giving way to April-like showers. The sky was one big sheet of gray. She tucked her hands under her arms and bent into the wind. At least her movement was keeping her warm.

The light at Seventy-second and West End turned yellow, and the Don't Walk sign flared red, but Gaia ignored it. She was dying to find out who was waiting for her near the entrance of the highway. Dying to find out if Loki were somehow free or if his men were still after her. She jogged across four lanes of road and was nearly nicked by the bent fender of a bagel truck. One inch from becoming roadkill.

As more raindrops hit Gaia's face, the little brick entryway at the corner of Riverside Park came into view, and Gaia instantly knew something was wrong. A couple of men hovered near the curb, intrigued by something they were watching but clearly ready to bolt if the need presented itself. All the other pedestrians were swinging wide the moment they arrived at the edge of the park. They were crossing the road at unsafe moments, checking over their shoulders. Clearly something was happening that they didn't want to get caught up in.

Which probably meant it was something Gaia would just *love* to join in on.

She jogged across Riverside Drive and skidded to a stop next to the two spectators. A man dressed in head-to-toe black had another guy, someone with mismatched shoes and very baggy sweatpants, pinned to the ground. On instinct, Gaia knew the man in black was the bad guy here. Maybe because black clothing meant villain. Maybe because he seemed too professional. Maybe because he seemed like he could easily be one of Loki's men. And if he was, then he was here for her. And if he were here for her. . .

Gaia took a running start, bent at the waist, and slammed into the assailant, tackling him to the ground. They tumbled, head over heels, away from his victim, and Gaia made sure she landed on top. She pushed herself up slightly, pulled back, and punched the man in black with all of her strength.

"Who sent you?" she shouted, pulling back and punching him again before he had time to recover from the first blow. His head snapped back and forth on his neck like it was on a hinge.

She shifted her weight, and he screamed—an agonized, screeching scream. That was when she noticed that his arm was in a sling. How perfect was that? She pressed her knee into his shoulder, and he screamed again.

"Who sent you?" she shouted.

"I. . . I don't know what you mean," he sputtered, spittle flicking her in the face. His eyes were wild with pain. His face looked like it had been put through a meat grinder. At least the mismatched-clothing man had held his own.

"You wanted to meet me here!" she shouted again, raindrops now dotting her arms, stinging her with their force. "Who sent you?"

He kicked up his leg and sent her sprawling away from his arm, then somehow staggered to his feet. Gaia stood quickly and lunged at him, but he was too fast. He backhanded her with his good hand and sent her reeling around. Definitely one of Loki's men. No one else would be able to function in that kind of pain. When the world stopped spinning, she was facing him again, and he leapt into the air, spinning with his leg outstretched. But Gaia saw it coming. She reached up and stopped his ankle with both arms before he could land his kick.

He crumpled to the ground but rolled over instantly, and as Gaia advanced on him, he thrust up his leg and caught her in the stomach. Gaia ricocheted back. She jumped up onto the step surrounding the monument as the man in black climbed to his feet.

"You're her, aren't you?" he said, then spit out a wad of blood.

"Like you weren't expecting me," Gaia shot back. The rain was driving faster and faster, soaking her through to her skin and making her hair stick in clumps to her face.

"I wasn't," he said. "But it will be my pleasure to kill you."

Damn, this guy was pretty full of himself, considering his condition.

Gaia smiled as he rushed her, then easily hopped out of the way. He stumbled forward and braced his good hand against the step, then spun around, throwing a punch in her general direction. Gaia ducked it easily. She pulled up her fist and swung down, pounding him across the cheek. He doubled over and she kneed him in the face, opening the cut in his already swollen lip. He tried valiantly to throw a right hook, but Gaia hit the ground and kicked out her leg, sweeping his legs out from under him. He hit the ground, facedown.

This was definitely easier than fighting Jake.

Gaia stepped around him, one foot on either side of his torso, grabbed his bad arm, and pulled it back.

The scream this time was not of a human nature.

"Who sent you?" she shouted again. She just wanted to hear it. She wanted to hear him say her uncle's name. She wanted it confirmed.

But then the arm went limp in her hand. The man in black had passed out from the pain. Gaia dropped the useless limb and looked around, her head still a bit dizzy from all the reeling. Dizzy from having gotten no answers.

Where was the guy the man in black had attacked? Maybe he had some answers. Maybe the man attacked him for a reason.

But before she could focus on anyone, she felt the blackout coming. The tingling sensation started in the back of her skull and crept forward. She fought to stave it off, but she knew it wouldn't work. It never did. She had to find the victim. She had to talk to him before he got away. . . .

Something moved at Gaia's feet. Someone was pushing himself up from the ground. One black shoe. One white. It was him. It was the guy. It was. . .

Gaia swallowed hard as he stood up and looked her in the eyes. She couldn't trust her vision, clouded by so many tiny prickles of black. By the raindrops that clung to her eyelashes. She had to be hallucinating. Those hazel eyes. Those laugh lines. That wavy brownish-red hair. That face. That face. That face.

And then he spoke. "Hi," he said. He smiled.

"Sam?" Gaia asked.

And everything went black.

Her hair is dirty and wet and matted from the rain. It's sticking to her forehead and her cheek in knotted tangles. She has a bruise just above her eye that is a swirl of purples and blues. There's dried blood under her nose. Her skin is pale, and her lips are flaking. She's wearing a T-shirt big enough for a linebacker and a pair of muddied, ripped cords with her ever present black boots.

She's the most beautiful thing I've ever seen.

All that time. All that time I was imprisoned, kept away from all human contact except the occasional roughing up by the guards, all I thought about was her. I thought about the first day I saw her in the park, playing chess—that look of concentration and joy on her face. I thought about the first time she smiled at me, the first time we kissed, the first time we touched. But after a while, with

SAM

nothing to look at but blank
white walls, and with no one to
see but those wrinkled, evil
faces, I started to wonder if I'd
made her up. If I'd imagined her
as a way to stay sane. Or at the
very least if I was building her
up to be something she wasn't. If
I was imagining this perfection
because it was all I had.

But now it's clear that I
didn't imagine a thing. She's
even more beautiful than I remembered.

THE FIRST THING GAIA FELT WAS

the water flicking against her eyelids. Splattering along her bare arms. Then a gust of wind whirled by, sending goose bumps over her chilled skin, and she pulled her arms around herself, nestling deeper into the arms that held her. She was outside. Why? How had she gotten—

Wait a minute? Arms holding her?

Gaia wrenched her eyes open with some effort, then blinked rapidly to clear the painful dryness that stung them. She shivered, and the arms tightened around her, holding her close. When she was finally able to keep her eyes open, finally able to see, she realized that she was actually still asleep. That all this rain and wind and cold and scratchiness was part of a very vivid dream. Because Sam Moon could not be holding her and smiling down at her. Sam Moon was long dead.

"Hey. You're awake," the dream Sam said. She felt his voice reverberate through his chest, beneath her cheek. It sent a pleasant shiver deep down into her body, and she smiled. Might as well enjoy this while she could. Before her subconscious took it all away.

"Hey," Gaia replied. "You're alive." It was an unmomentous thing to say, but this was an unmomentous moment. It was a dream, after all. And it wasn't as if she hadn't dreamed of Sam before. She had. She'd had nightmares almost every night since he died. This had to be another one. Any second now Josh would come along and shoot Sam in the head. And there would be nothing Gaia could do to stop it.

"That's all I get?" Sam said with a smirk. He touched her face, wiping a spot of rain away from her nose. His fingertips felt so real. "I go MIA for months, and all I get is your dry irony? Not that I mind, exactly. I mean, I'd hate to think you'd changed."

Any second now Gaia was sure she'd wake up. Sam would poof away as always, and she'd wake up in her bed at Natasha's to the annoying sound of her alarm clock bleeping.

She turned slightly, and a stabbing jolt of pain sliced through her temple from just above her right eye. She squeezed her eyes shut, and her hand flew to the bruise, her heart pounding.

That was real. That was real pain.

She stared up at Sam, amazed. She hadn't woken up when that jolt of pain had hit her. And if she hadn't woken up, then that meant Sam really was alive. In a flash it all came rushing back to her—the note, the subway ride uptown, the fight, the man with two mismatched shoes that had turned out to be—

"Sam?" she said through the throbbing in her head.

"There she is," Sam said. "Now you're awake."

"You're here? But how—how did you—" Gaia

broke off as tears threatened. She reached up and wrapped her arms around his neck forcefully, awkwardly, with all the grace of a mule. He squeezed her back so hard that for a moment she felt like she was going to crack.

He's alive! He's really here! Gaia's mind screamed through the million swirling images and thoughts and emotions that whirled through her head and heart. She was holding Sam Moon in her arms. She hadn't been responsible for his death because he wasn't actually dead. He was right here. As real and alive as ever.

She reached up and touched her fingers to his wet hair. Squeezed his back, his shoulders, then hugged him again, pressing her face into his rank T-shirt that smelled of stale sweat and ammonia. It was all real.

"But you died!" Gaia exclaimed when she pulled back, looking into his face to make sure he was okay. That it was actually him. The feeling of relief and happiness that washed over her was overwhelming. The shock almost paralyzing. How was any of this possible?

"Is that what they told you?" Sam asked, pushing her wet, clumpy hair away from her face and cupping her cheeks with his wet palms. "They didn't kill me. I thought they were going to, but they didn't. All I remember is fighting with this guy, and then I guess I was just knocked out, and then I woke up and I was in this compound in these different clothes and surrounded by guards. . . . I was kidnapped and I was held and no one ever told me why and I—" He cut himself off and laughed. "Sorry, I guess I'm babbling. I haven't talked to anyone in so long."

"It's okay. I want to know everything," Gaia said. "Where did they keep you?" It was just one of a thousand questions on the tip of her tongue, and it was the first to fall out. Sam shifted his weight, and Gaia suddenly realized that she was still cradled in his lap.

If Ed could see me now, her mind thought incongruously. She blushed and slid away from Sam, landing her butt on the wet bricks and turning to face him. Still, she couldn't seem to completely break contact. Letting go of him would be too dangerous. As long as she could touch him, `he was real`. So she held both his hands in hers, and they laced a few fingers together awkwardly.

"I was in some kind of compound in the Berkshires, I think," Sam said. "At least that's what I could tell from the route I had to use to get here." He uncrossed his legs to stretch them out, then crossed them again, looking at her almost forlornly, as if he missed having her in his lap.

"The Berkshires?" Gaia repeated. That was where she'd grown up with her parents. Had Loki had this compound there all along? Her parents had moved the family there to get away from her uncle, but of course he had followed. Of course.

Gaia had to swallow hard to keep the bile from rushing up in her throat. This was not what she should be concentrating on right now. Loki was out of the picture.

"I'm sorry about the weird note I left you," Sam said. "I wasn't sure what to do."

"So *you* left it," Gaia said. "When were you at the school?"

"A few hours ago," Sam replied, looking down at his chest. "That's where I got these clothes. They made us wear jumpsuits at the compound."

"How did you get out?" Gaia asked, shaking her head slightly in an effort to focus. There was so much to take in—so many clues to listen for. And all the while her brain was repeating, *Sam's alive! Sam's here! Sam's alive! Sam's here!* It was all a lot to deal with at one time.

"Well, I tried to escape a couple of times when I first got there, but let's just say they didn't like that very much," Sam said, looking away. A shadow crossed his face, and his grip on her hands tightened. Gaia's stomach turned. What had they done to him? What had they done to him simply because he'd made the mistake of knowing her?

"I gave up for a while, but a couple of days ago everything changed," Sam continued, his voice gaining strength. "The place had been a well-oiled machine, and then suddenly it was total chaos. So I took my chance, and I got the hell out of there." He looked to his left, his eyes growing distant.

"He was the last of the ones that came after me, I think," Sam said.

Gaia's eyes traveled over the body of the man she had just rendered unconscious. In all the confusion she'd completely forgotten about him. Rivulets of rain were running across the bridge of his nose and down the other side of his face. His back rose and fell slowly with his breathing. If he hadn't looked so worked over, Gaia would have thought he was just sleeping happily, knocked out from an all-night drinking binge.

This was not good. It wouldn't be long before one of those previous bystanders contacted the police. The cops were probably on their way here right now. Gaia stood up quickly and reached her hand down to Sam.

"We have to get you out of here," she said.

He grasped her forearm and allowed her to yank him to his feet. "Why?" he asked. "What's wrong?"

Before she could answer him, he swayed and his knees collapsed, and she had to wrap her arms around his back to keep him from hitting the ground. His eyes rolled back momentarily, and Gaia shook him to keep him awake.

"Sam?" she said. She reached up and slapped him a couple of times for good measure. He blinked rapidly, and it took him a moment to focus, but he finally did.

"Whoa. What was that?" he asked groggily.

"You almost passed out," Gaia said, her brow wrinkling.

"Oh. . . well, I haven't exactly eaten much in the last two days," he said weakly.

"Jeez!" Gaia exclaimed, covering her hand with her mouth. "What about your insulin? I totally forgot."

"Actually, I have plenty," he said, struggling for the Sharpie-like syringe he had in his pocket to demonstrate. "For some reason, back at the compound they were very generous about supplying me with insulin. I guess they wanted to keep me alive." He sluggishly dragged the back of his arm across his forehead. "What's the rush again?"

"It's him," Gaia said, pointing her thumb over her shoulder. "You really want to answer to the cops right now? Because I don't. Besides, you think he's the last one, but he's not. These people mean business, trust me."

In fact, Gaia realized as she was standing there, still holding on to Sam, if she was smart, she wouldn't take everything he said at face value. Loki and his men *did* mean business. And she couldn't imagine them letting any prisoner get away unscathed. Was Sam telling her the truth, or had he been turned by Loki? Was he here on a mission for him? Was he here to keep an eye on her?

"So, where do we go?" Sam asked, tucking his hands under his arms.

Gaia looked into his eyes, searching for a change. Searching for a hint of darkness, of watchfulness, of distrust. But there was nothing. Nothing but the same old Sam. Just a weakened, tired version of the guy she once loved. She had to trust him. She had to put her suspicions aside. She was just so glad that he was actually alive, how could she possibly think of anything else?

"I don't know, but you need to keep a low profile, at least until we're sure it's safe," Gaia said, grabbing his bicep. She turned him toward the street, and they walked into the rain, the drops stinging her face with their force.

"Well, I have no place," Sam said. "It's not like I can go back to the dorm."

"So you'll stay with me," Gaia said, before truly taking the time to think it through. Sam turned to look at her—she could tell from the corner of her eye—but she couldn't look back at him at that moment. She didn't want to know what he was thinking, if he was excited or took this as some sign that she still wanted him.

Right now she had to deal with logistics, not with emotions. And keeping Sam close by, while it did come with its own set of problems, seemed like the safest solution.

ED STOOD ON THE EDGE OF THE

Glutton for Punishment

sidewalk in front of the school, trying ever so hard not to turn around and look each and every time the big metal doors to the school squealed open and clanged shut again. He knew he was starting to appear pathetic. From now on he'd let himself look back every fifth time, maybe. Or maybe every third.

The last yellow school bus sputtered away from him, engulfing him in a cloud of rancid exhaust. He held his breath and tried to look unaffected as a couple of kids laughed at him through the windows. Perfect. Now he was going to smell like the Lincoln Tunnel for the rest of the day. Heather was gonna love that. If it was true that your other senses were heightened when you lost one of them, then she was going to smell him coming from ten blocks away. He pulled his Stussy baseball cap low over his eyes to keep the drizzle from his face and stared at the blue awning on the building across the street, watching it flap in the breeze. He concentrated on not turning around.

The squealing of the door sounded. *Okay, that was one. . . .*

It was followed by a lot of giggling and scurrying and multiple voices. Someone uttered the words *Justin* and *Timberlake*. Definitely not Gaia. He'd never in his life heard Gaia giggle, let alone talk to anyone who ever giggled. And he was categorically certain that she had no idea who Justin Timberlake was. He wished that *he* didn't know.

Another squeal. *Two*. . .

A blast of the latest Da Brat song from a boom box, accompanied by a few hand slaps. The guffaws of some guys trying to sound older and cooler than they were. Nope. Also not a `Gaia-type exit`.

Three. . .

Three was good enough. He turned and looked over his shoulder to find a couple of gawky freshmen boys walking out, poring over what was either the latest Spider-Man comic or a porn magazine stuffed inside the latest Spider-Man comic. A few more people spewed from the doors as Ed watched. He glanced at his digital watch and sighed.

He was definitely starting to get the feeling that Gaia was standing him up. And after the day he'd had—watching her roll around on the floor with that oily new guy, getting ribbed over it for the rest of the day—getting stood up definitely didn't feel good.

Okay, give her the benefit of the doubt, Fargo, Ed told himself, rolling up onto his toes and back down to his heels, marveling over the fact that he could even do that. Maybe Gaia had heard something about her dad and had left school early to go to the hospital.

Maybe he'd snapped out of it and she was by his bedside right now, laughing over the whole silly ordeal. He hoped so. He hoped that he had a message on his machine at home right now from Gaia, gleefully telling him that everything was going to be fine.

But knowing the way Gaia's unlucky life went, that probably wasn't the case.

She's not coming, a little voice in Ed's mind told him. *But why not? Where is she?* He felt a painful twist in his chest. The twist of insecurity he'd been feeling every five minutes or so ever since gym. But that was stupid, right? It wasn't like Gaia had gone somewhere with. . . what was his name again? Jackass?

He rolled his eyes and tipped his head back slightly, letting a few raindrops tickle his lightly stubbled chin. What had he been thinking, asking Gaia to go over to Heather's with him? Yeah, his intentions had been good. His heart had been in the right place. Heather needed company, and Gaia needed to get her mind off her father. But even if Gaia and Heather had reconciled their differences, was going to visit a blind girl really the best antidepressant? A recently blinded girl, no less? Actually, make that a recently blinded girl whose blindness, at least in Gaia's mind, was Gaia's fault?

"Real smooth, Fargo," Ed said under his breath. There was no way Gaia was going to show up for this.

The door behind him flew open and slammed

back against the brick wall. Ed's heart leapt. *That* sounded like Gaia. He broke his three-exit rule and turned around, only to find the oily moron himself loping down the steps, with two of Heather's BFFs flanking him. `Barf worthy.`

Well, at least he now knew that Gaia wasn't with him.

Ed watched Jake as he and his groupies passed by. What did everyone see in this guy that was completely invisible to the eyes of Ed Fargo? Did they not notice the liter of petroleum in his hair? Was he really fooling anyone with that brand spanking new Jeter jersey? It probably still had the little plastic tag holders in it. He'd probably just moved here from Boston and turned against his team in a lame-ass attempt to fit in. Be cool. Well, in Ed's opinion, it wasn't working.

Ed waited until oily boy and his women had disappeared around the corner and glanced at his watch again. He knew that if he didn't leave in the next two minutes, he was going to be late getting to Heather's. And he didn't want to be late because he knew she was looking forward to the visit, but he also didn't want to show without Gaia, because then he'd have to explain her absence to Heather, and that was going to be unfun. Heather would definitely think it was personal, and Ed would have a hard time convincing her it wasn't. Even though it definitely wasn't.

Heather would be hurt and Ed would be mortified, and it was all because Gaia had simply decided not to show for whatever reason. Ed loved her more than anything in the world, but even he could admit that she did have her flaws. Occasional disregard for other people's feelings topping the list.

She isn't coming, the little voice chided. *I don't even know why you're still here. Glutton for punishment, perhaps?*

"Ed!"

He whirled around, knowing it wasn't Gaia's voice but hoping he was wrong. He wasn't. Tatiana was strolling down the steps, little droplets of rain shimmering in her hair.

"Waiting for Gaia?" she asked, pausing next to him.

"Yeah. You don't know if she went to the hospital already, do you?" Ed asked.

"I haven't heard anything," Tatiana replied, lifting one shoulder. "She's kind of late, huh?"

"She'll be here," Ed said firmly, setting his jaw. Wow. He was really good at sounding sure of himself.

"You know, I envy Gaia," Tatiana said matter-of-factly.

"Why's that?" Ed asked, even though he was sure the answer would be a dig at him.

"She's the only girl I know with a man in waiting," Tatiana said. Then she smiled slightly as if to say, "Take it as a joke. That's how it was meant."

"Ha ha," Ed replied. "Very funny." His face burned against his will, and he turned away from her, pretending to look down the street as if Gaia might be coming from the back exit around the corner.

"I was just kidding," Tatiana cajoled. "Well, if you see her, tell her I hope her father is doing better. And if I see her at home first, I'll tell her to call you."

She's been acting weird all day, Ed noted as he watched Tatiana walk away. It wasn't like Tatiana to be catty like that. Maybe the pressure of Gaia's dad's coma was getting to her. Or maybe it was just starting to sink in that he and Gaia were really together. Either way, Ed had other things to think about.

Ed listened again for the doors. They were squealing open and slamming closed with much less frequency now. The school was emptying out. Soon the only people left would be the chess team and the chronic detention-getters. Gaia wasn't inside the school. Ed knew this. She wasn't going to show.

He pressed his teeth together and told himself he would wait one more minute. One more frustrating, annoying minute. Then he'd suck it up and walk very slowly over to Heather's. Hopefully there would be enough time to perfect his excuse for being late.

the tiny

lines around

his eyes

that **clearly**

shouldn't

have **delirious**

been there

for another

twenty years

The Little Hostess

GAIA OPENED THE DOOR TO THE apartment that she currently called home and was met by utter silence. There wasn't a light on in the place, and the shades were down, casting the entire living room in a soft, dusky grayness. Natasha, it seemed, was still at the hospital. Gaia wasn't sure whether to take that as a positive sign or a negative one. She had no idea where Tatiana might be, but it was good, for the moment, that she wasn't around.

Stealth missions were much easier when there was no need to be stealthy.

"Okay, come in," Gaia said over her shoulder to Sam, who leaned against the wall beside the door. His skin was pale, and there were big purple splotches under his eyes. He was looking dazed and very weak, and he hadn't said much in the last few minutes of the cab ride over. Gaia had to get him hidden away and then get some food into him or she was going to have another hospital run on her hands. And she was not going to let that happen. She'd already found and lost one of the men in her life this week.

Gaia stepped inside and held the door back for Sam, who managed to push himself away from the wall and into the apartment.

"Where are we?" he asked, glancing around the

large, sparsely decorated living room with heavy, glassy eyes.

"This is where I live now," Gaia answered. "With some friends of my father's." *My father, who's in a coma a few blocks from here,* she added silently. As stunned and psyched and elated as she was to see Sam, she had to get over to the hospital as soon as possible. She'd gone too long without being there. Anything could have happened to him by now.

"Thanks for letting me. . . ," Sam started, then trailed off. He brought his hand to his forehead and started to sway, but Gaia grabbed him before he could go down. He let her hold most of his weight as they made their way around the corner and down a short hallway. Behind the kitchen was a tiny bedroom, about the size of a walk-in closet, that years ago in some other reality had been the maid's quarters. It had its own three-foot-square bathroom, and it was half filled with boxes, but at least it was a place where Sam could stay. Where he would be safe.

And it was the only place in the apartment that Gaia could be certain Natasha and Tatiana would never go. Natasha wasn't exactly the nesting type. She hadn't been back there to unpack anything for as long as Gaia had known her. She wasn't even sure if Tatiana knew it was there.

Gaia half dragged, half walked Sam into the small room, and he immediately sank down on top of one of the shorter piles of boxes. He looked like a rag doll, slumped there in his mismatched clothes with his hair sticking out in all directions. His arms hung limp at his sides, his hands drooping open lifelessly.

"Don't move," Gaia said.

"Not likely," Sam replied with a slow smile. He still had a sense of humor. Good sign.

Gaia cracked a grin, then jogged back to the kitchen and ransacked the cabinets. She had no idea what Sam would want to eat, so she just grabbed things at random. She pulled out a loaf of bread, a sleeve of Ritz crackers, a can of macadamia nuts, a big bar of Toblerone chocolate, and two oranges. Cradling everything in her arms and holding the chocolate bar against her chest with her chin, she turned to the refrigerator and used her index finger to yank open the door. On the top shelf sat a six-pack of Coke with one can missing. Gaia hooked her finger through the empty plastic loop and pulled the cans out with a series of resounding, reverberating clangs.

She felt like such the little hostess. All she needed was an apron and a Martha Stewart haircut.

Sam couldn't even seem to focus on her when she hustled back into the room. Gaia's heart turned in her chest. He was fading fast. She couldn't believe he'd lasted as long as he had. How had he survived all this time by himself? Unlike her, he hadn't been brought up on loneliness and torture.

"Here you go," she said, going for chipper. She let everything tumble out of her arms onto the floor. "You even get room service."

Sam slid off the boxes, sank to the floor, and tore open the loaf of bread. He pulled out the first slice and shoved the whole thing into his mouth, jamming it in with his fingertips. The crusts, folded and torn, protruded from his lips and moved up and down as he chewed.

"Fank oo," he said through his bulging mouth.

"Uh. . . you might want to slow down," Gaia said, raising her eyebrows. "You're gonna puke if you do it that way."

Sam chewed slowly and swallowed, then reached for a can of Coke. "Good call," he said with his lopsided smile. He took a deep breath and let it out, then took a long swallow of soda. "Damn, that felt good," he said, wiping his mouth with the back of his hand.

"Okay, I'll be right back. . . again," Gaia said.

She ran across the living room and down the hallway to the bedroom she shared with Tatiana, dropping to her knees in the center of the hardwood floor. She ducked under the bed, shoving aside sneakers, candy bar wrappers, and an old, torn backpack to uncover the rolled-up sleeping bag she was looking for. Shimmying back out into the room, she flung out the bag and it slid across the floor, taking a few tumbling dust bunnies with it.

Gaia slapped the army green bag until her bedroom was thick with dust. The inside lining, a tan flannel material decorated with cowboys on bucking horses, was sticking out a bit at the end of the roll. Gaia ran her fingertip along it and briefly let her mind travel back to her childhood, when she and her parents used to camp out in her backyard, pointing out constellations and making up scary stories. This sleeping bag was one of her only keepsakes from that time. Gaia sighed and looked down at her own finger, still moving along the fabric.

Now she knew that it was all a lie, that feeling of security she'd had as a child. Loki had been there even then. He'd been there, just waiting for his moment to tear her life apart. Gaia felt a wave of sorrow well up inside her and fought it back.

What a loser, she thought, rolling her eyes. She grabbed an extra pillow from her bed and headed for the living room, shaking away her nostalgic thoughts. Her present bitterness. There was no point in going there. It was past, and there was nothing she could do about it. And Loki was paying for it now.

Natasha's bookshelves lined one wall of the living

room, bulging with hardcover classics, novels, and huge nonfiction tomes. Gaia reached up and slid a few titles from the shelves—*Moby Dick, Journey to the Center of the Earth,* and some random Tom Clancy novels just in case he went in for that kind of thing.

She walked back to Sam's new room and found him with his legs spread-eagled, all the food piled in front of him and an orange wedge suspended halfway to his mouth. His eyes were at half-mast, and his cheeks bulged like a chipmunk's.

"Are you okay?" she asked.

"Ate too fast," he said. "Taking a breather."

Gaia dropped her stuff and carefully removed the orange wedge from his hand. "Chew and swallow," she said slowly. "Chew. . . aaaaand. . . swaaaaalloooow."

Sam followed her instructions, and eventually the chipmunk cheeks went away. She pulled all the food away from him in case he got any stupid ideas about eating more, then untied her sleeping bag and snapped it open. She laid it down against the wall and tossed the pillow into the corner.

"It isn't pretty, but it's home," Sam said, lifting one side of his mouth.

Gaia smirked. "I'll get you one of those blow-up mattresses when I go out later," she said. "Of course, I don't know who's going to blow it up. . . ."

"This is fine," Sam said, crawling over to the

sleeping bag. "I had one just like this when I was a kid."

Gaia smiled at his butt, which was sticking straight up in the air as he buried his face in her pillow. This guy was clearly delirious. Not that she blamed him. He'd been on the lam for two days with no food or sleep after months of incarceration. She was lucky he wasn't licking the walls and speaking backward at this point.

Sam started to tip to the side to lie down, and Gaia dropped to the floor.

"Don't!" she said. "If you lie down right after eating all that, you'll *definitely* puke."

Sam glanced over his shoulder at her, his butt still in the air. "You know a lot about the rules of puking," he said.

Gaia shrugged, and Sam managed to turn himself around and sit down with his back up against the wall and his legs splayed out over the sleeping bag. Gaia got up on her knees, reached over and closed the door, just in case, then sat down next to him.

There was so much she wanted to say to him, so much she wanted to ask him, so much she wanted to apologize for, that the words suddenly seemed to get jammed up in her chest. The one thing that kept repeating itself in her mind was the one thing she wasn't sure she'd ever be able to bring herself to say.

Please forgive me. Please forgive me. Please forgive me.

"Thank you for all this," Sam said, reaching forward and dragging one of the books across the floor toward him. "I don't want to put you out."

Gaia snorted a laugh and felt herself flush with about a million emotions. "Please," she said. "It's the least I can do after everything I put you through."

"You put me through?" Sam asked, turning his hazel eyes on her.

"Yeah," Gaia said, staring in the direction of her knees. "None of this would have happened to you if it wasn't for me. You lost all that time. . . . You were in prison, basically. I can't even imagine what they did to you."

But she could. She could imagine a lot. And everything her brain came up with made her a little more sick to her stomach.

Sam's hand covered her own on top of the army green softness between them. "Gaia, I don't blame you for anything," he said, squeezing her palm and the back of her hand between his fingers. "I would never blame you."

"You're just saying that," Gaia said, pulling her hand away. She couldn't conceive of it. If she were in his place, she'd be out for blood. Revenge. She'd want to pummel anyone remotely connected with what she'd been through. In fact, she was practically seething on his behalf right now. If she could beat the crap out of herself, she would.

"I'm not just saying it, really," Sam replied earnestly. "I know you would never hurt me. The guys that held me were sick, and that's not your fault."

Gaia turned her head and looked at him. At the tiny lines around his eyes that shouldn't have been there for another twenty years. At the little scar along his hairline that advertised the position of former stitches. Something he'd probably gotten after one of his attempted escapes. She couldn't believe he didn't hold her responsible. But when she looked into his eyes, she knew. She knew he was telling the truth.

That was the difference between her and Sam. One of the differences, anyway. Sam had a forgiving side.

"Hey, c'mere," Sam said, his brow creasing.

He held out his arms, and Gaia leaned into him, draping one arm clumsily over his chest. It was still so unreal, the fact that she could hug Sam. That he was here.

"Everything's going to be okay now," Sam said. "I know it is."

Gaia felt a tear prickle at the corner of her eye but refused to let it fall. She wasn't going to get all weak and weepy right now. Now was not the time. And she wasn't going to let *Sam* comfort *her*. Whether or not he'd forgiven her for what had happened, she wasn't ready to forgive herself.

She pulled away from him, but Sam stopped her,

cupping the back of her neck with his hand. Gaia's heart caught in her chest. *He wants to kiss me,* she realized. Just what she needed right now. Another totally uncomfortable moment. How was she supposed to tell Sam that while he'd been imprisoned on her behalf, she'd been falling in love with someone else?

But she knew the answer to that question. She wasn't.

"I have to go," Gaia said, standing quickly and breaking the tension in the air. "My dad's in the hospital, and I have to. . . go."

She wiped her palms on the back of her cords and looked around to see if there was anything in the room that she needed.

"I hope he's okay," Sam said earnestly.

"He will be," Gaia lied. She had to. She didn't want to stay here any longer than she had to, and she would have to if she opted to explain. Explain why her father would never be okay. "So. . . if anyone comes home, just stay in here. I don't want to tell them about you until I know what's going on."

"Got it," Sam said with a nod. "I'm probably just gonna sleep, anyway."

"Good," Gaia said. She turned to go, pulling the door behind her, but before she let it shut, she stuck her head back into the room. "Sam," she said. "I'm glad you're back."

Sam smiled the smile that used to stop her heart. "Me too."

There's almost nothing Ed doesn't know about me.

He knows that when I wake up in the morning, my hair looks like a bird's nest. He knows that when I pass out after a fight, I drool like a slobbering infant. He knows that although it's incredibly difficult for me to tell him so, I love him. And he knows that until he was taken away from me, I also loved Sam Moon.

What Ed doesn't know is how I feel about Sam now.

And neither do I.

There was a point not that long ago when all I thought about was Sam Moon. He came along at the perfect time to be my obsession. My father was gone to who knows where. I was living with people I barely knew—a woman I couldn't stand—in a city about as familiar to me as Budapest. I was at a new school where everyone was predisposed to hate me. (At least it felt that way.) And I was a freak of nature.

GAIA

And then there was Sam.

He was beautiful. And kind. And so smart and sure of himself and unsure of himself. He was the first person who ever caused the air around me to sizzle. To crackle with some kind of weird, bizarro electricity. He was Sam. He was everything I wanted. Or so I thought.

All along, all that time, Ed was there. He listened to everything, suffered through everything. He was my friend in a way no one had ever been before. He saw me. He saw right through me. And I didn't care.

It feels wrong to keep the truth about Sam's return from Ed. He deserves to know. I just don't know when would be the best time to tell him.

Telling him now would be the safer route. Because if he finds out a few weeks from now or even a few days from now, it'll be like I was keeping something huge from him. No, it won't be *like* that, it'll *be* that. And Ed hates that. He loathes secrets.

But if I tell him now, there will be so many questions that I'm not ready to answer yet. Questions like, how is it possible for someone to come back from the dead? Did he, like Elvis before him, fake his own death? And when will he follow in Elvis's footsteps and leave the building? (Or, more accurately, leave *my* building?)

And other, more difficult questions, like, do I still have feelings for him?

Actually, there's nothing difficult about that question. Because the answer doesn't even matter. It makes no difference whether I have feelings for Sam, because I love Ed and he's who I'm with now. And as far as telling him about Sam goes, I think it's best to wait. The fewer people who know that Sam is alive and that he's here, the better. Secrecy is the best way to keep him safe. For now.

Even if it's not the best way to keep my relationship safe.

HEATHER GANNIS LOOKED LIKE A

different person. She was as poised as ever. As self-aware. As impeccably put together. But she was also entirely different. Her thick brown hair was pulled back in a neat ponytail, exposing more of her face than Ed had ever seen in all the years he'd known her. Her skin was perfect—not a blemish in sight—and she was

Tangible Sense of Peace

wearing no makeup. She smiled easily. And when she laughed, her eyes seemed more alive than they ever had when they had sight.

There was an almost tangible sense of peace around her.

Ed sat on the couch across the table from her, and when he spoke, she lifted her eyes in his direction, but they didn't fall on him. Her gaze seemed to be aimed somewhere just up and to the right of his shoulder. As if she gave him credit for more height than he deserved. Instead of making Ed feel like Heather could see nothing, it made him feel like she was talking not to him, but to someone behind him. Someone who he couldn't see himself. The effect of this new Heather and this invisible person was more than a little disconcerting. He had no idea how to talk to her, and he had to concentrate to keep from looking over his shoulder.

It's just Heather, Ed reminded himself. *She used to carry a Hello Kitty backpack. She used to read Nancy Drew during science class. She once sent you a note asking you if you liked her a lot, a little, or not at all. You used to hold her hand when you walked home from school. She's still that person.*

"So, are you excited about tomorrow?" Ed asked, sitting on the edge of the couch with his back hunched, clasping and unclasping his hands. He felt conspicuous, like he was going to be graded on his performance, and it was making him sweat.

"Yeah. Excited and scared," Heather said lightly. "At least the whole what-to-wear problem isn't an issue. I usually spend a few weeks on that before school starts, but this time no one's going to be able to *tell* what I'm wearing."

She laughed at her joke, and Ed let out a somewhat strangled sound. He wasn't sure how PC it was to laugh at a blind joke made by a blind person. What was the rule there?

"Time to break out those leg warmers I know you've been just dying to wear," Ed replied in an affected voice, trying to play along.

"I'm thinking pajamas," Heather said with faux seriousness. "Maybe a nice muumuu."

"But hey, you never know. There may be some hot sighted janitor or teacher who'll need impressing," Ed added.

"Good point," Heather said with a mock-thoughtful frown. "Better go for cleavage."

Ed smiled and leaned back slightly into the couch. *See? Just relax,* he told himself. *It's just Heather.*

Just Heather, who in the last few days had proven to be even stronger than Ed had originally thought. Who'd managed to surprise everyone by taking her new disability and facing it head-on, enrolling in school and learning to cope, instead of curling up in a ball and feeling sorry for herself.

"It's amazing, what you're doing," Ed said, his heart pounding a bit at the risk of making an intimate statement. "I'm really. . . well, I'm proud of you."

Heather smiled, looking at that point over his shoulder. "Thanks, but I'm taking my cues from you," she said.

Ed flushed and looked down at his once useless legs, amazed at how far they had both come since the day he'd been injured. Back then Heather couldn't stand to look at him. Now here she was, telling him he was her role model.

"It's going to be so weird, learning everything all over again," Heather said, taking a deep breath. "I have to learn to *read* again. Isn't that bizarre? It's like tomorrow I graduate to the first grade."

"Hey, on the upside, first grade means nap time," Ed replied, earning a laugh. "Ooh! And free snacks!"

Heather pressed her palms into her thighs and

turned her head. "Okay, I can't talk about this anymore or I'm gonna lose it," she said. "I've been obsessing all day. Let's talk about something else."

"Okay. Like what?" Ed asked.

"Like. . . how's Gaia?" Heather asked, raising her eyes again. "What happened to her? I thought she was coming with you."

"She wanted to," Ed put in quickly, almost as a reflex. "She just—"

"Don't tell me, another trauma?" Heather said with a good-natured smirk.

When Ed stayed silent for a moment, the smirk fell right away from her face.

"Oh, come on! I was kidding! What happened now?" Heather asked in disbelief, her brow crinkling just over her nose.

"Well, her dad's kind of. . . in a coma," Ed said, still unable to believe the words himself. Last night—not twenty-four hours ago—everything had been fine. He had been talking and laughing with this man, who was now catatonic without explanation.

"Omigod," Heather said, paling slightly. "Is he going to come out of it?"

"No one knows," Ed replied.

Heather shook her head, her eyes trained in the direction of the coffee table. "Poor Gaia. It's nonstop with that girl."

Tell me about it, Ed thought.

"Is she okay?" Heather asked.

"I don't know. You know Gaia," Ed said. "She's not exactly one for emoting. I thought that coming over here would be a good distraction, but she didn't even show up today after school."

"Oh, well, it's okay. I mean, if her father's in the hospital, I wouldn't expect her to come here," Heather said, lifting both shoulders.

"I know, but she wanted to come," Ed said. "I was going to go over to the hospital with her before we came here. It didn't even occur to me that she wouldn't show."

"Maybe she went straight over to see her dad," Heather suggested.

"Maybe," Ed replied. He left out the fact that he'd called the ICU on his way over here and talked to Natasha. The fact that Natasha had told him she hadn't seen or heard from Gaia all day. The fact that he really did have no clue where she was. Or who she was with. Or what she was doing. And that it was eating him from the inside out.

"I'm sure she's okay," Heather said.

"Yeah, I'm sure she is, too," Ed said. "It's just—"

Don't say it, don't say it, don't say it. Don't be that guy. Just don't.

"What?"

Don't don't don't don't don't—

"It's just that there's this new guy at school and—"

Damn!

"Ed!"

"What?" he blurted, his voice cracking. "You don't even know what I was going to say!"

"Yes, I do!" Heather protested, a blush lighting her cheeks and her mouth open in a teasing smile. "You think Gaia likes some new guy! You do! Omigod! You are not happy unless you are jealous!"

"That is not true!" Ed replied, incredulous. "How can you say that? Who wants to be jealous?"

"Ed Fargo," Heather replied. "Let's see, when we were going out, I was *constantly* cheating on you with other guys. There was John Brooks. . . Bobby Cook. . . Enis Totaj. . . that foreign exchange student from Pakistan. . . . Oh! Mr. Christopher, that cute math teacher."

"See! You *did* like him!" Ed exclaimed! Ha! He *knew* it!

"I don't believe you!" Heather said, her whole face lighting up in triumph. "I don't care who this guy is or what you *think* Gaia sees in him: She does *not* like him."

"How do you know? He could be Brad Pitt," Ed pointed out.

"Brad Pitt is so not Gaia's type," Heather replied. She shook her head, smiling. "Ed, Gaia loves you. You know it. I know it. Everyone at school knows it. You guys were, like, made for each other. Two total freaks."

"Oh, thanks," Ed said with a smile. He liked this reassuring thing. This was good.

"Sorry. Had to throw that in there," Heather replied.

She leaned forward a bit, and her eyes traveled up the wall behind him. Then she cast them down to her hands and toyed with the fingers she couldn't see. It seemed like she was wishing she could look into his eyes to reassure him and the fact that she couldn't was throwing her off.

Slowly she stood up, and Ed instinctively sprang forward. "Don't get up," Heather said, hearing the motion. She put her hand out flat and paused. "I'm fine." Then she inched her way around the coffee table, giving it a wide berth, and sat down next to Ed. "Is this okay?" she asked.

"Fine," Ed replied. He cleared his throat and tried not to stare at her eyes. It was so hard to believe that she couldn't see him. That she was sitting right there and he could study every inch of her, but she couldn't even tell how close or how far he was from her.

Heather reached out her hand and laid it on top of Ed's. Perfectly, flatly on top of his hand in one shot. It was like she could hear his thoughts and wanted to prove him wrong.

"Everything's gonna be fine," Heather said, facing the room. "Gaia's going through something really hard right now, and we all know that she isn't Little Miss Share girl even when things are seminormal. You've just got to let her deal with things in her own way. I know that if my parents hadn't given me some breathing room, I'd probably be psych-ward bound right now."

Ed took a deep breath and let it out slowly, turning his hand over so that he could entwine his fingers with Heather's. It felt good to touch her. It felt like she could see him now, in a way. It helped him relax.

"You're right—I just have to be patient," he said.

"And understanding," Heather added pointedly.

"Damn, you girls ask a lot," Ed deadpanned.

Heather laughed. "Give her some space," she said. "She'll come around."

Ed squeezed her hand and repeated her words in his head, trying to let them soak in. Unfortunately it wasn't the easiest thing to do, deciding to give Gaia space. He'd been doing that ever since he met her. . . and obsessing about her from afar. Now that he had her, he was *still* supposed to give her space? It hardly seemed fair.

Well, you can't spend every waking minute with her, Ed, he told himself. *Especially when you have no idea where she is. . .*

I really don't like the person I became in the wake of being stood up this afternoon. I was like this jealous, paranoid, self-effacing little twit with no trust. The thing is, I *know* on some level that I'm being stupid, but that doesn't stop me from feeling this way. So I've come up with some ideas to keep it from happening again. I mean, to keep from being stood up by Gaia again, not to keep from feeling this way, because I know that's not going to happen.

Okay, here's the list of possibilities:

1. Buy Gaia a cell phone.
Pros: She'll be able to get me
anytime, anywhere.
I'll be able to get her
anytime, anywhere.
Cons: She is rabidly anti-cell
phone.
She'll probably break it,
and if not, she'll never
use it.

2. Buy us both beepers.

Pros: She'll be able to get me
anytime, anywhere.
I'll be able to get her
anytime, anywhere.
It's less offensive and less
expensive than a cell phone.

Cons: She'll probably break it, and
if not, she'll never use it.
The whole drug-dealer stigma.
They're so 1998.

3. Get my hands on one of those
house arrest bracelet things.

Pros: I'll always know where she is.

Cons: People will think she's an
ex-con.
She's not one for acces-
sorizing.
If I suggest it, she'll
definitely kick my ass.

He
seemed
like **her**
someone
she **complete**
cluelessness
could
trust.

GAIA SAT IN THE CUSHIONED CHAIR

Hospital-Issue Soap

next to her father's bed, holding his cold hand. Her eyes were trained on the small television that was suspended by a metal arm over his bed. *Jeopardy* was on, and Gaia was already in the lead. It was unbelievable what the people on this show didn't know. If Gaia ever got the chance to take on Alex Trebek and two numb-nuts contestants, she'd clean up.

She wondered what kind of questions he'd ask her in the short get-to-know-you part of the show. "*So, Gaia, I understand you were born without the fear gene. . . . Tell us about that.*" At least it would make the questions about latch-hooking hobbies and law degrees pale in comparison.

"The only two men to win the Best Actor Oscar twice, in successive years," Alex Trebek intoned, looking to the contestants. The chubby guy on the end attacked his buzzer.

"Come on, Dad, you know that one," Gaia prodded her father, squeezing his hand and looking at his peaceful face. She swallowed hard. "Um, how 'bout I just give you the five hundred dollars."

She stared at her father's now stubbly profile, scrutinizing every inch for a tick or a blink or even a

153

deeper breath than the rhythmic, shallow, in-out, in-out she'd been listening to for the last hour. There was, of course, no movement. But Gaia knew if she stared long enough, she'd find something. She'd imagine something. And then she'd be elated for no reason. She made herself look away.

Gaia turned her heavy eyes toward the open door across from her, wondering where Natasha and Tatiana were right now. Natasha hadn't been here when she'd arrived, which was a mixed blessing. It meant that she wasn't in Gaia's face, but it also meant that she might be home, finding Sam.

Sam. Just thinking his name sent a half-eerie, half-pleasant thrill over her skin. She still couldn't believe that he was alive. That he'd shown up in her life again. She'd let him go so long ago, and now he was back. Part of her expected to go home and find the maid's quarters empty save for all the dusty boxes. That she had imagined the whole thing as some kind of shoddy defense mechanism in response to her father's coma.

Letting out a long sigh, Gaia leaned back in her chair, never letting go of her father's hand. She looked down at the pink hospital scrubs she was wearing and shook her head. She couldn't remember the last time she'd let anything pink touch her skin. Maybe never. But after all that fighting, with no bathing, she'd been so disgusting when she'd walked into the ICU that when the idiot nurse suggested she use the shower, she actually took her up on it.

It had felt amazing, that shower—fresh hospital towels, hospital-issue soap and shampoo with no frills, all that hot water. Gaia had almost relaxed in there, enclosed by turquoise ceramic tile, listening to salsa on the transistor radio some janitor had left on in the hallway. And now that she was clean and unsmelly, now that she was wearing the softest clothes she'd ever felt against her skin and had her hair pulled back in a neat ponytail, she almost felt human again.

But she was exhausted. It seemed like every muscle in her body was crying out for sleep. As if they'd gotten a taste of comfort and wanted more. Gaia felt her grip on her father's hand relax, but as long as she didn't lose contact, she didn't mind. Her eyes slowly started to close. Seconds later she was walking along the edge of the woods near her old house in the Berkshires with Ed, hand in hand, smiling. Ed was twirling her around in his arms, and she was laughing. But when he put her down again, the sky turned dark. The trees behind her morphed into a hundred soldiers, clothed in black. They stood in a circle like sentries, screams sounding from behind their backs. Familiar screams. Screams of pain.

Suddenly Sam appeared between two of the guards, making a break for it. Gaia caught one glimpse of his anguished face before he was thrown back into the circle. Then Jake appeared, tortured and weak, only to be thrown back as well. Gaia tried to rush the guards, but her feet wouldn't move. When she looked down at her ankles, Ed was lying on the ground, his hands clamped around her ankles, holding her fast.

"Ed! What are you doing!? Let go of me!" Gaia shouted, trying to kick him away from her and get free. All Ed did was tighten his grip and glare up at her, smiling maniacally. Gaia's heart tightened. Why was he doing this to her? Why wouldn't he let her help her friends?

Gaia looked desperately at the sentries. "Sam! I'm sorry! I'm sorry!" she shouted. "Jake!" But their screams were too loud. There was no way they could hear her over their own wails of pain.

Then her father's face appeared as he tried to break free as well. He looked at Gaia pleadingly, reaching his hands out to her from between the bodies of two sentries, grasping at thin air.

"Dad!" Gaia screamed. "Dad. Don't go! I'll help you! I'll help you!"

Gaia stretched forward until her fingers hurt, until she felt like she was going to stretch herself out of her skin, but she couldn't get to him.

"Help me, Gaia! You're the only one who can help. . . *meeeeee*!"

Just as her fingertips grazed his, her father was ripped away from her, his screaming louder than that of all the others, slicing through her heart.

"Ms. Moore?"

Gaia started awake, gasping for breath. It took her a moment to get her bearings. Her father's hand had slipped from hers while she slept, and she grabbed it up, wrapping her fingers around his tightly. His screams still echoed in her head from her dream, and she had to show herself that he was still here with her. Not entirely *here*, but at least physically. She hadn't lost him. Not yet.

"Ms. Moore?" someone said again.

Gaia blinked groggily and finally focused on a man who was standing in front of her, holding yet another metal clipboard. Another chart. Another doctor.

"I'm Dr. Sullivan," the man said, holding out a large, freckled hand. "I'm the specialist assigned to your father."

Gaia, not wanting to let go of her dad's hand again, reached up with her left. Dr. Sullivan paused, smiled, and switched his chart from one hand to the other so they could share a proper shake. He had a firm grip. A kind smile. Gaia decided to keep an eye on him. Thanks to Sam, she now knew that Loki's men were, in fact, still out there. Anyone in this hospital could be on her uncle's payroll.

"What's going on with my father?" Gaia asked,

looking directly into Dr. Sullivan's light green eyes. His thick red hair was peppered with gray, and he had plenty of laugh lines around his eyes and mouth. His freckled skin had a pink tint to it, like he'd recently spent too much time in the sun. These were not traits shared by most of Loki's men. They were usually too clean, too perfect, too sheltered. They were automatons who never saw the daylight and never learned to laugh like a real person.

Gaia started to relax.

"I've got to be honest with you, Ms. Moore—"

"Call me Gaia," she said.

"Okay, Gaia," Dr. Sullivan said. Another smile. "Your father's condition is an anomaly."

Why am I not surprised? Gaia thought. "Highly irregular," she muttered.

"I'm sorry?" Dr. Sullivan prompted.

"That's what the other doctor said," Gaia replied. "His condition was highly irregular."

"The other doctor was right," Dr. Sullivan agreed. "But that doesn't mean there's no answer to why this is happening. There's always an answer in science. That's why I like it."

Gaia smiled in an attempt to be polite. She didn't have the heart to tell him that he was wrong. That there was an anomaly in the genes of the girl sitting right in front of him that defied explanation. Sometimes science disappointed.

"So what's next?" Gaia asked.

"I'd like to run a few more tests," Dr. Sullivan said. He walked around the bed and picked up her father's wrist, holding it between his thumb and forefinger and consulting his watch. "There may have been a hormone released into your father's system as he choked—something that could put him out like this. It's rare, but it happens. If that's the case, we can give him some injections that will restore the proper levels."

"And then he'll wake up?" Gaia asked, raising her eyebrows.

"But don't get your hopes up yet," Dr. Sullivan said, the corners of his eyes wrinkling. "I'll run some tests and get back to you by the end of the week. I assume we have your home number?"

"Yeah," Gaia said. "It's in there somewhere."

"Great. Well, it was nice to meet you, Gaia," Dr. Sullivan said, holding out his left hand this time. Gaia grasped it gratefully and forced a smile. "I'll be in touch," he said. And with that, he swept out of the room.

Gaia sat back in her chair again and sighed. Dr. Sullivan seemed like a good guy. He seemed like someone she could trust.

The *Jeopardy* theme song was playing, and Gaia stood up and flicked the TV off. She'd missed final *Jeopardy,* so she'd never know if she won. She decided to just assume she had since she'd been kicking so much butt before she drifted off.

Drifted off. A vague memory of her dream tried to present itself to her mind's eye, but it was too foggy and disparate. All Gaia could remember was that Jake was in it. Jake. What was that about? She'd just met the guy, and already he was crashing her dreams.

"Well, Dad, I should go," Gaia said, standing. "I gotta go make sure my houseguest hasn't been found."

She smiled and leaned over to give her father a quick kiss on the forehead. When she pulled back, she looked down at his closed eyelids, imagining that she could see into his eyes. What she wouldn't give to be able to bring her father home to meet Sam. To be able to say, "Dad, this is my friend who I thought was dead. Sam, this is my father, who was missing." To have them both at the same time.

Apparently that kind of luck was too much to ask.

Gaia took a deep breath, gave her father's hand one last squeeze, and grabbed her balled-up clothes and her messenger bag. She turned and walked out of the ICU, her thoughts turning entirely to Sam. She had to get him something to eat for dinner.

Jeez, that sounded so maternal, she could barely stomach it. But still, somehow, a smile played across her lips. He was alive. She had to keep reminding her-self. Sam was alive. And he was waiting for her at

160

home. Bringing dinner home to Sam. Who ever would have thought it possible?

ED STARED DOWN AT HIS FEET,

Unhealthy
Mix

lifting one set of toes, then the other, then the other, then the other, trying to distract himself. If nothing else, he always had his feet. His movable feet. They were good feet. They were.

The hospital elevator door made its loud, obnoxious *bing!* and slid open, rattling all the way. Ed took one step, still concentrating on his feet, and saw himself almost step on another pair. Another pair in combat boots.

Ed looked up into Gaia's surprised eyes.

"Hey!" he said, his heart pounding like he was on speed. His stomach twisted nervously, and his mouth went dry. . . until he saw what she was wearing. "Have you been playing doctor without me?" he joked.

"Hey!" Gaia blurted energetically. She planted a fast, firm kiss on him with such enthusiasm, he almost thought it wasn't her. "When did you get here?"

"Just. . . now," Ed replied, wondering exactly how

much coffee Gaia had imbibed that afternoon. She seemed nervous, jittery. Her eyes were all over the place. Maybe she just felt guilty about ditching him and wasn't sure how to act.

"Everything okay?" Ed asked as she stepped into the elevator and he stepped back so the doors could close.

"Yeah, I guess," Gaia said, reaching out and lacing her fingers through his. She looked at him and twitched a quick smile, then averted her gaze, focusing intently on the elevator buttons as they raced toward the ground floor.

Okay, what, exactly, was going on here? Gaia seemed to be in a semimanic state, and she'd initiated not one, but two forms of physical contact in the space of five seconds. And now she was bouncing up and down on the balls of her feet as if all she wanted to do was escape. To get away from him.

You're just imagining things, Fargo, he told himself. *You're just paranoid because she ditched you this afternoon.*

Ed felt a lump forming in his stomach, made up of a nice unhealthy mix of guilt, anger, uncertainty, sorrow, and sympathy. How could he feel all those things at one time?

He waited for her to mention it. Waited for her to explain or apologize or explain or ask about Heather or. . . *explain.* By the time they reached the lobby, he was almost bouncing up and down himself. The worst part about it was that she didn't even seem to notice the almost palpable tension in the air. Here he was, stressing out, and she was just staring straight ahead at nothing.

"So, how's your father?" he asked, just as the door opened.

"They're gonna do more tests," Gaia replied. She had already released his hand and started across the lobby. "They still don't know what's wrong."

"What kinds of tests?" Ed asked, feeling like he was a little kid trying to keep up with his mom in a crowd.

"Blood tests. Something about a hormone." Gaia finally paused in the center of the carpeted lobby and looked over her shoulder at the exit. Away from Ed. She *did* want to get out of there. She wanted this conversation to come to a quick close so she could flee. But where? Why? What had happened between their sweet morning together and now to make her want to avoid him?

Was it that wrestling match with Jake? Had something shifted in her at that point that suddenly made her not want to be in his presence? Maybe she'd realized that she did want someone Affleck-esque. The anti-Ed. Maybe that was why she seemed to want to get out of here so badly. So much for all Heather's reassurances.

Ed couldn't take it anymore. He wasn't going to let

her make a quick getaway. Not after all the waiting he'd done today. Waiting for her to talk. Waiting for her to show. Waiting for her to mention Heather. Now it was her turn to wait. He walked over to one of the plush couches and sat down.

Gaia just stood in place for a moment, then walked over and stood right in front of him.

"Ed... I'm sorry, but I kind of have to go," she said apologetically.

All right. If she was going to make him do it, then he would do it. She was getting the blunt treatment.

"Where were you this afternoon?" Ed asked, resting one elbow on the arm of the couch and lacing his fingers together. He went for total innocent curiosity. *All the better to guilt you with, my dear.* Childish, he knew, but this was what happened to him when he was feeling insecure.

Gaia just looked at him blankly for a moment, and Ed tucked his chin and looked at his feet, waiting for her to remember. He was actually hurt by her complete cluelessness. So she hadn't blown him off because she had to come to the hospital right away because the doctors had called her in. She had simply blown him off.

Finally Gaia brought up her free hand and slapped her forehead, closing her eyes. "Oh God. Heather! I completely forgot," Gaia said. She sucked in air through her teeth. "I'm so sorry! Was she mad?"

"Not really," Ed replied. *But I was.* The words were on the tip of his tongue, but he couldn't make them come out. For all the wishing he'd done that she would share her feelings, he couldn't share his own. He was too scared. Petrified. He didn't want to be the person he was inside. The lovesick, pathetic, insecure whiner.

"Are *you* mad?" Gaia asked, her brow furrowing.

Say it, say it, say it!

"Not really," he repeated. "But you can make it up to me by hanging out with me now." He stood up, reached out, and took her free hand in his. His pulse raced when he touched her skin. She really did look pretty in pink. "Want to go catch a movie or something? I'll get you a huge popcorn, and we'll buy them out of Sno-Caps."

Please just say yes.

When Gaia's face scrunched up, his heart took a nosedive. She couldn't actually be preparing to turn him down. . . .

"I'm sorry, I can't," Gaia said, glancing at the door again. He wasn't imagining this. She really was having trouble keeping eye contact with him.

"Why? It'll take your mind off things," Ed said, grasping at straws. Grasping at her. "There might even be something with a talking dog!" he said, waggling his eyebrows.

Gaia laughed, but it was a short laugh. "Can I take a rain check?" she asked. "I really have to get home."

Her hand slipped from his, and she took a step back. Ed felt like he was going to hurl right there in the middle of the swank hospital lobby, with all the little old lady volunteers looking on.

"Come on," he said gamely. "You can't tell me you want to hang out with Natasha and Tatiana more than you want to hang out with me. What's so great about home?"

Then Gaia's face actually reddened. She looked at the floor, then at the door again, then at the floor again before looking into his eyes. He couldn't believe it. He'd thrown her. Something was definitely going on. Ed felt all the hairs on the back of his neck stand on end.

What's going on!?

"I just. . . I really need to be alone right now," Gaia said, an almost pleading look in her eyes. She pressed her lips together, and Ed knew she was irritated that she was blushing. He knew that she knew that he was reading her like a book. Unfortunately he was only getting half the message.

"Gaia, why do I feel like there's something you're not telling me?" Ed asked.

She blinked. He was right. He'd thought they were beyond this. He'd thought things had changed and there would be no more secrets. He'd thought she was ready to tell him everything. The fact that she was still hiding something made his heart feel sick.

"You always feel like there's something I'm not telling you," Gaia said, trying for flip but failing miserably.

"And I'm always right," Ed replied. He was starting to harden. He couldn't take this anymore. There was no way he could endure being shut out again, but he could already see the wall building back up around her. The wall it had taken him so long to break through.

"Well, you're not this time," Gaia said. She leaned over and gave him a quick kiss on the cheek. She was a bad liar. Always had been.

"You're really not going to tell me?" Ed asked when she pulled back.

"Ed—"

"Whatever. I'm too tired to do this right now," Ed said, shoving his hands into his pockets so hard, they almost came right through the seams. "I guess I'll just see you in school tomorrow."

Before she could respond, Ed crossed the lobby and was out the door. On the sidewalk, with the cool evening air bathing his face, he instantly felt the immaturity of what he'd just done and was humiliated. But his pride had gotten the better of him, and he couldn't turn back. Not even when he heard her calling his name over the din of the city.

He'd obviously managed to stay in shape at that compound. Just what she needed—a nice big dose of half-naked Sam.

skin

GAIA WALKED INTO THE DARKENED

Pink Pants

apartment, her arms full of takeout bags and groceries. She took one quick look around and used her hip to quietly push the door shut. She had to get rid of all the loot before anyone saw her with it and asked too many questions. She paused and held her breath, listening. A Britney Spears song bopped its way down the hall from the room she shared with Tatiana. The girl did so love her top 40.

A door opened, and Britney grew louder. There was a creak in the hallway. Gaia sprinted into the kitchen, threw her bags into the pantry, and slammed the door.

"Mom?"

Gaia whirled around just as Tatiana appeared at the kitchen doorway.

"Hi," Tatiana said, rolling a pencil between her two palms. Her forehead crinkled. "What was that noise?"

"Just. . . looking for a snack," Gaia said, making a big show of opening one of the cabinets and pushing boxes and bags around inside. She wondered what Sam was doing at that moment. Imagined him with his ear up against the wall, trying to hear if it was she who'd just come home.

"How's your dad doing?" Tatiana asked, sliding

onto one of the stools that stood next to the high breakfast counter.

Oh, so now she cares about my dad.

Gaia paused. Tatiana's nonchalance was befitting of someone making a health inquiry about a gerbil. Maybe she was in a rare form of advanced-stage denial. It was fine with Gaia, though. Her roommate's lack of sincerity coupled with her outrageous display of self-centeredness in the gym this afternoon justified Gaia's plan to blow her off. She just couldn't deal with conversing right now. Sam was two doors away, probably a little scared, probably hungry, probably wondering when she was coming back.

"Gaia?"

"Oh. . . sorry," she said, pulling out a bag of chocolate chip cookies and popping one into her mouth. "I spaced. I guess I'm just hungry," she said through a mouthful.

"You probably haven't eaten all day," Tatiana said sympathetically. She reached for the phone on the wall next to her. "You want me to call Golden Wok? We can have dinner, and you can tell me what the doctors had to say and—"

"No, thank you," Gaia blurted a little too quickly with a little too much edge cracking through her voice. "Actually. . . I'm kind of tired," she added.

"Do you want to go to bed?" Tatiana asked,

hanging up the phone again. "I'm studying, but I can go in the den. . . ."

This is a nightmare, Gaia thought. The apartment was too small. Wherever Tatiana went, she was going to know where Gaia was. They could hear each other's every movement no matter where they were in the apartment.

"I'm probably going to be up for a few more hours, so if you want to pass out, feel free," Tatiana said, slipping off the stool.

Gaia forced a strained smile. "Yeah, I guess that's what I'll do," she said. It was as good a solution as any. At least if Tatiana thought she was sleeping in the bedroom, she probably wouldn't come in. Probably, maybe.

Glancing at the pantry, Gaia followed Tatiana from the kitchen back to their bedroom, where Tatiana started to gather her books. Gaia sat on the edge of her bed, holding her messenger bag on her lap, and watched her. She felt bad about tossing Tatiana out for no reason, but she didn't know what else to do. She couldn't let anyone find out about their houseguest. The bedroom was the only place she had any chance of being undisturbed. If she was going to be in it, of course.

"Did you talk to any of the doctors?" Tatiana asked as she shoved her notebooks into her canvas bag. "Have they come up with anything?"

"Not yet," Gaia replied. "But I met this one guy who seemed to know what he was doing."

"Yes?" Tatiana said, raising her eyebrows hopefully. She seemed almost intrigued. "Does he have an explanation?"

Gaia shrugged. "He said something about a rare hormone release," she explained. "They're testing my dad's blood again."

"Good. Maybe this doctor will find the answer and soon this will all be over," Tatiana said. She clicked the edges of a few papers against the desk as if to punctuate her point.

I hope so, Gaia said to herself.

Tatiana finished gathering her things and picked up her portable radio, which was still blasting Britney. "Sleep well," she said with a sympathetic smile.

"Thanks," Gaia replied guiltily. Here Tatiana thought she was emotionally exhausted, when in fact she was planning a secret rendezvous with a fugitive on the other side of the apartment.

Tatiana turned to leave, then paused and looked over her shoulder, her nose scrunching. "Do you smell hot dogs?" she asked.

Gaia colored. She lifted one shoulder and glanced down at the messenger bag in her lap, cursing Gray's Papaya for their pungent eats. "Must be coming from outside."

Tatiana frowned. "Okay. I'll see you in the morning," she said.

Gaia waited until she heard the den door close, muffling the pop princess, then crept over to the bedroom door and closed it almost all the way, stopping just before it could click shut. She kicked off her boots and crossed to her bed, rearranging the pillows and blankets to make it look like someone might be sleeping there. It wasn't the most convincing job, but it would suffice if someone decided to glance in.

Back at the door, she turned off the light and slipped out of the room, closing the door loudly so that Tatiana would think she'd gone to bed. Then she tiptoed quickly down the hall, across the living room, and over to the kitchen. As she pulled the bags out of the pantry, she knew Tatiana was going to hear. Each crinkle of a plastic bag seemed to be `amplified a thousand times.` But there was no sign of her roommate. Gaia hugged the bags to her chest and headed for Sam's room.

She smiled. *Sam's room.*

She paused outside the door, reached out one hand shakily, and turned the knob. Sam shot up like a dart as the door swung open.

"Oh, it's just you," he said, his bare chest heaving as he clutched a book in one hand.

She'd scared him, she knew. She knew what it looked like—she just didn't know what it felt like.

Gaia ripped her eyes away from his skin, resisting

the urge to tell him to get dressed. He'd obviously managed to stay in shape at that compound. Just what she needed, a nice big dose of half-naked Sam. She already felt guilty enough for ditching Ed. For not telling him Sam was back. For keeping her ex in her apartment right under Ed's nose and not sharing. Now he was sitting around half naked and looking good. Damn good.

"Just me and a ton of provisions," Gaia whispered, dropping to her knees and putting down her bags. She turned and closed the door quietly, then sat back as Sam went through the bags, watching him with her teeth holding her lower lip like she was watching her parents open Christmas presents.

"Gaia, what the heck did you do?" Sam asked, his eyes wide.

He pulled out the blue-and-white box that held the mini-TV she'd purchased at 6th Avenue Electronics.

"I didn't want you to get bored," Gaia said with a shrug, even though she was giddy from his surprised reaction.

"Please! This place is like a funhouse compared to where I was," Sam said, lifting the Tom Clancy book he'd chosen from the stack Gaia brought in earlier. "You didn't have to do this."

Gaia blushed and shrugged again, as inarticulate as ever.

She waited as Sam unpacked all the food—everything

from pretzels to soda to peanut butter and bread. He stacked everything up in a neat pile along the wall as if he were making a little home for himself. When he turned away from her, she saw two fleshy pink circles on his back, wrinkling with scar tissue. She had to gulp to keep from groaning aloud. Bullet wounds. They were right there. Sam Moon had been shot. Twice. All because of her.

He turned around again, and Gaia looked away so he wouldn't catch the pain and guilt in her eyes. She didn't want him comforting her again. She wasn't sure she could stand it, especially after what she'd just seen. He smiled at her and then pulled out the inflatable mattress from the last bag. They both just looked at it, overwhelmed.

"I guess we could take turns blowing it up," Gaia said. "I can't exactly bring the vacuum cleaner in here. I don't even know if we have one."

"Gaia, this is great. Thank you," Sam said, putting the box aside. He looked at her and scrunched up his nose. "Do I smell hot dogs?" he asked.

Gaia grinned and pulled her messenger bag from her shoulder. "This is our dinner," she said, lifting out the white Gray's bag. When she opened it, the entire room filled with the smell of boiled hot dogs and relish. Gaia breathed it in, closing her eyes. She hadn't eaten real food in twenty-four hours, and her stomach responded with a painfully loud grumble.

"Oh my God. I forgot about those," Sam said, his mouth almost visibly watering.

Gaia pulled out the loaded hot dogs one by one and flattened one of the shopping bags to use as a table. She laid everything out, then looked at Sam and nodded.

"So, dig in," she said.

As she and Sam ate, Gaia told him all about everything that had happened since he'd disappeared. She left out the gorier, more disturbing details but filled him in on the greater points—her father's return (he was happy for her), her father's hospitalization (he was sad for her), Heather's blindness (he was thrown and stopped eating), and Ed's ability to walk (he was surprised and glad). She didn't tell him that she and Ed were a couple. That she and Ed had had sex. That she and Ed were in love. All greater points. All left unsaid.

"So. . . how are things with you? Other than your dad, I mean?" Sam asked when she was done with the storytelling.

Ed's face floated before her mind's eye, and her body felt thick with guilt and longing, but she couldn't tell him. She wasn't sure if it was for his sake or her sake or if it somehow made things even in her mind—Sam didn't know about Ed, Ed didn't know about Sam. But somehow she knew she didn't want to see his face when she told him, so she didn't.

"Things are fine, you know," Gaia said, lifting her shoulders and letting them fall. "As fine as ever."

Sam smiled and pushed himself up off the floor, then crawled over to Gaia's sleeping bag. He leaned up against the wall just as he'd done earlier that day when he'd finished eating. He was starting to look better, with more color in his cheeks and less color under his eyes.

"I called my parents before," he said.

Gaia's eyes nearly bugged out of her head as she shoved the last bite of hot dog into her mouth. "You left the room?" she asked.

"I'm sorry, but I had to," Sam replied. "No one saw me, I swear. No one was home. I just. . . I had to talk to them."

Gaia's heart turned for him, and she stopped chewing and made herself swallow. It wasn't like she could blame him. She was sure she would have done exactly the same thing.

"What did they say? What did *you* say?" she asked.

"I told them that I was okay and I was sorry and I couldn't come home yet. I mean, I'd kill to go home, but they might find me there," Sam said, looking down at the sleeping bag. "I told them it was for their own safety, and they freaked out—wanted to know what I'd gotten myself involved in." He looked at Gaia, his hazel eyes laughing sadly. "Imagine trying to explain that."

Gaia looked away, guilt permeating every pore of her body. He'd gotten involved with her, that's what he'd gotten involved in. And it had torn him away from his family.

"Anyway, I'm sorry," Sam repeated. "I just really needed to hear their voices."

"I understand," Gaia said, wiping her hands on her pink pants.

"It's weird, but ever since I hung up the phone, I've been dying to see them," Sam said, putting his head back against the wall and looking up at the ceiling. "It's like there's this sucking black hole where my heart used to be."

"I know," Gaia said. She got on her hands and knees and crawled over to sit down next to him. "Just spending that little time with my father. . . it's like it made me miss him even more."

"Like a tease," Sam said, looking at her.

"Yeah. Like a tease," she replied. "I just hope this doctor I met today was right. He said my dad might be able to come home soon."

Or that they may never figure out why he's in a coma, she added silently.

"Really? That's great," Sam said.

Yeah. . . great, Gaia thought. She looked down at her hands, at her chewed fingernails and her bruised knuckles, and sighed. A chunk of hair fell forward from her ponytail and grazed her cheek, tickling her skin. She thought of pushing it back behind her ear, but her arms suddenly felt very heavy.

Gaia felt Sam shift, and before she could move, his fingertips grazed her cheek, sending a pleasant chill down the side of her body. How could his touch still do that to her? After all this time. After everything. After Ed. He tucked her hair back slowly, softly, watching her face the entire time. Gaia froze, her heart pounding in her chest, watching him out of the corner of her eye.

He was still beautiful. There was no denying that.

And he was doing it again. Looking at her that way. That way that used to send tingles to parts of her body she shouldn't be thinking about in his presence. She crossed her legs and concentrated on feeling nothing. But she could remember now—remember how much she used to want him. And it was clear that he still wanted her. It made her feel sorry for him. And confused. And even more guilty than she already did.

"I'll always be here for you, you know," Sam said, still watching her closely. "I'm back, and I'm not going anywhere."

Gaia trained her eyes on her hands again and willed him to turn away. Willed him to stop staring at her like that and to stop feeling the way he was feeling. It was all so confusing. So complicated. It was too much for her to sort out with everything else that was going on.

If Ed knew where she was right now, he would kill

her. No, he'd kill himself. No, he'd probably just have an embolism.

"I know," Gaia said.

Finally Sam turned away and closed his eyes, slumping down a bit farther against the wall. "Eating makes me so tired now," he said sleepily.

Gaia scrambled to her feet. "I'll let you sleep," she said, happy for an excuse to escape.

Sam's hand shot out and grabbed her wrist. "You don't have to go," he said, his eyes at half-mast.

"I have a lot of work to do for school," Gaia lied. "So I really do."

"Oh. Okay."

She was pretty sure he was asleep before his head hit the pillow. Gaia gathered the garbage from the hot dogs and crept out of the room, shutting off the light behind her. She kept her eyes on Sam's sleeping face as she closed the door and closed herself off from him. Then she turned and leaned back against the door, her full stomach turning dangerously.

It was all so confusing. Sam was back. He seemed to have been thinking of her while he was gone. What if he was expecting to pick up where they left off? There was a time not long ago when Gaia would have prayed for that. But now, with Ed in the picture, things were so different. What a difference a kidnapping made.

It didn't happen the way it was supposed to. In my mind there was a lot of kissing. I mean, sure, there would have to be explaining first. Apologies, forgiveness, laughter over how silly we'd been to let each other go. But that part was never all that fun to imagine. It was the other stuff. The stuff that would come afterward. The thought of Gaia weeping with joy in my arms. Her telling me she never gave up hope and kissing me like one of those classic movie heroines. She'd wear a low-cut red dress with matching lipstick on her full lips, and her hair would be billowing in a soft, tropical wind. . . .

Or some other slightly more real- istic scenario, untainted by the pathetic fantasies of a twenty-year- old guy locked up in prison without a woman in sight. When Gaia and I saw each other again, I wasn't sup- posed to be getting the piss beaten out of me. I wasn't supposed to be saved by her. I wasn't supposed to be wearing clothes that would make

S
A
M

the reject pile at the Salvation
Army. I spent months envisioning how
it would happen, and not one of the
above details ever appeared in my
daydreams.

And now it's been a whole day
and we still haven't even kissed.

That is something I never would
have predicted. I mean, I figured
after everything that happened,
we would let bygones be bygones.
And I know it has to be weird for
her. She thought I was dead, so
the whole thing must take some
adjusting. But I know she loves
me. I know she still does. And I
know she wants to kiss me. I can
see it in her eyes.

And she's right down the hall.
Sleeping. I bet she looks so beautiful right now, all curled up in her
bed, her hair spread out on the pillow, her bare feet kicked out from
under the blankets. She's right. . .
down. . . the. . . hall. . . .

But I'm not going to push it. We
were meant to be together, and we
will be. We will be. I just hope
it's sooner rather than later.

Swallowing Back the Sobs

GAIA SAT UP STRAIGHT IN BED, her heart pounding from being ripped so quickly from a state of slumber to a state of hyperalertness. She rubbed at her eyes, which refused to focus, and realized the telephone was ringing. She blinked at the clock. 5:02 A.M. If this wasn't an emergency, she was going to have to crack some skulls.

"Who is that?" Tatiana asked groggily from the next bed.

Gaia flung out her arm and whacked the phone from its cradle, then brought it to her ear.

"Hello?"

"May I speak to Ms. Moore, please?"

The voice was male. Older. Tired but efficient. Gaia gripped the phone tightly and swung her legs over the side of the bed, her adrenaline flowing. For some reason, she had the distinct feeling that this phone call was going to send her flying out the door.

"This is Gaia Moore," she said.

Tatiana sat up at the intense sound of Gaia's voice. She knew it meant trouble. Gaia glanced at her and then looked down at her knees. Her body seemed to be producing an unusual amount of heat. So much so

183

that she wanted to peel off her clothes and jump in a cold shower. A trickle of sweat ran down the side of her face.

"Ms. Moore, this is Dr. Sullivan. We met yesterday?"

Instantly every muscle in Gaia's body contracted. Dr. Sullivan. She liked Dr. Sullivan. But still, if he was calling her at this hour, odds were he had some serious news to share with her.

"I told you to call me Gaia," she said as lightly as possible, hoping to keep the conversation from taking the negative turn she was sure it was going to take. Hoping to keep it peppy even though she was allergic to pep of all kinds. Unfortunately it came out sounding like an order from a drill sergeant.

"Yes. Of course. Sorry, Gaia," he replied. He was distracted. Exhausted. His laugh lines were most definitely not crinkling on the other end of the wire. Gaia's free hand clutched the top sheet on her bed into a tight little ball.

"*What is it?*" Tatiana mouthed. Gaia shook her head ever so slightly.

"What's going on?" Gaia asked.

"Well, I'm afraid I have some bad news," Dr. Sullivan replied. He took a deep breath that seemed to take forever.

Out with it! Gaia wanted to scream. *Just tell me already! Enough with the dramatic pause!*

"We found a disturbing irregularity in your father's

tests," Dr. Sullivan continued. Gaia could hear papers flipping in the background.

"What kind of irregularity?" Gaia asked, the fingers on her free hand curling even tighter on the sheet. Tatiana was now on the edge of her bed, her skin as pale as the white USA T-shirt she'd worn to bed.

"It's a very rare blood disease, Ms. Moore," he said grimly.

"What!" Gaia blurted. *But he choked. Wasn't that what started this?* How had they gotten from choking to a *blood disease*?

"Luckily, though, the situation is not entirely without hope," Dr. Sullivan continued. "I've had your father transferred to St. Augustine's Clinic in Switzerland, where they've made magnificent strides in—"

Gaia felt like her train of thought had just hit a brick wall. What had he just said? "You *what*!?" she shouted, erupting with a force previously unknown to man. Tatiana's blue eyes filled with fear and she stood up, one hand holding the fingers on the other, her knees pressed together like a toddler's.

"What? What is it? Gaia?" Tatiana asked desperately.

But Gaia was too busy listening to the silence on the other end of the line. She could practically hear Dr. Sullivan's mind reeling. Switzerland. He had not really just said that he'd sent her father to Switzerland.

"Now, Ms. Moore—"

"You sent my father out of the country without

talking to me first?" Gaia shouted, standing now, all the heat in her body rushing straight to her head. Her veins and arteries felt like they were going to explode. "What the hell kind of procedure is that? Without my permission? Without my consent? You can't just ship sick people all over the world without telling their families! Who the hell do you think you are?"

"Ms. Moore. . . Gaia. . . please calm down—"

"Don't tell me to calm down!" Gaia shouted, burning tears coming to her eyes and slipping down her cheeks. "You can't do this!"

Natasha appeared at the door to the bedroom, her hair sticking straight up in the back as she pulled on a silky pink robe. She looked at Gaia, and her face went slack.

"What's going on?" Natasha mouthed to Tatiana. Tatiana shrugged in response, her hand held over her stomach as if she were nauseated.

Gaia saw this but didn't register what Natasha had said. She couldn't comprehend anything at the moment. Her father was on a plane traversing the Atlantic Ocean unbeknownst to him and everyone he knew. This could not be happening.

"Gaia, transferring your father to St. Augustine's was the only hope we had of saving him. Trust me, he'll be in good hands there. They are the foremost pathology experts in the world," Dr. Sullivan continued.

186

"I don't understand," Gaia said, reduced almost to a whimper. She felt like her life was slipping away from her. And in a way it was. Her father—her only family—was in the hands of people she didn't know in a country half a world away. "How can you do this without telling his family?"

"Your father has no living adult kin," Dr. Sullivan said. "There was no one to sign off on this, but believe me, Gaia, I would not have sent him if I didn't believe the situation was dire."

"You should have called me," Gaia said, trying to be firm. "You should have—"

"What. . . oh. . . yes. . . one moment," he said, holding the mouthpiece away from him. "I'm sorry, Ms. Moore, I'm needed in emergency," he told her. "I will call you as soon as I've had confirmation of your father's arrival at the clinic. And don't worry. As I said, he's in good hands."

Before Gaia could respond, the line went dead. She held it for a moment, staring down at the glowing green buttons, then pulled back and hurled the phone across the room, where it smashed against the wall and exploded into a hundred pieces all over Tatiana's bed.

Natasha gasped and held her chest, her eyes wide. "Gaia! What is wrong?"

"They took my father to Switzerland," Gaia replied, wiping in vain at her eyes.

"What!" Tatiana and Natasha exclaimed in unison. Neither of them moved a muscle. It was as if this news had frozen them in time.

"I knew I shouldn't have left him there. I should never have left him!" Gaia turned and brought her hands to her head, pushing her fingers into her hair.

The tears were coming freely now, choking her words and soaking her shirt. Gaia hated showing this weakness in front of Natasha and Tatiana, but she couldn't help it. She couldn't stop herself. This was her father, and she'd let him down. Again.

"Switzerland," Natasha said, her eyes searching Tatiana's as if she might find some explanation there. "Switzerland?"

"He said there was some special clinic there that could deal with his particular irregularity. Some blood disease," Gaia said, throwing up her hand and letting it slap down against her thigh. She sniffled and got almost no air through her stuffed nose. "What blood disease? He choked!"

"Who told you this?" Tatiana asked, taking a step across the room. She sounded indignant, ready for battle. As if she were going to go over to the hospital and hunt this person down. Gaia knew the feeling.

"Dr. Sullivan," Gaia said, crossing the room and flinging open the door of her closet. "I trusted him!" she spat, yanking a gray wool sweater down from the top shelf. "When am I ever going to learn? I can't trust anyone!"

"Gaia, that is not true," Natasha said, coming to the door of the closet. "You can trust us."

A lot of good that *does me,* Gaia thought. Clearly she wasn't even sure that was true, considering she had a certain secret houseguest asleep across the apartment. Gaia wasn't ready to trust Natasha and Tatiana yet. Not fully. Otherwise she would have told them all about Sam. She just hoped her tirade hadn't woken him. If it had, he was probably sitting in his cave right now, petrified and dying to know what was going on.

She yanked out her favorite, most functional army green cargo pants and ripped off her scrubs. As Gaia dressed, she forced herself to stop crying, swallowing back the sobs that threatened to keep coming forever. She could not arrive at the hospital looking like a scared, sad little girl.

She needed to strike fear into people's hearts.

"I'm going over there," she told the hovering women, shoving her feet into her boots.

"I will come with you," Natasha said, turning toward the door.

"No." Gaia cut her off and trudged from the bedroom ahead of her. "You stay here in case he calls back."

"But Gaia," Natasha protested as she and Tatiana followed her down the hallway.

Gaia took a deep breath and turned to look at the woman who, for all intents and purposes, was her functioning stepmother. The woman who loved her father.

"Please," she said. "I'll call you as soon as I know anything more. I need to do this alone."

Tatiana put her hand on her mother's back, and Natasha's expression became resigned. "All right," she said, reaching out to grasp Gaia in a tight hug. "Good luck. Find out all you can."

"I will," Gaia said, pulling away awkwardly.

She glanced at Tatiana, who shot her a confident smile, then raced from the apartment. She was going to make Dr. Sullivan tell her everything, show her every chart and test result he had. No more of this middle-of-the-night, clinical phone call crap. If he was going to ship her father out of the country, he was going to have to look her in the eye and explain.

GAIA RAN ACROSS THE DESERTED

streets of the Upper East Side, this time with nothing to chase. She wished she were running against time—running to catch the transport ambulance before it could take her dad to the airport. Wished she'd gotten the news in

Too Pathetic

time to attempt to save the day so that something other than sheer anger was driving her. But she hadn't even been given the opportunity to stop this. It was all out of her control.

A tear escaped Gaia's eye and traveled backward from her temple toward her hairline. She shoved it away with the heel of her hand. It was just the running that had caused it, that was all. She wouldn't allow it to mean anything more. She would not break down again.

The morning was cool and dark, and virtually no one was on the sidewalks other than the occasional overly motivated jogger. Gaia caught sight of the hospital ahead and slowed her pace a bit. She didn't want to arrive completely disheveled and out of breath. She wanted to make sure that she didn't set off the security guy's radar in the lobby. There would be no point to any of this if she never made it upstairs.

Suddenly something huge and heavy hurtled past her, right in front of her face, so fast, it left a breeze behind it. If Gaia had kept up her speed, it would have flattened her. She looked left and saw an old-fashioned metal garbage can hit the middle of the road with a clatter that could have woken the dead. Or even the slumbering little old ladies that peopled the neighborhood.

"Well, look who it is."

Gaia wheeled around, knowing exactly who she was going to see. Behemoth Man. And there he was in all his grimy glory, wearing a floor-length leather coat that probably cost the life of at least ten cows. He looked every bit as grungy and angry as he had the last time she'd seen him. But there was one difference. This time he'd brought friends.

Taking an instinctive step backward, Gaia took a moment to assess her adversaries. The man to Behemoth's right was short but broad, with next to no neck. He held his head back with his chin thrust forward like those guys who spent way too much time in the windows at Crunch, showing off their bulging muscles for the passersby. To his right was a man that could only be Behemoth's brother. He was almost as tall and could have weighed in with him pound for pound, but he looked a lot more solid. A lot less clumsy. And this one was wearing rings. Big rings that would definitely hurt.

"This the bitch you told us about?" Mr. Crunch said with a smirk. "She don't look that tough."

"Yeah, Tommy, you couldn't take her?" the brother said with a laugh, slapping Behemoth on the back.

"Shut up, Ricky," Tommy spat, backhanding his brother's shoulder.

"You shut up," Ricky shot, shoving Tommy.

"No, you shut up," Tommy said, shoving right back.

Great. Thugs with sibling rivalry issues, Gaia thought. *Maybe I should just run. By the time they're done with the atomic wedgies, I'll be long gone.*

"Hey!" Mr. Crunch shouted, grabbing Tommy by the back of his coat and pulling him away from his brother. "I thought we were here for the girl."

Tommy yanked down on his coat and shook off the argument, glaring at Gaia. Then, ever so slowly, he pulled a long, shiny knife from his inside pocket. This was no switchblade. It was more like a kitchen knife. A steak knife. He turned it around, grinning sadistically at her, making sure she was taking it in.

Gaia arched one eyebrow. She was not impressed.

"I woulda brought my gun, but it woulda been over too quickly."

And then he lunged.

Gaia stopped the knife-wielding arm with one hand and thrust her knee up into his gut, using his own momentum against him. He doubled over, and she grabbed the arm with the other hand, twisting his wrist until the knife clattered to the ground. Again it was almost too easy. But this time there was someone else to pick up the knife.

Out of the corner of her eye she saw Ricky dive for the weapon. She gave Tommy another swift knee and he let out a half groan, half gasp. Tossing him to the ground, Gaia whirled on Ricky, who was clutching the knife and looking down at his coughing brother with uncertainty. Mr. Crunch was somewhere behind her, but he wasn't making a move. He was simply hovering. And as long as she could sense where he was hovering, she was fine.

Ricky let out a kind of strangled battle cry that almost made Gaia laugh. These guys had to be kidding. He lunged at her just the way his brother had. Gaia sidestepped him, turned, and flung out her leg, right into his midsection. He stumbled, tripped, and sank the knife right into his brother's calf.

Tommy screamed out in horrified pain and Ricky got to his knees, trembling. "Oh my God, Tommy. Oh. . . I'm so sorry!" He covered his mouth, then moved a hand as if to grab the knife, thought the better of it, and covered his mouth again.

The knife was sticking out of Ricky's leg like a stake. Mr. Crunch looked like he was going to be sick. How did these guys think they were going to pull off a stabbing murder if they couldn't even handle a little stick to the leg?

"I'm gonna kill you, Ricky!" Tommy shouted, red faced and sputtering. He twisted himself around and pulled the knife from his calf, letting it drop to the ground, covered in blood. Ricky took one look at it and ran, loping off down the street and disappearing around the corner. Apparently he took his brother's threat seriously.

"Tommy?" Mr. Crunch said uncertainly.

"Kill her!" Tommy growled, clutching his leg.

Mr. Crunch picked up the knife, narrowed his eyes, and approached Gaia slowly, his arms down straight at his sides. He wasn't going to make the same mistake his friends had and come on too quickly. Of course, if he came at her like this, with no defense, he was pretty much toast.

He and Gaia circled each other, and Gaia never took her attention from the knife. Its position would dictate her moves. She had to know where it was at all times.

Finally Mr. Crunch lifted the knife and swiped at Gaia, straight across her chest. She jumped back, the blade narrowly missing her sweater. He tossed the knife to the other hand and brought it down with a slashing thrust. Gaia blocked his motion with her forearm and hit him with an uppercut, right under his chin. Mr. Crunch's head snapped back and he dropped the knife. It skidded across the sidewalk and fell over the curb, lying on the side of the street.

Mr. Crunch glanced at the weapon, then made a move for it, but Gaia threw herself forward, tackling him to the ground before he could reach the blade. They tumbled over and over each other down the sidewalk until they finally rolled right into Tommy. He let out another pained cry, and Gaia used Mr. Crunch's distraction to crawl out from under him. He never saw the first punch coming—a nice sharp jab to the face. She heard something crack, and his nose started to bleed.

Gaia made a move to crawl over him and grab the knife, but he shouted and pulled up his legs, shoving her off him with his knees, away from the street. Gaia struggled to her feet and Mr. Crunch did the same, clutching his nose. When he brought his hands away, his face was covered with blood and it dripped down onto his jacket, leaving a dozen spreading stains.

"You broke my nose, you bitch!" he shouted.

Gaia shrugged, which only served to incense him.

He came at her like a madman, with wide, lunging punches. A left to her shoulder, a right to her jaw, all the time staying between Gaia and the street. He was strong but had no moves she hadn't seen before. She ducked another left and spun around on the ground behind him. By the time he'd realized what happened and turned around, Gaia had the knife clutched firmly in her hand.

She lunged for Tommy, who was still prone on the ground, and brought the blade up under his chin.

"Call him off," she ordered.

"Piss off!" Tommy shouted.

She pressed the knife into his skin, and he let out a strangled cry. Gaia glared up at Mr. Crunch. "Go," she said. "Get out of here or I'll kill him."

Mr. Crunch looked down at Tommy, touched his fingers to his nose, and winced. "Screw this," he said finally, making a decision. He turned and ran toward the hospital, no doubt headed for the ER with some grand story about a mugging he'd just single-handedly broken up.

Gaia stood up, walked over to the street, and tossed the knife into the sewer. Then she straddled Tommy's legs, standing over him as he covered his calf with his bloodstained hands.

"If I ever see you in this neighborhood again, that leg wound is gonna feel like a paper cut," she said, making sure he could read in her eyes how very serious she was.

Tommy attempted a defiant expression for a moment, but it didn't last. He finally rolled his head back on the ground and looked away. *"Fine,"* he said through his teeth.

Gaia turned and started down the street, happy to find that the fog wasn't coming on. Those guys were too pathetic. It hadn't been enough of a fight to completely wipe her out. And luckily, she hadn't been cut or bruised. She took a deep breath and smoothed back her hair, realizing she was a lot more calm than she'd been ten minutes ago. Pummeling Tommy and his friends was just what she'd needed.

She was more ready than ever to confront Dr. Sullivan.

GAIA WALKED UP TO THE DESK IN
the ICU, the picture of seren-
ity. She'd moved through the
lobby with nary a glance from
security or the volunteer personnel. Now all she had to do
was get these people to page
Dr. Sullivan. She was going to
find him, and she was going
to get her answers.

Vegetative and Half Dead

"Can I help you?" the elderly
nurse asked, her eyes watery behind her thick glasses.

"I need to see Dr. Sullivan," Gaia replied, going for
nonchalant.

"Oh. Well, you're in luck! There he is!" The elderly
woman pointed with her pen over Gaia's shoulder,
and Gaia's heart caught in her throat. This was it.
He was standing right behind her. The man who had
taken her father away.

Gaia turned slowly and saw Dr. Sullivan walking
out of one of the ICU rooms, making some notes on
his chart. He was concentrating and hadn't seen her
yet. Part of her, a very primal part, wanted to just run
over there and tackle him, sending him into the glass
wall behind him.

"Dr. Sullivan?" she said, stepping back from the
desk. Her voice came out shakily.

He paused and looked up from his notes, and a

cloud of confusion crossed his face. "Gaia! What are you doing here?" he asked. And he smiled. The man who had taken her father away smiled right in her face.

"I came to see you," she said, staring directly into his eyes. How could he just be looking at her with that open, pleasant expression? Half an hour ago, on the phone, she'd been out for blood and he had known it. Were all doctors really this cocky and detached?

"Well, I was going to call you after my rounds," Dr. Sullivan said, crossing over to her and placing the chart he was working on down on the ICU desk. He folded his hands on top of it and looked at her sorrowfully, calmly. "We ran those tests on your father."

Gaia clenched her hands into fists in an effort to keep from exploding.

"I know," she said, impatience swelling within her chest.

His bushy red brows knitted. "What do you mean, you know? Nurses aren't supposed to divulge this information." He glanced over his shoulder at the two nurses on duty, and they just looked back at him blankly. What the hell was he talking about? Was this all some kind of game to him? If it was, she wasn't playing.

"The nurses didn't divulge anything," Gaia spat. "You told me."

"I'm sorry?" His eyes narrowed, and a small

bemused smile crossed his face. The man was genuinely confused. How could this be?

Gaia felt her knees weaken slightly, and her stomach seemed to drop out of her body. Either this guy was a very good actor, or he had a split personality, or something was very wrong here.

"Gaia, what do you mean? I haven't spoken to you since we met yesterday," Dr. Sullivan said.

Gaia was suddenly very, very weak. Her vision clouded over like it did before her blackouts, and she leaned her side into the ICU desk, clinging to consciousness. She pressed her palms into the cool surface of the desk, hoping it would serve to ground her.

"But you. . . you called my house," Gaia said, her mouth completely dry. "You told me you sent my father to Switzerland. . . ."

Dr. Sullivan chuckled. He couldn't know how his laughter cut through her heart. Gaia knew for certain at that moment that he hadn't made that phone call. That whoever had called her hadn't been Dr. Sullivan. It had been someone else. Someone who didn't even work here. Someone who now had her father strapped to a bed and shoved in a plane, headed to a destination unknown.

"I think you've been having some very vivid dreams," Dr. Sullivan said kindly. "But what I would have told you if I *had* called your house was that your father tested negative for the hormones I mentioned to you."

Gaia closed her eyes as the ICU spun around her, trying to breathe evenly. Trying to block out the familiar taunting voices in her head. The ones calling her stupid, gullible, moronic.

"My father is gone," she whispered, letting the reality of it sink in.

"I'm sorry, I don't know what you're—"

"I mean he's not here anymore. They've taken him to Switzerland. Check his room," Gaia said, opening her eyes and glaring at him, her jaw clenching.

Dr. Sullivan pulled back his head. "Check his room? What are you talking about? I just saw him a—"

Gaia stood up straight, ignoring the head rush, and walked right by Dr. Sullivan. For a moment he didn't move. He clearly thought she was a lunatic. Talking about phone calls and Switzerland and making no sense to him whatsoever. But as Gaia approached her father's room, she knew that in moments it would all make sense. At least to her.

Maybe it was a joke, Gaia thought, a flicker of irrational hope spawning irrational thought. *Someone's idea of a sick joke. Or maybe I did dream the whole phone call.* When she opened the curtain, her father would be there, `vegetative and half dead,` but there. The last hour would be reduced to the status of bad dream.

She reached up, grasped the curtain, and flung it aside. Her father's bed was empty.

Gaia's stomach turned inside out over and over and over again as she stood there, clutching the curtain against the wall, staring at the twisted sheets, the IV tube that hung limp, the blank monitor on the heart machine.

Her father really was gone. And Gaia had no idea where he was, who had taken him, or why.

To: Y
From: X22

Extraction of subject complete. There was no
interference. Takeoff time was 3:37 A.M. No
weather complications are reported. Flight will
arrive on schedule, runway 1-A. Pilots have been
briefed as to procedure.

From: Y
To: X22

I commend you on a job well done. We are on
our way.

Sometimes I wonder what
we all did to deserve this. Even
now that I know most of the story
of my parents, of my uncle, of my
birth, it still doesn't seem
right or just or fair. What was
it, really, that got us all
started on this path? Was it the
moment my father and Oliver
decided to join the CIA? Was it
the moment my father met my
mother? Or the moment Oliver met
my mother? Was it the moment my
mother left Russia? Was it my
uncle's illness, diagnosed when
he was just a kid—when my mother
and I didn't even exist in the
Moore reality?

Which thing would have had to
be different to make the course
of my life change? All of them?
Just one? There are so many
things that I can point to and
say, "If this had never happened, I
would have had a normal life."
I would have two parents. I would
have a father who wasn't constantly disappearing. I would

live in a house with a family who loved me.

I might still be fearless, but it wouldn't matter. It wouldn't apply. Because all there would be is happiness. Normalcy. Football games and snowball fights and sleepover parties and laughter. You don't need fear to live a life like that. You just need to know how to be.

I guess it doesn't really matter what the moment was when it all changed. When my life veered from the line it could have followed onto the jagged path it's taken. What matters is what I do now. What I choose to do at *this* moment to change my path again. Who I choose to take with me. How I choose to get there.

Because I am going to change my future. I am going to find my father, and we are going to leave this path. And I don't care what I need to do to make it happen.

Enough is enough.

here is a
sneak peek of
Fearless™ #26:
ESCAPE

Gaia suddenly realized that she was talking a mile a minute, like some **fake** hyperactive **mothers** five-year-old who'd neglected to take her Ritalin.

FAKE MOTHERS ARE THE ENEMY.

This had been Gaia Moore's credo for the better part of the last year. It was like a physical law of sorts. A mantra that had been engraved in her brain ever since she'd suffered through

Emotionally Baffling

her prison sentence in that brownstone on Perry Street with the most fake of all fake mothers, Ella Niven.

Ella had been as fake as they come. Fake nails, fake red hair, fake eyelashes, and an inflatable chest faker than those of Britney and Mariah combined. But the fakest thing about Ella Niven had actually been hidden under that fake chest. Her fake heart. No, not just a fake heart. A murderous heart. Yes, in Gaia's limited experience, fake mothers, for the most part, tried to kill you.

All right, maybe that wasn't fair. Ella, as it turned out, hadn't been *all* bad. In fact, she really hadn't been anything other than a victim. Just another one of Loki's helpless victims. But still, take away those last forty-eight hours of redemption in Ella's life, and all you had left was a jealous, vindictive, all too fake mom who had spent her last days on this earth trying to order a hit on her own adopted daughter.

Obviously the odds of Gaia ever trusting another fake mother after that were pretty goddamn slim. But nonetheless, here she was, stomping her way down the hall of her apartment, headed for Natasha's bedroom, with one very simple goal in mind: She had to forget absolutely everything she believed about fake moms.

Natasha Petrova was fake mom number two, and now, more than ever, Gaia needed to trust her. Not only did she need to trust Natasha, but she actually needed her help. And Tatiana's help, too. Because Gaia's father was obviously in serious danger, more serious than any of them had even imagined. And Gaia had learned an essential lesson in the last few weeks—perhaps the most essential lesson of them all. She had learned that she wasn't alone.

She did not have to face all this impending doom in a vacuum. Now there was this *thing* in this apartment on East Seventy-second Street that was starting to look and feel more and more like a family. And not even a fake family. Gaia had to admit that each day, the nagging sensation that Natasha and Tatiana were nothing more than cheap and nefarious imitations of a mother and sister had faded a little farther into the distance. And now, after everything they had been through together, Gaia was beginning to remember one of the best things about a family—something she hadn't even thought about since her mother had died.

If Gaia's father really was in serious trouble, now at least *one* other person would care as much as Gaia did. That person always used to be her mother. Her *real* mother. But now that person was undoubtedly Natasha. And whatever doubts Gaia might have had about Natasha in the past, one thing was for damn sure. Natasha loved Gaia's father. She truly loved him. And they were probably headed for marriage. She was the closest thing Gaia had to a real mother. Closer than Gaia was even willing to admit. And when Natasha heard about Gaia's encounter with the *real* Dr. Sullivan at the hospital, she was going to be just as shocked and infuriated as Gaia was. And just as ready to kick someone's head in.

Gaia knocked loudly on Natasha's bedroom door, barely waiting for her faint and groggy invitation. She slipped through the doorway and crouched down next to Natasha's bed, glimpsing the flashing clock on the bedside table. 7:03 A.M. Natasha had somehow managed to fall back asleep since Gaia had rushed off to the hospital, though Gaia couldn't imagine how. But Gaia's news would surely send her flying up from the bed and straight to the phone to check in with all her Agency contacts.

That's what they needed now. They needed to call in the entire cavalry and send out a worldwide APB. They needed the kinds of answers Gaia couldn't possibly obtain alone.

"What. . . what's going on?" Natasha croaked sleepily. Her eyes slammed shut when Gaia flipped on the bedside lamp.

"Something's wrong," Gaia said sharply. "With my father. Something is really wrong."

Natasha squinted her eyes and tried to get a better look at Gaia. "What are you talking about? What time is it?" Natasha leaned toward the clock and then fell back on her pillow. "Did something happen at the hospital? Did you talk to Dr. Sullivan?"

"I did," Gaia said. "You need to be awake for this. Are you awake?"

Natasha propped herself up against the headboard and brushed her hair clumsily from her face. She pulled the covers up over her silk nightgown and tried to focus her eyes on Gaia's. "I am sorry," she uttered, clearing her throat before speaking again. "It has been such a horrible morning, I think I was just trying to recover. To. . . recharge for when you got—"

"Well, the morning just got worse," Gaia interrupted, sitting firmly down on the bed. "That call we got this morning, from Dr. Sullivan. . . That wasn't Dr. Sullivan."

"What?" Natasha tilted her head quizzically. "What do you mean?"

Gaia looked deeper into Natasha's eyes. "He was a fake. He was a goddamn *fake*. Dad is gone."

A long silence took over the room. Sounds of morning traffic and the muted chatter of New Yorkers snuck in through the barely opened window. Gaia couldn't tell if Natasha was just dumbfounded or if she had already begun to think countermeasures. She prayed it was the latter. Wherever her father was, there was no time to spare on drawn-out explanations. Not that Gaia really had any explanations.

"What do you mean... a 'fake'?" Natasha asked.

Gaia's hand clenched with frustration, bunching up the covers, but she quickly relaxed it. She was being ludicrously unfair. Obviously Natasha was going to need a little more than that to go on. Even a clairvoyant genius would have needed a little more information.

"I'm sorry," Gaia said, dropping her head momentarily. "I'm sorry, I'm moving too fast. Listen. The phone call—the call we *thought* was from Dr. Sullivan—it was a complete fake. All that stuff he was spewing out about some *clinic* and sending him off to *Switzerland*? I thought it all sounded so ridiculous, so *stupid*, but... but *he's* the doctor, right? He knows *everything*. But he *wasn't* the doctor. That's why we need to put out an APB. That's why we need to call in the Bureau or, you know, Interpol, or—"

"Gaia, Gaia, shhh. . . ." Natasha placed her hand gently on Gaia's shoulder. Gaia suddenly realized that she was talking a mile a minute, like some hyperactive five-year-old who'd neglected to take her Ritalin.

"I know I'm not making much sense," Gaia muttered, driving the palms of her hands deep into her eye sockets. She hadn't even realized how wound up she was until she'd started to speak. "I'm sorry, but we've got to do something. We've got to do something *now*."

"Gaia, I am not understanding you," Natasha said calmly. "Did you speak to the real Dr. Sullivan or not?"

"*Yes.* At the hospital. I *saw* the real Dr. Sullivan. I *talked* to him. He told me that all of Dad's tests had come back negative. There was no hormonal. . . *whatever*, and he didn't know a damn thing about Switzerland or anywhere else. He didn't even know Dad was gone from the hospital. Dad is *not* in the hospital, Natasha, he's *gone*. Now I don't know if *anything* is true. I don't know if they took him to Switzerland or if he's still in New York somewhere or *what*. I don't even know who 'they' are. Who was I talking to on the phone? 'They' could be a million different people. I'd say it was Loki for sure, but he's practically dead. So then *who?* Who is doing this to my father? Where the hell is he? You've got to make some calls. We've got to figure out who the hell *they* are and how we're going to—"

"*Gaia.*" Natasha clamped both her hands around Gaia's shoulders and pressed down firmly. "You have *got* to *calm down*."

Gaia locked her eyes with Natasha's and tried to collect herself. She was a little out of control, she knew that. But what exactly did Natasha expect? After everything they'd gone through just to have a few calm and happy minutes as a family, how could Gaia be anything other than a basket case? How could Natasha stay so calm after hearing all of it?

"How can I calm down?" Gaia complained. "How the hell can I calm down right now? How can *you* be so calm? We don't know where he is. We have *no idea* where he is now. Why are we even still sitting here? We should be moving on this *now*."

"Gaia." Natasha's tone was soothing but patronizing. She loosened her grip on Gaia's shoulders, but she didn't let go. "Listen to me now. If all this information is true . . . then of course I would be out of my mind, like you. If someone has really taken Tom in the state he's in, then I would be beside myself. Absolutely *beside myself* with worry, *of course*. But Gaia. . . we don't know *anything* for sure. All you have right now is a prank phone call from a man you cannot even identify. Perhaps Dr. Sullivan is misinformed, uh? Or perhaps he is simply not aware of a decision to send Tom to this clinic in Switzerland? There are *so many* possibilities right now. Believe me, Gaia. I have been doing this for a very long time. If I went running around with my head spinning every time I got a false lead or prank phone call, they would have locked me away long, long ago, you see?"

Gaia stared defiantly into Natasha's oddly vacant eyes. "No, I don't see," she said. "I don't see why we're not—"

"A few calls, of course, I will make a few calls, Gaia. But what we need to do now is stay calm. What we need to do now is *wait*. Wait for more information. Do you understand?"

Gaia turned her head toward the window with increasing frustration, watching as a tiny beam of light cut through the room like a laser beam—like the sun was trying to break in and light the carpet on fire.

She turned back to Natasha and examined her face, trying to sift through the condescending kindness, and the sage wisdom of an experienced agent, and the generic innocence of her big brown eyes. Gaia wanted to see some of the desperation that she was feeling. The desperation that came with loving someone so much that the thought of losing him actually damaged your sanity. That was half of what she'd come into this room for. Not just the help, but the empathy. The empathy that only a family member could feel. . .

But she couldn't find it. These simply were not a mother's eyes. And they weren't a wife's eyes, either. Gaia didn't even know what these eyes were.

Maybe Natasha was just an incredibly disciplined agent. Or maybe she was just nothing like Gaia. Maybe she handled the traumas of her life with total passivity. Gaia tended to handle her traumas with a well-placed kick to the groin area. They were just. . . different. That's all. That's what was going on here. Two different people coping in two very different ways. This "new family" thing was going to be a long road.

"No," Gaia said finally. "No, I don't understand. If you need to wait it out, then you wait it out. But I'm not waiting for anything. I want to know what's going on. And I want to know now."

"We need patience now, Gaia. Patience is the best way to—"

"Where's Tatiana?" Gaia interrupted. "I didn't see her in our room."

Tatiana wouldn't be talking any of this "patience" bullshit. The more Gaia thought about it, the more she realized how much better she knew Tatiana than Natasha, anyway. She'd hardly spent any real time with Natasha, at least not without being in a completely delirious fever state. But Tatiana. . . Gaia and Tatiana had been to hell and back together. Tatiana didn't waste time. She didn't tiptoe around a problem waiting for "more information." When Tatiana heard about Gaia's trip to the hospital, she'd sprout claws and fangs and go to work with Gaia on finding her father. Tatiana had guts. She must have gotten them from her father.

"She left early," Natasha explained. "She said something about having coffee downtown before school. Gaia, please. Don't worry, okay? I will make a few calls, all right? I will try to find out what we really know. We have to believe that Tom is okay. We have to—"

"I have to go." Gaia shot up from the bed and headed for the door.

"Gaia, come on, now, don't do that."

"Let me know how the waiting goes for you."

Gaia was out the bedroom door before she could even hear a response. *Believe that Tom is okay? What a load of crap.* So much for her newfound faith in fake moms.

She shot over to her room, shoved a few random books into her bag out of habit, and slipped right back out and down the hall toward the front door. She needed to get downtown and find Tatiana. But first, there was one more door she needed to open in the house. One more emotionally baffling, still barely believable, highly complicated door.

. . . A GIRL BORN
WITHOUT THE FEAR GENE

FEARLESS™

A SERIES BY
FRANCINE PASCAL

SIMON
PULSE

FROM SIMON PULSE
PUBLISHED BY SIMON & SCHUSTER

3029

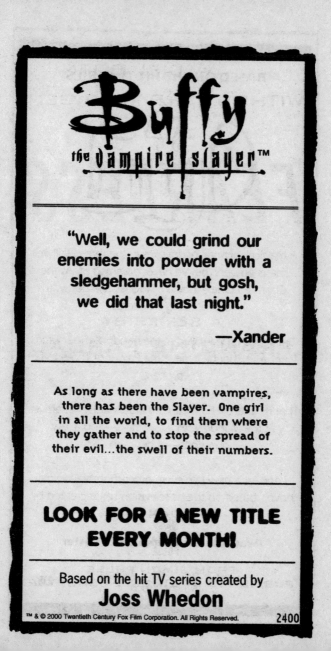

Buffy
the vampire slayer™

"Well, we could grind our
enemies into powder with a
sledgehammer, but gosh,
we did that last night."

—Xander

As long as there have been vampires,
there has been the Slayer. One girl
in all the world, to find them where
they gather and to stop the spread of
their evil...the swell of their numbers.

LOOK FOR A NEW TITLE
EVERY MONTH!

Based on the hit TV series created by
Joss Whedon

™ & © 2000 Twentieth Century Fox Film Corporation. All Rights Reserved.   2400

BASED ON THE HIT TV SERIES

Charmed ™

A magical incantation invokes in the three Halliwell sisters powers they've never dreamed of. As the Charmed Ones, they are witches charged with protecting innocents.

But when Prue is killed at the hands of the Source, Piper and Phoebe believe the Power of Three to be broken.

That is, until their half-sister, Paige Matthews, arrives at the Manor, with a few tricks—and a few questions—of her own....

Look for a new title every other month! Original novels based on the hit television series created by Constance M. Burge.

Available from Simon & Schuster

™ & © 2002 Spelling Television Inc.
All Rights Reserved.

2387